Memphis
Underground

Snowbooks

2 4 6 8 10 9 7 5 3 1

Copyright © Stewart Home 2007

Book design by James Bridle

Proudly published in Great Britain by
Snowbooks Ltd.
120 Pentonville Road
London N1 9JN
www.snowbooks.com

A CIP catalogue record for this book is available
from the British Library

ISBN 9781905005420

Memphis Underground

Stewart Home

snowbooks

LONDON

About the Author

Stewart Home has worked across a variety of media including performance, music, film, writing, installation and graphics. He is the author of the novels *Pure Mania, Defiant Pose, Red London, Blow Job, Cunt, 69 Things To Do With A Dead Princess, Down & Out In Shoreditch & Hoxton, Tainted Love* and a number of other books.

www.stewarthomesociety.org

"Tho' obscured, this is the form of the Angelic land."

William Blake, *America*

"My life was a wandering. I never had a home-land. It was a matter of being constantly tossed about, without rest. Nowhere and never did I find a home."

Johan Amos Comenius,
The Labyrinth Of The World

Contents

Contents

PART 1

INNER CITY BLUES

Is It In?

I don't start work until two in the afternoon. That is, when I've paid drudgery to do. Right now I'm grinding on Tuesday and Thursday. There isn't much demand for people in my line of work. I'm a freelance librarian. Although acquiring specialist skills can pay dividends in the job market, my big mistake was opting for the wrong type of information management. I should have gone into computers. I studied philosophy at London University and like my peers emerged with a singularly useless qualification. Most of those who graduated with me went on to work in information technology. My failure to accompany the majority of my class into employment where there was at least an outside possibility I might be promoted was utterly predictable since I'd only ever played at being middle-class. Put me back on a council estate like the ones I'd known as a boy and I'd almost revert to my original working class social type. My education half removed me from the proletariat and although I can now pass myself off as a bourgeois, whenever I do so I feel like I'm faking it although no one else seems to notice. Given my inability to properly assimilate to the social norms of the privately educated types I met at college, I guess I'm lucky to have regular work. Certainly my situation could be a lot worse. When I was sixteen an Oxford Street department store offered to gear me up in a red suit and white beard. Fortunately, I turned down this golden opportunity to be trained in the rare art of operating a Santa Claus grotto. While the employment was regular, it only came up once a year.

I am most often known by my given name of John Johnson. I come from south London, and right now I'm based at the head office of Dreadnought Insurance, located conveniently close to The Barbican's Silk Street entrance. Silk Street used to be the south end of Whitecross Street, but companies on what had once been a road that was synonymous with poverty, successfully lobbied to have their end of the boulevard renamed. I'd imagine Silk was chosen for its not so austere legal connotations of taking silk. Personally, I prefer to think of it in terms of silky skin, and the way watching money buy influence is a form of pornography. I usually have a mooch through Whitecross Street before I clock on at Dreadnought Insurance. Thursday is my better day at the street market. On Monday and Tuesday trading is slow and not all the stall holders bother to put out their wears. There are three separate record and CD trading operations in Whitecross Street, spread over two market stalls and three indoor premises.

I wanted to get out of librarianship and into music futures, which is why I was busy catching up with the hits and misses of yesteryear. The population of the British Isles is ageing. Teenagers are in a real minority when it comes to laying out wedge on youth culture. Music in Whitecross Street was being sold to office workers who wanted something to lift them when they got home from a hard day in the city. We're not talking about company directors here, but people on 20K doing punishing clerical jobs. Some of those shopping in Whitecross Street were in their twenties but the bulk were in their thirties and forties. Despite the existence of glossy life-style monthlies for ageing hipsters such as *Later*, I figured there was still a lot of potential for increased market penetration amongst those enjoying a premature second childhood. Disenfranchised punters enjoying a resurgent youth instead of mid-life crisis needed a champion, and I'd convinced myself I had the vision to sell them back their teenage obsessions. These were people who needed a dream but would only buy into one if it was offered at a bargain basement price— after all, most of them had mortgages to pay and kids to support. Since quality mattered, I'd have to shift a lot of units if my prices were to be competitive. What I needed was a lump sum to set up a slick merchandising operation. I figured my flatmate Captain Swanky was my most likely source for this.

I met Swanky in The Trader on Whitecross Street. The Captain worked, or rather didn't work, in his dad's degree mill. Students sent in cheques and got worthless diplomas by return post. The University Of Cripplegate operated out of a cramped and shabby office above a newsagent. For reasons I'd never been able to fathom, most of the space was taken up by row after row of recycled filing cabinets. The Captain's parents lived in Spain and since maintaining middle-class appearances meant that their child—who was unemployable—had to have a job, they'd provided him with one. Or rather, The Captain's parents had provided him with a position and a wage, they didn't actually expect their indolent youngest son to do any work. Swanky oversaw the day to day running of The University Of Cripplegate, which meant watching the legs of the two young secretaries who were paid a minimal wage to make sure the cheques got banked and diplomas sent out. The Captain was happy to ogle skirt from nine in the morning until the pub opened. He rarely returned to the office once he'd left for his lunch time meeting with

3

a barmaid who chatted to him if there was nothing else to do, which was just as well because in an inebriated state he'd have raised the already rather brisk turnover of staff in his father's lucrative business. Whenever anything out of the ordinary required sorting out at the University Of Cripplegate, Swanky's brother, who ran a stud farm, would come up from Hampshire to attend to it.

Having dragged him kicking and screaming from the bar of The Trader, I made Captain Swanky look at the music that was being sold in Whitecross Street, and then at the people who were buying it. The punters were fully-fledged adults, and I suggested to The Captain that if we could get through to them as well as the younger club crowd, then crossover into the mainstream was a virtual certainty. I wanted to set up a dot. com music merchandising operation. I had to explain to Swanky that capitalism works in cycles, that bust is followed by boom. He'd fallen for the lie that cyber-investments were dodgy. We spent some time chatting with a stall holder at the bottom of the market. Dave was in his forties and drove down to London from St. Albans with his stock five days a week. He was into everything as far as dance went, jazz funk through to house, but what utterly obsessed him was northern soul. He figured that rare groove recordings really meant something to people since they were still being listened to more than thirty years after they'd been made. Dave shifted a lot of garage but didn't think anybody would be interested in it in ten years time. He'd priced up his northern stock to start with. Normally he knocked recently acquired CDs out at a fiver, then shifted down in price if the product didn't walk. The boxes of northern soul compilations he'd picked up as bankrupt stock had gone out at eight knicker.

When things slowed down, he'd reduced this to a blue note. He hadn't had to duck beneath this benchmark to sell the lot.

"I love this stuff," Dave enthused. "I've got northern CDs all over the house, because maybe all I want to listen to on a compilation is one track. It's driving the missus crazy. That's why I've got to index all the tracks on my computer. That way I can find the songs I want on these compilations without having them strewn all over the place. It'll keep the missus happy and maybe she'll let me go to the Togetherness weekender in Stoke. A lot of the blokes I grew up with are divorced now, so they don't have to get permission to go out all night. My mate told me you won't see anyone under thirty-five at the northern soul revival clubs. It's all changed since we were young. We thought you had to get married and settle down. These days there's no reason why a bloke in his forties shouldn't stay out all night. That's why the northern scene hasn't died. People thought it was dead in the eighties but it has come back now. It's as strong as ever. My mates are going to all the revival events, the stuff up north and the all nighters at the 100 Club here in London. Now my daughter's teenage I don't see why I shouldn't be going along with them. Get a bit of my youth back. It's gotta be better than dancing to machine music."

Nostalgia ain't want it used to be, I informed Captain Swanky. Nostalgia, I reiterated, was the future. We just had to work it like there was no tomorrow. We had to buy up the rights to deleted records and then turn them into club hits. We had to get teenagers and their parents into the same sounds. We needed to learn our lessons from dance music crazes like Acid Jazz. We should aim to create peace, love and unity in the clubs—while making ourselves rich at the same time.

Then I corrected myself. Captain Swanky had money falling out of his derrière, so cash incentives meant nothing to him. The Captain's ruling passion was fame. How he was perceived by other people meant a lot to Swanky. He'd set himself the impossible task of making the perception of his peers match his own self-image. He was the Citizen Kane of Old Street. So I told him he'd be a street credible star if we worked the teenage and post-mortgage brigades into a frenzy of unity and love. The Captain was almost convinced, so I arranged to meet him at The Purple Haze later that evening. Swanky had invested in the club with the sole intention of reserving himself a deejay slot. After saying good-bye (or rather see you later), I left The Captain and made my way to Silk Street.

June Gregory was on reception as I wandered in to work. I asked her if she wanted to go to The Purple Haze after she knocked off. June didn't like rock music and suggested we go to a soul club instead. Unfortunately, I had to postpone any such arrangement until another night. I wanted The Captain's money, so I wasn't going to let him down. At least, not quite yet. Moments after taking my leave of June, I was at my work station with the pile of newspapers I was supposed to clip in front of me. The phone rang. I picked it up, and at first I thought there was no one on the other end of the line. Then I realised some joker had put sellotape over the part pressed to my ear. I tore the tape off. I'd been belled by my boss Michael Martin. He asked me for a summary of how the international standard book numbering system worked. On his way into work he'd been going through what Aleister Crowley had to say about books as talismans and it had occurred to him that a system of numerology based on ISBN numbers would be a very potent form of magick. Martin's interests were, to say the least, arcane. Although officially I was paid to track reports about financial matters and human disasters, I'd have been out of a job had it not been for Martin's life-long pursuit of the esoteric. Of course, Martin's wiccan activities were a source of much amusement behind his back. A wag in the office had recently used a computer graphics programme to mock up a picture of Martin and the comedian Tommy Cooper (dressed in nothing but a fez) performing sex magick at Stonehenge. The image had been anonymously e-mailed to everyone who worked for Dreadnought Insurance, including the boss.

As I explained the ins and outs of the international standard book numbering system to Martin, he became increasingly excited. From what I'd told him, he was sure he'd cracked a way of winning the National Lottery. Martin instructed me to look up the ISBNs of Crowley's books in various editions. I went to grab a pen from my drawer, but the joker who'd sellotaped the phone had evidently made off with my stash of biros too. I was reduced to cradling the telephone headset against my shoulder and imputing Martin's queries directly into my computer. As soon as I put the phone down, I got onto the internet and entered the name Aleister Crowley into a search engine. However, before I had a chance to look at any of the 666 results that came up, the phone went again. It was Colin from marketing. He wanted photocopies of all the recent clippings I had about home insurance deals offered to council and housing association tenants. This information was needed urgently, so I had to drop Crowley and dive into the stacks. Everything went smoothly until I tried to xerox the clippings. The person who'd sellotaped the phone and stolen my biros, had also interfered with the photocopier. They'd slapped their member onto the machine and xeroxed it double-sided onto the one remaining ream of plain paper. Afterwards they'd put their rude copies back into the feed tray.

Colin, it must be said, had a sense of humour. Admittedly, it was one I didn't share. I like my humour dry, Colin preferred jokes that were sick. Therefore, I knew it wouldn't offend him if he got his press cuttings copied onto a xerox of someone's willy. Especially if, as I strongly suspected, it was his own middle-wicket. After all, it was Colin who'd introduced a number of the younger men in the firm to that ever popular game known as Cheapskate. The blokes would go out for a drink after work, and having armed themselves with Dutch courage, they'd compete to see who could have sex with a prostitute for the least money. Colin came into work one day claiming that the previous night he'd found a girl who needed the foil from a sweet wrapper to cook up her junk, and so he'd managed to do the business with her for thirty-six pence. Or rather, for a Yorkie. Having been caught shop-lifting from the nearest late-night store, the smack ho was banned from entering it. Colin had bought her the chocolate sweet wrapped in silver foil, and had his evil way for it. Arguments about whether this story was true raged around the office for weeks. Now that a few years had passed, it was the stuff of work place legend.

I knew I couldn't give Colin his photocopies on the spoiled paper. There was a strong probability he'd need to show the clippings to someone else. In any case, when montaged onto the priapic image with which the paper had been defaced, the cuttings were difficult to read. I buzzed Sandy in the stock room. She was out of copier paper and Everything Direct weren't making another delivery for days. She suggested I ask accounts for a few hundred sheets of plain white, since they'd had her last five reams. I knew Sandy was trying to be helpful, but her advice pissed me off. The type of people who worked in accounts would have evicted a stricken toddler from an oxygen tent if their family was ten pence short on a credit repayment. When I'd started at Dreadnought my wages had been held back until some paperwork was sorted out. I was desperate for money but trying to get it out of accounts was like extracting teeth. Everything had to be done by the book or else they'd have the combined force of the tax man, the company directors, the shareholders and every con artist in London on their back. They did, however, suggest that I go to my bank manager and arrange an overdraft. Tight-fisted was too benign a term to describe accounts. There was no way I was going to get a few sheets of paper out of them.

Since I didn't have any money of my own to spend on paper (I'd left my wallet at home, or rather I hoped I'd left my wallet at home because it wasn't in my pocket), the easiest thing to do was pop over to the University Of Cripplegate. The secretaries knew I shared a flat with Captain Swanky, and I told them he'd asked me to go in and fetch him a ream of plain white. Unfortunately, I was seen leaving the Dreadnought building by both June Gregory and our janitor Winston Smith. June gave me a couple of quid to get her a sandwich, while Winston wanted a bottle of cider. That meant a detour via Safeway. The queue at the check out wasn't particularly long, but each of the five people in front of me paid by credit card. Added together what they spent didn't amount to twenty knicker. Plastic made them feel good, saved them the aggravation of ruining the hang of their clothes by weighting themselves down with spare change, while simultaneously assuaging their fears of being mugged. Those who asked for cash back had it counted out in ten pound notes. I suffered a further delay at the University Of Cripplegate. The secretaries had never had a chance to speak to me alone, and they hoped I might be able to resolve their long running speculations about Captain Swanky's sexuality. They were aware that The Captain ogled them, and were deeply puzzled by his inability to make an effective move. Since he was filthy rich, the dolly birds were prepared to overlook some of his more unsavoury qualities. The secretaries had noticed that Swanky spent a lot of time hanging out with a lipstick lesbian. They wanted to know if he was gay, latent or swung both ways. I tried offering them a simple explanation—brewer's droop—but it didn't wash. In the end, I made my getaway by saying The Captain was deejaying at The Purple Haze later that evening, and they'd have all their questions answered by checking out his act.

When I got back to the office, our Time and Motion specialist Ruth wanted to know what I'd been doing. It was nearly four o'clock and I didn't appear to have done any work. I explained that the photocopying paper had been spoiled and I'd had to go out to get more. Ruth insisted I give her a flash of the mysterious member that had caused me so much bother. She thought it a tad on the small size, and insisted on taking the ruined paper away with her. Fortunately Ruth had found the episode sufficiently amusing to overlook the time I'd spent out of the office. That is, on the condition I stayed late to catch up with my work. I checked my voice mail and there were fourteen messages all requiring immediate attention. I should have checked my email when I got in, but I was so behind with everything I decided to leave it until later. As it was, I was unable to get anything done until after most of the staff had gone home. Ruth had passed the photocopied phallus around the office, and one visitor after another passed through my door to speculate on which plonker was responsible for my troubles.

Nowhere To Run

Scapa Loch didn't exist, or rather it didn't exist as it appeared on late twentieth-century maps. There wasn't a large loch or lake in the centre of Hoy, a sparsely populated island off the north coast of Scotland. What had been marked on maps as fresh water was actually an American military listening base with a sixties housing estate abutting it. After the end of the cold war the listening base had been decommissioned, and the spooks and their families who lived in the houses that had been built to service it were deployed elsewhere. There were 138 houses on the estate, plus a pub which had been run by the military and closed down when they moved on. There was also a community hall which had been temporarily decommissioned but was to be reopened now that I'd been installed as the first Scapa Loch Housing Estate artist-in-residence.

Land was cheap in the islands and the estate had been generously laid out with both gardens and trim communal areas. Access onto the housing estate was by Martin Luther King Street, with entry from the east—and since the same patch of tarmac functioned as the exit—escape was to the west. Martin Luther King Street had no housing placed directly on its east-west axis, but half way along this ingress a branch of the

11

road ran to the north, with twenty-two houses flanking it. Immediately south of the non-residential section of Martin Luther King Street was an imposing eight foot high mesh fence, topped with barbed wire and festooned with black lettered notices on white plastic boards. The message they displayed was short and severe: "NO PHOTOGRAPHS. BY ORDER." On the other side of the fence stood the decommissioned listening base, the buildings boarded up but not yet derelict nor dismantled.

At the far end of the non-residential portion of Martin Luther King Street and running northwards from it, was Washington Road. There were six houses on the west side of Washington Road which were divided up between a block of two and a block of four dwellings, all located towards the south end of the street. On the east side there were twenty-four houses in four blocks of six. Running eastwards off Washington Road were two cul-de-sacs each with twelve houses ranged in two blocks of six on either side of the closes; they were named Oswald Court and Ruby Court respectively. The former lay immediately to the north of the latter. Abraham Lincoln Street ran alongside or parallel to the east-west axis of Martin Luther King Street, with one of its three sections strung between Washington Road and the housed and northwardly oriented portion of Martin Luther King Street. Another fragment of Abraham Lincoln Street ran north off the part already described between the housed section of Martin Luther King Street and Washington Road; the other segment bore west parallel with much—but not quite all—of the western portion of the part of Martin Luther King Street that was oriented westwards (in other words, the housing on this section of Abraham Lincoln Street faced the north-western section of the listening base, although since this section of Abraham Lincoln Street came to an abrupt end it would be more accurate to say it faced the eastern half of the north-westerly section of the listening base). There were sixteen semi-detached houses on the more westerly parts of Abraham Lincoln Street, with twelve of these being to the west of the housed section of Martin Luther King Street and four to its east. The remaining eighteen houses on Abraham Lincoln Street were of a different design to those at its western end. There were four blocks of four terraced houses and one block of two semis all similar in design. Some, but not all, of these houses had a utility room built onto the back, creating differences in their external appearances when seen from certain angles. Leaving aside this feature, furnishings and decoration, all the houses were otherwise identical inside.

John F. Kennedy Drive ran from not quite half way-up Washington Road across to not quite half-way up the housed and northwardly facing part of Martin Luther King Street, then after crossing Martin Luther King Street it ran west for one block of semis, before curving south-west for six blocks of semis, then took a sharp turn south for three blocks of semis and finally ended where the street met the far-western extremity of Martin Luther King Street, immediately prior to the point at which the latter allowed cars to enter and/or leave the estate. As well as the twenty semi-detached houses already mentioned, there were six terraced homes on John F. Kennedy Drive located immediately to the east of the northwardly oriented section of Martin Luther King Street. All the houses on John F. Kennedy Drive were on the same side of the street, which apart from the most westerly section of the road, was its south cum south-east side. On the far-western section of the housing estate, this side of John F. Kennedy Drive lay to the

13

east. On a baroque cul-de-sac running northwards off the eastern side of John F. Kennedy Drive, immediately west of Washington Road, was the abandoned Ship Inn. Behind the boarded up pub lay the Scapa Loch Community Hall. This latter structure was to act as the base of my professional operations during the period in which I was artist-in-residence on the Scapa Loch Housing Estate. It made no sense to me, but the pub and community hall were located on a close that was officially considered to be a part of John F. Kennedy Drive. If I'd been responsible for naming the roads, I'd have called this section of the estate Kennedy Close.

Going To A Go-Go

I arrived at The Purple Haze late. I'd gone back to the Stanton Drew Estate to change into my glad rags and get a bite to eat, only to find myself held up. The first thing I'd had to do was open all the windows in the flat. Swanky had obviously been home before me, and he had a habit of leaving unlit gas rings on. As far as I could make out, what happened was that he'd decide to make himself an espresso, put the gas ring on, change his mind before the gas was lit, then go out without remembering to put the gas off. It happened all the time. Swanky had told me he was terrified he was going to walk in one day with a lit fag in his mouth and blow the place up. Fortunately, I didn't smoke and it was usually me who had to sort out the chaos Swanky created. Turning the gas off wasn't a problem, but opening the windows made me a little irate. Mrs. Inconsiderate had dumped a bag of household rubbish and an unwanted carpet onto our balcony. She didn't like leaving her flat, so rather than put waste down the communal chute, Mrs. Inconsiderate would dump it onto my balcony. I cleared up the trash, then headed upstairs to complain. I could hear Mrs. Inconsiderate moving around the flat, but she wouldn't answer the door. I kept shouting at Mrs. Inconsiderate to come and speak to me, but she flatly refused to do so. Her husband was at work, so she phoned up a friend in a neighbouring block and got her friend's husband to come over and accuse me of harassing her. This led to a long and rather heated argument on the landing outside Mrs. Inconsiderate's flat. I tried to explain that I didn't like rubbish being dumped on my balcony, but Mrs. Inconsiderate's family friend was having none of it. In his view, I'd moved up from South London long after the Inconsiderates had established themselves in their flat. Therefore, I had no right to constantly disturb them by hammering on the door.

By the time I got back into my flat, enough air had blown through it to clear the worst of the gas, so I figured it was just about safe to cook my tea. The meal was nothing special, scrambled egg on a couple of slices. I just put a little butter in the pan with the eggs, where most people go wrong is by adding a dash of milk. The best way to make scrambled eggs is without milk. So I had my eggs and I had some coffee. Then I found some Greek yoghurt in the fridge and I ate that too. Having overdone it on the cholesterol, I figured I ought to eat some fruit, so I munched on a peach. I wanted to have a bath but I needed to let what I'd consumed digest, so I slapped a CD entitled *Big In Wigan* onto my hi-fi system and put my feet up. An hour later I was ready for a bath. When I got out of the water I decided to shave. The heat from a hot bath opens up the pores

15

on the skin, which makes the period immediately after bathing the best time to shave. Having shaved, I
found some fresh clothes, and after picking up a bag of
records I was ready to head out.

The Purple Haze is, when all was said and done, a
heavy metal club. Hendrix I could dig, particularly
when he was acting as a talented side-man to soul
acts like the Isley Brothers. Hendrix got played at the
Purple Haze, but the rest of what went down there
was almost exclusively white. Captain Swanky was
behind the decks when I walked into the club and he
was spinning Hawkwind. It seemed like an inevitabil-
ity when this was followed by Black Sabbath. If the
punters were lucky, Swanky might slap something on
by the Stooges or the MC5, but Deep Purple (and I'm
not talking about the band's early pop-psyche recordings circa *Hush* here) was more likely. Those present
were ninety-five per cent male and their average age
must have been around twenty. None of which made
for a particularly pleasant atmosphere. There was too
much testosterone about. I bent the Captain's ear and
he let me take over at the decks. I thought I'd ease
the crowd into something more soulful. I kicked off
with the Johnny Jones and The King Casuals cover
of *Purple Haze*, which with its William Bell production went down pretty well. It was, after all, almost
familiar. Next I tried The Temptations' *Message From
A Black Man*, a superb example of psychedelic soul
crossover. As soon as the vocals kicked in with their
politically conscious message, bottles and cans rained
down on me. The all white crowd were happy enough
to listen to a soul cover of a Hendrix song, but black
power messages were something they simply would not
tolerate. Order wasn't restored until Captain Swanky
slapped *Radar Love* onto the decks.

I don't have a clear memory of the rest of Captain
Swanky's set. As far as metal went he was pretty much
fixated on the seventies, which was when he'd first
got into what might very loosely be called music. It
certainly wouldn't have been an unusual night if he'd
played The Blue Öyster Cult and Judas Priest. What I
did take in, or rather knew from previous visits to The
Purple Haze, was that there was something very wrong
about the club, or at least with its clientele. The kids
who were the mainstay of the place were too young to
remember the dreadful metal sounds of the seventies
from the first time around, but that was what they dug.
The Purple Haze didn't cater for those who wanted to
hear speed metal, or thrash metal, or death metal, or
black metal. Sure you'd hear at least one Motörhead
track most nights, and that must have been the beginnings of the punk metal crossover (at least if you're not
trying to make a case for reviving releases by the likes
of the Groundhogs or Third World War). Motörhead
got played because they'd evolved from Hawkwind, but
you wouldn't hear Iron Maiden. The whole idea of the
club was to go back to the original hard rock sound of
yesteryear. However, the punters weren't dressed as if
punk had never happened, Instead of the denim jackets
that had dominated the seventies heavy scene, most of
those present were geared up in leathers, and they also
had tattoos and piercings. The main thing that differen-
tiated this crowd from twentieth generation goths and
punks was the fact that they really didn't have haircuts.
Their barnets were a freeform nightmare of dandruff,
and an utter lack of grooming. The hair at The Purple
Haze hadn't been teased into mohawks or silly fringes,
on the whole it hadn't even been dyed. It simply hung
limply down shoulders and over backs. It was about
the only thing that those present had got right in their

attempts to recreate the anti-sartorial inelegance of an authentic seventies hard rock crowd.

When Swanky finished his set, his co-promoters hauled both of us into a back room where they proceeded to rant about the disco shit I'd tried to play. Explaining that neither Johnny Jones nor The Temptations were disco acts proved fruitless. The heavy metal assholes who worked alongside Captain Swanky appeared utterly incapable of appreciating the difference between CJ & Co. and Jimmy McGriff. For these bozos, disco was a term of abuse and they applied it indiscriminately to any black musician who didn't play Hendrix-style guitar licks. Calling what I'd spun disco was simply a shorthand way of suggesting I should be banned from their club. The Captain, who I thought might stand up for me since he underwrote the ongoing losses The Purple Haze was sustaining, wasn't even interested in debating the matter. Swanky has never been one to take a position on important issues and since by this time his friend Jasmine had shown up like a proverbial bad penny, it didn't surprise me when I was barred from the venue. Jasmine, I should perhaps explain, doesn't like me. She is what used to be known as a lipstick lesbian, and she sure as hell had The Captain pussy whipped. Jasmine slept with Swanky, she rolled around in bed with Swanky, she snogged Swanky, but she insisted she was gay, so she wouldn't have penetrative sex with Swanky. Jasmine stayed at our flat five nights out of seven and she was constantly complaining about my presence. In her opinion, I ought to go and find some other place to live. Since Jasmine was always happiest when she didn't see me, once she was on the scene, my being banned from The Purple Haze was a forgone conclusion. I walked out of the club and straight into some night time refugees from Dreadnought Insurance.

Colin from Marketing was ushering Mr. Martin around various Shoreditch lapdancing joints, whilst simultaneously assuring him that the entertainment was every bit as good as that found in the West End but it came at a fraction of the price. Although Colin knew where to find strippers, Mr. Martin had become intrigued by the music the girls used for their performances, and the man from Marketing looked blank when asked to name the tunes. Once the two men spotted me, I was dragged along to Brown's. I refused to go inside because Colin would put it around the office that I'd taken part in their girl crawl and thereby ruin my chances of getting a date with June. So we stood on the street outside Brown's and I was pretty amazed by what I heard. The girls appeared to be dancing to *Holy Magick* by Graham Bond, which is like Sun Ra crossed with Aleister Crowley at a happy Hammond party. I explained to Mr. Martin that Bond had started off playing rhythm and blues with Jack Bruce and Ginger Baker before they joined Cream. Later on, Bond got a little weird and he'd made some records for punters interested in the occult including *Holy Magick*. It had, of course, all ended tragically for Bond in 1974, when he died under the wheels of a London Underground train.

Once I'd promised to make tapes of my Graham Bond records for Mr. Martin, I was led south down Shoreditch High Street. There seemed to be some kind of bizarre jazz funk revival going on in most of the strip joints. Standing in the street outside the Rainbow Sports Bar I discovered the girls were dancing to Eddie Harris. We headed for the White Horse and I explained that what Mr. Martin could hear was Herbie Mann's classic 1969 soul jazz crossover album *Memphis Underground* (the title track had been widely covered, and my favourite versions were by S.O.U.L. and the J. J. All Stars). At The Norfolk Village I identified the body odour boogies as the psychedelic soul jazz guitar sound of Boogaloo Joe Jones. Moving on to The Crown & Shuttle, I found that the girls were stripping to Richard "Groove" Holmes. Colin wanted to hurry on to The Ten Bells, but I told Mr. Martin to give it a miss. The girls got their kit off with Jack The Ripper memorabilia plastered across the walls behind them. It was too tacky for a man of Mr. Martin's refined tastes. Mr. Martin decided to call it a night and hailed a taxi, I decided to go home. Colin went to look for crack hos in Wentworth Street.

It Hurts So Good

I'd been allocated a three bedroom house on Martin Luther King Street. There was a spacious porch running across the left half of the building as one faced it, and it was through this that I entered the dwelling. Behind the porch was a hallway, which provided access to a water closet and the stairs by which one reached the first floor. The downstairs of the house had been built on an open plan design and there was no door between the hallway and the living area to my right, which was light and spacious since it ran the entire length of the building and had windows at both the front and the rear. I had to pass through the living room and veer left to get into the kitchen, which was located immediately behind the water closet and the stairs. As I've already said, the downstairs was laid out on an open plan design, so there was no door between the living area and the kitchen. The kitchen was spacious and fitted with modern units, with plenty of cupboard space and ample work top areas. The cooker was electric with two ovens and ceramic hobs. A back door gave access to the rear garden, which like that to the front and on the free standing side, was turfed.

The master bedroom upstairs was, as I expected, at the front of the house. The window was on the opposite side of the front wall to the porch. It was ranged symmetrically above the front living room window. The room had two built-in cupboards, the smaller one being beside the door, utilising space that if it had not been blocked off by plasterboard would have run continuously with the built-in cupboard in the second bedroom. The master bedroom had been allocated one-third of the total built-in cupboard space that had been divided between these two rooms. The second and third bedrooms only had a single built-in cupboard, whereas the master bedroom had two. The other built-in cupboard, which ran between the front facing wall and the bathroom, was considerably larger than the cupboard by the door. The bathroom was installed with a three piece white suite consisting of a bath, wash basin and water closet. There was a shower curtain that could be drawn on a rail around the bath, and a shower that had been built into the white tiling that ran from the tip of the bath to the ceiling.

The main walls of the property were of cavity concrete block construction. A damp proof course was incorporated within the dwelling, as was adequate sub-floor ventilation. The roof was of pitched timber construction externally clad in concrete interlocking tiles with tiled ridging and cement skews. The gutters were black and of modern PVC design. The windows were of white uPVC sealed unit double glazed design.

There were thirteen-amp power outlets throughout the house, with metering for the system located in an external wall box. Space and water heating was provided by a full oil-fired system. The modern insulated hot water cylinder was located within a hall cupboard. The radiators of the central heating system were served with copper piping and there was a wall-mounted boiler in the kitchen. Access to the loft was via a hatch in the upper hallway. The internal walls were of timber stud overlaid in plasterboard, the ceilings of plasterboard throughout. The flooring was of suspended timber construction. The internal doors were of timber, the external doors of glazed timber.

The walls throughout the house had been papered with wood chip and painted in various shades of orange and brown. There were fake paper dado rails in both hallways and all the rooms, except the bathroom and kitchen. The curtains and furniture were of traditional chequered design, and rendered in clashing shades of canary yellow and lime green. There were table lights in each of the bedrooms, and side lighting to illuminate various work surfaces in the kitchen. The illumination in the living area consisted of two overhead hundred-watt bulbs that were barely covered by frilly pink shades. There was a hi-fi system in the living room, comprising of CD, speakers, amp and tape deck. A half-dozen CDs had been stacked beside it—popular orchestral selections of Mozart, Beethoven and Brahms, alongside hit collections by The Beatles, The Beach Boys and Abba. There was a wide screen television with a VCR beneath it, and three factory sealed blank video cassettes. Fortunately the fridge was empty, and the kitchen cupboards and draws contained only utensils and crockery. When I put away the food I'd brought with me, I was half afraid I'd find that scampi ready meals had been left out waiting for me.

"I think you'll be happy here," Jim Fletcher, the man employed by Retro-Americana (Suburban) Homes to site manage this particular estate, beamed. We shook hands and Jim strode out of the house, leaving me alone to settle into my new home and my new role as Scapa Loch Housing Estate artist-in-residence. Since Fletcher appeared to know nothing about culture, I had few worries about him working out that I was not exactly the man he took me to be.

Singing In The Rain

I got back home not long after midnight. I was tired and felt like going to bed, but there wasn't any point. My neighbours constantly disturbed me, and the gang of teenagers who hung out on the estate were being particularly noisy. I could tell they were hopped up on drugs. The youths were annoying at the best of times, they lived on a neighbouring estate and came onto ours because it enabled them to misbehave without their parents knowing about it. They liked to speed, and when doing sulphate the boys in question were particularly snotty. They were deep into an argument about a mobile phone. They probably wouldn't have viewed what was going on as an argument, more like horseplay. One youngster had shown another his mobile, and now it was being passed around the gang with the owner becoming increasingly anxious to get it back.

"Give me my mobile!"

"Fuck you, man!"

"Give me my mobile!"

"Fuck you, man!"

A window opened: "Could you be quiet?"

"We're not disturbing anyone!"

"Yeah, there's no need to shout at us!"

"Yeah, fuck you man!"

"Yeah, fuck you!"

The window closed and the argument went on.

"Give me my mobile!"

"Fuck you, man!"

"Give me my mobile!"

"Fuck you, man!"

Then the door to one of the blocks opened: "I'll fucking kill you if you damage my car! You're leaning on my fucking car! I'll fucking kill you!"

"What car?"

"That fucking silver car! I'll fucking kill you if you touch my car!"

"We haven't touched your car!"

"What car?"

"That silver car. Look at all the marks on my car! If you go near my car again, I'll fucking kill you!"

"Fuck you, man!"

"I'll fucking kill you!"

"Give me my mobile!"

"Fuck you, man!"

"Give me my mobile!"

"Fuck you, man!"

"You touched my fucking car!"

"Fuck you, man!"

"I'll fucking kill you!"

"Give me my mobile!"

"Fuck you, man!"

"Give me my mobile!"

"Fuck you, man!"

"He fucking hit me!"

"Let go of me you cunt!"

"I'll fucking have the lot of you!"

"Fucking hell!"

"Fuck!"

The sounds died away. The door to one of the blocks slammed. The teenagers had left the estate at a remarkably early hour by anyone's standards. Aside from loud music, revving car engines, the sounds of domestic ultra-violence and children crying, the estate was almost peaceful. It was too good to last.

"We're nearly there Michelle," the woman who said this had a voice like a fog-horn.

"I can't go on mum."

"Lean on me Michelle, we're nearly there."

"I'm freezing mum."

"We're nearly there."

Five minutes later, there was the sound of the bell ringing on a neighbouring block.

"Daniel! Daniel!

25

Daniel! Daniel! Daniel! Daniel! Daniel! Daniel! Daniel!
Daniel! Daniel! Daniel! Daniel! Daniel! Daniel! Daniel!
Daniel! Daniel! Daniel! Daniel! Daniel! Daniel! Daniel!
Daniel! Daniel! Daniel! Daniel! Daniel! Daniel! Daniel!
Daniel! Daniel! Daniel! Daniel! Daniel! Daniel! Daniel!
Daniel! Daniel! Daniel! Daniel! Daniel! Daniel! Daniel!
Daniel! Daniel! Daniel!"

"He's not in Michelle."

"Daniel! Daniel! Daniel! Daniel! Daniel! Daniel!"

I could hear the sound of the bell being rung, and someone pounding on the door to the neighbouring block with their fists.

"Daniel! Daniel! Daniel! Daniel! Daniel! Daniel! Damn you, damn you, damn you, Daniel!"

"He's not in Michelle. They're out fucking them slags."

"Damn you, damn you, damn you, Daniel!"

"They're out fucking them whores."

"Damn you, damn you, damn you, Daniel!"

"He's not in Michelle. They're out fucking them slags."

"Daniel! Daniel! Daniel! Daniel! Daniel! Daniel!"

"They're out fucking them whores."

"Damn you, damn you, damn you, Daniel!"

"We should have stayed in the fucking pub. We could be having another fucking drink."

"I'm freezing mum."

"We should have stayed in the fucking pub, Michelle. At least we'd be fucking warm."

"Daniel! Daniel! Daniel! Daniel! Daniel! Daniel!"

"He's not in Michelle. They're out fucking them slags. We should have stayed in the fucking pub. We could be having another fucking drink. He's your fucking boyfriend. Why hasn't he given you a set of fucking keys? They're out fucking them slags."

"Damn you, damn you, damn you, Daniel!"

"We should have stayed in the fucking pub. We could be having another fucking drink."

"I'm freezing mum!"

"We should have stayed in the fucking pub. At least we'd be fucking warm."

"Damn you, damn you, damn you, Daniel, damn!"

"Michelle, oh Michelle, you've fallen over Michelle."

"I'm freezing mum!"

"Let me get you up."

"Daniel! Daniel! Daniel! Daniel! Daniel! Daniel!"

"Michelle, you're all wet Michelle. You've fallen in a fucking puddle. Let me get you up."

"I'm freezing mum."

"Here, have my coat. Oh Michelle, you're all wet. We should have stayed in the fucking pub. At least we'd be fucking warm. We could be having a fucking drink."

"Daniel! Daniel! Daniel! Daniel! Daniel! Daniel!"

"Where's your fucking mobile. I'll fucking call someone. Tell me the number of one of your fucking friends. Oh Michelle answer me. You must know somebody's fucking number. We should have stayed in the fucking pub. At least we could be having a fucking drink. Tell me somebody's fucking number so that I can fucking call them."

"Daniel! Daniel! Daniel! Daniel! Daniel! Daniel!"

"Hello, is that the police? I've come down from Clacton to see my daughter and we're locked out of her boyfriend's flat. I know this isn't an emergency. I know I'm not supposed to dial 999 unless it's an emergency, but we're cold and we're locked out of my daughter's flat. My daughter's only nineteen and we can't get in. Can't you send someone down to help us get in? Yes, I know I could have phoned the local police station but

I didn't know the number. Yes. Okay, yes. Look, yes, I'm sorry."

"Daniel! Daniel! Daniel! Daniel! Daniel! Daniel!"

"Oh Michelle, you've fallen over."

"Damn you, damn you, damn you, Daniel!"

"We should have stayed in the fucking pub. We could be having another fucking drink. They're out fucking them slags. They're out fucking them whores. I should have fucking stayed in Clacton. I'm not coming to fucking London again. We should have stayed in the fucking pub. We could be having another fucking drink. Why did you fucking move to London? Why didn't you fucking stay in Clacton? They're out fucking them whores. They're out fucking them slags. They're fucking them whores."

"Damn you, damn you, damn you, Daniel! Damn you, damn you, damn you, Daniel! Damn you, damn you, damn you, Daniel! Damn you, damn you, damn you, Daniel!"

"They're out fucking them whores. They're out fucking them slags."

And so the drunken conversation continued for the next three hours. Call me sad if you like, but after about an hour curiosity got the better of me and I twitched the nets. Michelle was a big girl in a short skirt. Her hair was long and dyed honey blonde. When I first looked she was pounding the bonnet of a car with her fists, then she toppled off the bonnet and rolled into a puddle. Michelle's mother had shorter hair and a peroxide bleach.

She looked about forty and had the beginnings of a stoop. She tried to pull her daughter out of the rain water, but Michelle appeared determined to wrestle with the puddle. Eventually, two meat wagons and a squad car pulled onto the estate. Michelle was arrested. Her mother had to ride to the police station in a separate vehicle. Shortly afterwards Captain Swanky arrived home with Jasmine. He slapped the first Led Zeppelin album onto our shared record deck and proceeded to party. I gave it about five minutes, then went through to the living room.

"It's half past four in the fucking morning, you're disturbing the neighbours, turn that down."

"If it bothered anybody, they'd complain."

"Yeah, why are you always hassling The Captain?" Jasmine put in. "You're a killjoy. You ought to find somewhere else to live. The Captain deserves this place to himself. He doesn't need to put up with a creep like you."

The conversation was killed by a knock on the door. One of the neighbours had come around to complain about the noise. I let Swanky deal with it. He'd created the problem. I went to bed. I had to make the most of the few chances there were of getting any kip.

I Know The Score

The Scapa Loch Housing Estate was being sold off in eight phases, with new home owners moving into sections of demilitarised property while other portions were still being refurbished. I was being paid from a mixture of private and public money to make the entire proposition more attractive now that the sales were entering their penultimate phase, and there were still a fair number of properties remaining unsold from earlier stages. Fortunately workmen were still about to help me with the realisation of my art pieces. To be honest, I couldn't really see how an artist-in-residence would attract buyers from the project's natural constituency, the skilled working class. There was little work on Hoy, and while the houses were being sold for not much more than the annual salary of an ordinary school teacher, their main appeal was to those who had already retired or for men working at the oil refinery on the neighbouring island of Flotta. It was a beautiful home base for family men working in the oil industry. Given the lack of interest I expected to encounter from the new home owners on the estate, I'd built various web projects into my residency. The developers Retro-Americana (Suburban) Homes had liked this, because they thought it was a way of attracting potential buyers from around the world. For my alter-ego it was a means of ensuring he was attracting at least one constituency (even if it was virtual) that had some interest in what I was doing on his behalf. My work was, of course, being monitored by those who were paying for it, but that didn't mean they had any real commitment to the artistic projects from which I'd be scamming a living. There were forms to be completed, and they were explicitly designed to ensure I didn't sit on my backside supping whisky.

The first piece of work I attended to once I was installed in the job, was putting up a metal sign at the entrance to the estate which read: "Welcome To The USA. America is a state of mind, not a geographical location." A couple of workmen called Billy and Mark were assigned to assist me, and I directed them as they erected the sign. Once we'd finished, I invited Billy and Mark back to my place for a cup of tea.

"What's it all aboot then?" Billy asked.

"What?" I queried.

"That sign we just put up, what's it all aboot?"

"Surely it's obvious," I replied.

"It may be obvious to you pal, but it isnae to me."

"Well," I said and then I paused to think through how I might explain this. "We're all Americans now, or at least we're all a product of the Black Atlantic, we all have a stake in modernity and America is the Utopia of modernity."

"I'm nae sure I follow pal."

"Well isn't that the perennial problem of the artist, the problem of expressing himself, of communicating beyond the immediate milieu of his peers and making himself understood?"

"I'm nae with you pal."

"What, you don't care to immerse yourself in the problems of the artist?"

"It's not that, it's that I cannae understand what you're saying."

"Artists cannot make themselves understood."

"Well, I can nae understand what you're saying."

"But that's what I just said is the perennial problem of the artist, that you cannot understand them."

"Aye, but why would that be a problem, it's nae like I go to art galleries or buy paintings. Why is it a problem for artists if I can nae understand them?"

"America," I said, "America gave us rock and roll."

"Aye."

"And if we didn't have rock and roll, then not only America, but the British Isles, even Orkney and Hoy, would be a very different place."

"Aye, I can see that. My grandson, he's not yet a year old, but he loves it when my daughter plays U2. Billy, he's called Billy because my daughter named him after me, loves U2."

"Listen to this," I said and I put on Pucho & The Latin Soul Brothers.

"Aye," Billy said, "aye, nae bad but I prefer The Beatles."

Let's Groove

I wouldn't have been late arriving at my desk if June Gregory hadn't stopped me on my way in. June was excited because Mr. Martin had promised he was going to make everyone in the office rich if they joined his lottery syndicate. I told June not to waste her money and the upset this caused was what really delayed me. When I got to my work station, Ruth from Time and Motion was sitting on my desk, she seemed to have a real downer on me.

"You're late, and what's more, you're late for work. This isn't a kindergarten or a play group, this isn't a college or an art school. You don't need to tell me what you've been doing because I know how you waste your time. You've been in the Cut Price Music Store, and you've probably also been in Golden Grooves, come to think of it, it's more than likely you've been wasting your breath talking about northern soul with that bloke Dave from St. Albans, who doesn't even have a shop, only a stall."

"Ruth," I said, "I've been doing all those things, but in my own time. I got into the building before two, I just haven't been at my desk."

"Not at your desk? I don't see how you can get any work done if you're not at your desk. What's more you've wasted your lunch time on records when you could have gone out for a light meal with a lonely woman like me."

"Well, I'm sure there are lots of people in the office you could go to lunch with, there's Colin from Marketing, he's always looking for people to wine, dine and sixty-nine."

"Colin! Colin! I wouldn't be seen dead with that man! Now since you claim to have been in the building on time, what have you been doing?"

"June on reception stopped me on my way up, she had some questions about the press archive!"

"More likely she was holding your hand and asking for a lunch date! I hate that trendy little trollop. I'm sure she's had implants, her breasts and bottom can't be that large naturally. I'm issuing you with a formal warning about slackness. You're being watched: screw up again and you'll be out of a job."

As I was receiving this warning, Colin from Marketing walked in. He had his usual shit eating grin on his face, but it seemed to get broader as he took in what was happening.

"Okay John," Colin said once Ruth had left, "I've some important and secret things to ask you, they require discretion. I want you to come along to the toilets with me, so we can pass notes under the divides between the cubicles."

"Couldn't we do it by email."

"Not secure enough."

"We could encrypt the messages."

"No way, the programmers who make the encryption software are employed by criminal gangs who are immediately alerted to the fact that whatever it is you're saying, it is well worth their while taking a look at it."

"How do you know."

"It said so in the hacking section at the back of Women's Wear Weekly."

"Why would Women's Wear Weekly run a hacking section?"

"It provides a lot of the nancy boys who buy the magazine with a legitimate excuse for making a purchase, while pretending to their friendly neighbourhood newsagent that their interest is in computing rather than flouncy underwear."

"So when you're out curb crawling, have you got silk panties on underneath your business suit?"

"Certainly not, I'm interested in computers, and to make male purchases of their journal credible to newsagents and suspicious wives, Women's Wear Weekly now runs the best hacking section to be found in any commercially published magazine."

So off we went to the toilet without so much as a further word about flouncy underwear, and the first note I got read as follows: "I've been having an affair with June Gregory and beneath her demure exterior she is into really wild sex. She wants to know if you'd let her sit on your face while I put on her silk slip and panties, and after I've watched you bring June to orgasm while simultaneously jerking myself off, June and I could then take it in turns to suck you off? Whoever got you to come in their mouth would then have the pleasure of pissing in your gob. I know it's sick, but this is the sort of thing June is into and having got my dirty hands on her, I just can't keep them off. Indeed, she got me and Mr. Martin to do the very thing I'm now asking you to do."

The idea that June was screwing Colin and Mr. Martin was so unlikely that it might just be true. I needed time to think about this and said so to Colin.

"Give me time to think." I said.

"You're not supposed to talk, you should have slipped a note under the divide."

"Sorry, I forgot."

"Okay, but if you need time, I'll have to go and make an urgent phone call. I want you to stay here, I'll be back in ten minutes."

I waited twenty minutes and Colin still hadn't returned, and by this time I figured I really ought to get out of the toilet and back to my work station. Ruth from Time and Motion was standing outside the door.

"Colin alerted me to the fact that you were hiding in the toilets to avoid doing any work. I know you've been in there for at least twenty minutes, and that is considerably longer than calls of nature require. I gave you a warning earlier this afternoon. Now you're fired."

I'd been set up. On my way out of the building June asked me what had happened. I explained and she slapped me across the face.

"I thought you were a nice boy, the type I might marry, but you're sick if you'd believe I'd have a three-in-a-bed romp with Colin and Mr. Martin."

Shaky Ground

The centrepiece of what was in all but name my exhibition at the Scapa Loch Community Hall was a huge white-on-white canvas, onto which I'd sprayed a dollar sign in white. The dollar sign was visible but thanks to the way I'd organised the lighting, would be missed by a casual observer. The title of the show was Comparative Vandalism, I wanted to illustrate the shortcomings of the many recent physical attacks on works of art, and simultaneously provide pointers as to how the quality of cultural hooliganism might be improved.

"What's it all about then?" Steve Smith asked as he pointed at my anti-Malevich. Smith was one of my neighbours in Martin Luther King Street.

"Well," I said. Then I paused to take a deep breath before plunging in: "The problem with vandalising art is it tends to reinforce the idea that it is the works themselves, rather than the complex process of their emergence from a network of social relations, that should be our primary concern. To vandalise an art work is to revalorise it, since within the gallery system physical attacks on objects function as a kind of anti-potlatch, whereby partial destruction draws attention to their value and brings into play the repressive apparatus of art restoration."

"I don't understand, and I don't see what its got to do with the picture I asked you about. As far as I can see, you've primed a canvas but you've yet to actually paint anything. I like looking at pictures, myself."

"What I've done is make a copy of Malevich's famous white on white painting Suprematism, a classic piece of Russian avant-gardism from the nineteen-twenties. Then I've..."

"But I don't get what that has to do with vandalism," Smith interrupted.

"I was just about to move on to vandalism. You see there is this contemporary Russian artist involved in ethical avant-gardism called Alexander Brenner, who as a gesture of disillusionment with all political systems returned to Moscow from Israel, where he'd emigrated with his seventeen year-old girlfriend."

"How old is this guy if he's got a seventeen year-old girlfriend?"

"I dunno, but he's not teenage, he's a good deal older than seventeen."

"Are you sure his girlfriend is only seventeen?"

"Well, I heard she was only seventeen. It's probably gossip, it's more likely she is twenty-three but looks seventeen."

"Seventeen! Jesus fucking Christ, you artists have all the luck! Even if I wasn't married, I'm sure no girl that age would be interested in me. Getting a twenty-three year-old girlfriend would be a real stroke of luck for any of the guys I work with at the oil refinery on Flotta. There's a load of us moved up here for the jobs and money, and our wives aren't getting any younger you know. But even if I was back home in London, I'm sure I couldn't pull a seventeen year-old bird."

"Anyway, Brenner is famous for going into the Stedeljik Museum in Amsterdam and spraying a green dollar bill sign onto Malevich's *Suprematism* as a gesture against the commodification of art."

"What! You mean that's all you have to do to get a seventeen year-old girlfriend? I could do that! A three year-old could do it!"

"What I'm suggesting here is that Brenner would have done better to spray a white dollar sign on the famous white on white painting. It would have been more subtle, the damage would have been very hard to reproduce in newspaper photographs, thereby avoiding valorising the very thing he wanted to decommodify. So I've remade his vandalism in my *Suprematism After Brenner (Modification)*, by spraying white on the white on white. By doing this I'm simultaneously materialising the fake invisibility of the working class after the collapse of Bolshevism in the former Eastern bloc. Clearly, this is a higher form of vandalism and the...."

"Have you got a can of green spray paint?" Smith asked.

"Yes," I said, "I'll get it for you if you want, but what are you intending to do?"

"Well if this Brenner chap can get a seventeen year-old girlfriend by spraying a white painting with a dollar sign, I don't see why I shouldn't get to shack up with a twenty-year old art history student if I vandalise your white on white with a green pound sign. I'm sick of family life, the wife drives me nuts with her nagging, and I don't rate my chances of winning the pools that highly. This could be my passport to pussy heaven."

"I don't think so."

"What do you mean you don't think so? Are you going to call the cops if I spray a pound sign over your painting? I thought you were into vandalism."

"It's not that, the problem is I'm not particularly famous and my paintings aren't worth very much. It's unlikely I'll ever sell *Suprematism After Brenner* because very few art collectors pass through Hoy. However, for insurance purposes the painting is valued at a thousand pounds. I'd love you to vandalise it, because I'd get an insurance pay out and maybe a paragraph or two as a news story in Art Monthly."

"Okay, I'll vandalise the painting, if you'll split the insurance money with me."

So we shook hands, and I left the building, since I was worried that if I hung around and witnessed the vandalism without intervening then it would have constituted fraud. Nevertheless, I was pleased that despite Smith's difficulties in understanding my work, through discussion we had eventually found common ground and common interests. Proof indeed that even in the twenty-first century sham artists could still communicate with members of all social classes, if—and it is a big if—after the butchery of the previous century art still had anything left to say.

No Money Down

What with the value of metal plummeting, these days if you want a motor scrapped, instead of being paid a few quid for your wreck, you have to part with a score to get it crushed. That and the couldn't-give-a-toss culture which superseded the welfare state, meant that London was littered with abandoned cars. Perhaps rather unsurprisingly, these bangers don't end up in the more desirable parts of town, instead most are to be found where there is run down social housing. So clapped out Fords and dumped stolen cars were considered among the best toys going by many of the kids on the Stanton Drew Estate. I looked out of the kitchen window. Ten teenagers were standing at the entrance to the block opposite mine arguing, while some younger kids were pushing an abandoned car around the green in front of my flat.

There was a boy in the drivers' seat of the wreck, and one in the front passenger seat. Another kid was sitting on the bonnet, and there were a couple on the roof. Other juveniles were pushing the car from behind and both sides, while yet more were running around the moving vehicle. The driver decided it would be fun to crash the car into the wall of a neighbouring block, fortunately the kids on top of the car didn't look like they were too badly hurt when they fell off the roof. One boy was nearly crushed between the car and the wall, but he got out at the last minute. There was a lot of laughing and the teenagers said something to the younger boys which I didn't catch. Not long after the children and youths had disappeared, I went out and slashed the tyres on the wreck. A couple of teenagers sloped around the corner of the block as I finished my work.

"You're such a bastard, you always want to ruin everyone's fun."

"Yeah, you're a batty man, I know shit leaks out of your arse and makes a mess of your pants!" the second put in.

I ignored them and went back to my flat. I called up the council to tell them to get rid of the wreck, but knew from experience this might take them weeks or months. They rarely did anything about abandoned cars until they'd been burnt out. At least if the kids were unable to push the car around, there was less chance of one of them getting injured.

The car was set alight a few hours after I'd deflated the tyres, badly damaging one of the uPVC double glazed windows it had been rammed beneath. It was more than a month before the wreck was removed.

Crumbs Off The Table

I fell out with Steve Smith a few weeks after he vandalised my *Suprematism After Brenner (Modification)*. There were a couple of things that had really pissed him off. Firstly, when the insurance payment came through he was incensed that I only gave him £250. I explained that under the conditions of my residency any proceeds of sales I made from work created at Scapa Loch were to be split fifty-fifty between me and my employers. The terms of my contract stated that for legal purposes insurance payments made against damaged art were to be treated as sales. Since the painting was valued at £1000, I received a £500 cut of this, which I split with Smith. He grumbled that he wouldn't have risked going to jail for £250, but took the cash and continued speaking to me. The vandalism didn't make the art press, although it was reported on local radio news.

What really offended Smith was the interest my *Bedtime With Adam* performances were attracting. These pushed forward the critique of an art student couple who'd entered The Tate and had a romp on Tracy Emin's *Bed* when it was on display as a Turner Prize candidate. Under instructions from my employers, I had my romps with Adam when the Scapa Loch Community Hall was closed. However, I was allowed to display written documentation of what I was doing, and Adam—my blow up sex doll—was left sprawled across the bed at all times, with dried semen clearly visible around his mouth and backside. Although there was a media black out on what I was doing, news of my performances quickly spread around the highlands and islands, and people from all over the place began beating a path to the Scapa Loch Community Hall. Smith was present when three teenage girls turned up to see "the gay sex art freak"—as I was now known locally—for themselves.

"What's the matter, don't you like girls?" a redhead asked as she grabbed my nuts and squeezed them hard, before adding: "I'm much better than a male sex dolly. Ooh, I think I feel the beginnings of an erection!"

"Don't turn your back on him," a brunette put in, "or he'll be straight up your bottom!"

"I like girls!" Smith pouted as he moved towards us with a leer on his face.

"You would, you dirty old man," a blonde snapped.

"We're queer converters," the redhead cackled, "we're not interested in smelly straight men like you, so fuck off."

Smith did as he was told and never spoke to me again.

"Girls, girls," I said seizing an opportunity to extricate myself from what could have become a sticky situation, "you've got me all wrong, Let's go back to my place, so that I can shag the lot of you."

"But I thought you liked men!" the redhead said as she removed her hand from my crotch.

"I think you're mistaking cultural hooliganism for reality," I shot back, "because what I'm doing here is suggesting ways in which critiques of art can be made more effective. To me it is a matter of indifference whether I'm making love to a male or a female sex doll. At the end of the day it is only a piece of latex. The point is real human communication is impossible in art galleries where culture is treated as an adjunct to profit capitalism. Attempting to bring warm and loving human relations into a museum is a mistake, what I'm doing is showing the essential inhumanity of the art system."

"But I thought you were a faggot," the redhead objected.

"Yeah, aren't you supposed to be a shirt-lifter?" the blonde added redundantly.

"A shit stabber," the brunette echoed.

"But isn't that the fundamental problem of the artist, the fact that their work is misunderstood and misrepresented as a direct consequence of its commodification?"

"You mean," the redhead lisped incredulously, "that both you and your mate like girls?"

"Yes," I replied.

With that, the three teenagers ran screaming from the Community Hall.

Wicky Wacky

I went to see the Welfare people and told them my business had failed. They said I was self-employed as a freelance librarian and that the only way my business could fail was if I'd not been out hustling work. In other words, I'd voluntarily given up my employment and therefore I wasn't entitled to any benefits. I had to pay the rent, so I pawned my collection of *Buffy The Vampire Slayer* DVDs and my grandmother's jewellery. After this, I had money to eat but I needed more, so I continued looking for work. In the end I landed on the night shift at a cuttings agency just off Shoreditch High Street. My job was simple and tedious, I had to watch various editions of each day's television news which were recorded on video—terrestrial, digital, satellite—and if any one of a long list of specified clients was mentioned in a news story, I had to make a transcript of the piece. Everything was going smoothly, until the Time and Motion expert turned up at the tail end of my third shift. It was Ruth from Dreadnought Insurance.

"What are you doing here?" I asked her.

"Moonlighting, or rather taking on a second job, if I hadn't we'd end up financially stretched getting the bigger house we'll need when I have your babies."

"What do you mean when you have my babies?"

"Well, if I don't have your babies, you'll be out of another job because I'm the Time and Motion expert here now and if I say you're not pulling your weight you'll be sacked."

So on my first night off I had a candle lit dinner with Ruth in Brick Lane, then we travelled by train to her two bedroom semi in the suburbs. Everything seemed to be going smoothly until I tried to undress her.

"I'll do mine, you get your own clothes off," and immediately after saying it, Ruth flipped the light switch.

After I'd got under the blankets with Ruth, I ran my hands down her body, She still had her T-shirt and panties on.

"Well then," Ruth said, "aren't you going to do it?"

There didn't seem to be any point in explaining that one didn't just do it without foreplay. I turned over onto my side. It was a long and sleepless night. I got home early the next morning, knowing I needed to find a new job.

Raise Your Hand

I'd established a rapport with Diana who lived across the road from me. We'd sit on her porch and watch the world go by. Not that there was much to look at. You didn't see many people on Martin Luther King Street. Mainly it was cars passing by, they were heading to the harbour where the male driver—it usually was a male driver—would catch a ferry to the Flotta oil refinery. You had the odd woman out walking a dog, and kids riding around and around the Scapa Loch Housing Estate on bicycles. I'd sit with Diana on her porch and we'd drink beer and wine, or sometimes I'd drink whisky and Diana would drink gin. We'd get drunk and we'd talk.

"I used to have this friend who was gay," I said, and as I said it I knew I was inebriated.

"A lot of people think you're a bender, Tony," Diana interrupted. At first I thought she'd said on a bender, but as she proceeded I realised my mistake: "the lack of sexual interest you show in women, even when both you and they are tipsy, leads me to suspect that, like my brother-in-law, you are indeed a friend of Dorothy."

Since I'd moved to Hoy there had been mornings of beer, followed by afternoons of wine. I'd made fewer art works than most professional artists, but I had drunk far more than the average pisshead. There had been whole days devoted to drunkenness, indeed, I had lost all track of time.

"You wouldn't choose to kill yourself in that way," I was trying to pick up the lost thread of our conversation. "Can you recall the details of how Stephen Milligan died? I remember the James Rushbridger case better. Rushbridger tied his feet together and he had straps on his hands. He put a rope around his neck and leant forward, and once he got past the point of no return, he couldn't regain his balance, and he quite deliberately went slowly forward and topped himself. It was suicide in a gas mask and oil skins."

"Milligan, Milligan, I remember Milligan," Diana was doing her level best to engage with me despite being sozzled. "Milligan, turned up at The Whipping Club, didn't he. I used to tell Charlie I was going to see my father and I'd go to The Whipping Club instead. Yes, Milligan is living on John F. Kennedy Drive and Rushbridger is in Ruby Court. We met at those sado-masochistic clubs, but I didn't want to bow out of public life with a segment of orange in my mouth. I chose a car crash for my fake death, because I wanted to become an icon of the modern age like John F. Kennedy and Jayne Mansfield. As for Milligan and Rushbridger, all they wanted was to disappear."

"Did they?"

"Yeah," Diana spat, "we got the idea the night we saw that funny American man singing at the club, what was his name? Boyd Rice, I think. He was supposed to play a concert in Clapham and it got cancelled because anti-fascist protesters threatened to bomb it, so he played a secret gig at The Whipping Club instead, and it was that night we all decided to fake our deaths and disappear. The establishment wanted us out of the way so they were very happy to help. We were an embarrassment, me much more than the others."

"Didn't a judge or someone die at that club, some bloke aged about sixty?"

"Yes. How do you know about it? Did you ever go to The Whipping Club?"

"Once or twice."

"And for a moment you had me believing you weren't interested in sex. Are you a top or a bottom? Would you like me to force you to suck somebody's dick?"

"It's unbelievable, that place, a lot of the people just look really sad. I remember going in the toilets and there was some geezer tied up in a cubicle, with his feet sticking out from underneath. It's undignified. It reminded me of an American science fiction writer who got a timing device, and he tied himself up in a dustbin using the timing device as a release, but it jammed. He was found about three weeks later, dressed in women's clothes and doubled up in the bin. The cops thought he'd been murdered, but an investigation proved he'd just been getting his jollies, and it had gone horribly wrong. Poor sod."

"At least that way one dies with a hard on."

"It was funny when I went to The Whipping Club. I remember this girl done up in rubber gear just coming and standing next to me for ten fucking minutes. I just turned my back on her, because I knew all she wanted was for me to force her to her knees before sticking my dick in her mouth, she kept telling me to do this."

"I knew you were a bottom, I knew you were, the rubber girl wanted you to act like a top and you couldn't do it."

"I mean, I'd read about Jim Morrison when The Doors were a top rock attraction, and he'd just be standing at a bar and groupies would fellate him, and he'd just carry on talking oblivious to what was going on down there. What a strange life. What was that film of The Stones?"

"Oh God, *Cocksucker Blues*."

"Have you actually seen it?"

"I got hold of it but the copy was bloody awful, the picture was so fuzzy it wasn't worth watching."

"Is there a clean print or is the original really crap?"

"I wouldn't know, you'd do better to ask my father-in-law!"

As morning gave way to afternoon, and beer gave way to wine, we spoke about jerking off in toilets; and about men who electrocute themselves pissing on railway tracks; and about suicides on the underground; and about finding human turds on tube trains. Then there was a pause in the conversation and I started thinking about what Diana had been saying. I'd always found her good company and wondered why she had that cloned Princess look. Then it struck me with the force of revelation, I wasn't boozing with a copy, I was getting pissed with the real thing. Life was weird when you were artist-in-residence on the Scapa Loch Housing Estate.

Shoreditch Low Riders

Captain Swanky didn't just have a car, he had an urban assault vehicle. Or rather he had a couple of low riders, which caused me no end of grief with several families in our block, who were involved in running an illegal mini-cab business. The late-night cabbies didn't seem to appreciate that Captain Swanky saw himself as a real john for having the flashest motors on the estate. What bothered them was the fact that the council hadn't assigned anybody parking spaces, and Swanky regularly parked in places they wanted for themselves. The Captain didn't seem bothered that his windscreen wipers were regularly broken, and tyres occasionally slashed. What annoyed me was the verbal abuse I received from disgruntled mini-cab drivers who couldn't get their head around the fact that there were two blokes living in the same flat, and therefore had me down as the owner of the low riders.

The bell rang, and being a light sleeper I was disturbed by it. Captain Swanky could sleep through anything and as it turned out, he was already up and ogling the legs of the secretaries at his dad's degree mill. I hauled myself to the entry buzzer in the hallway of my flat.

"Hello."

"Come down and move your car."

"Look I've been through this with you before. The car in question isn't mine, and besides there are no assigned parking spaces on this estate. A consultation process about parking is supposed to be underway, but for the time being anybody can park anywhere they like."

"I'm a private tenant. I pay one pound seventy a week for that space. Move your car."

It was Mr. Bullshit's usual bullshit. I knew full well he

wasn't a private tenant and that he didn't pay one pound seventy a week for a parking space. In the past I'd asked him to provide proof of these assertions and he'd been unable to do so, but he still stupidly claimed if I went to the council they would confirm what he had to say. The local estate office branded him a liar. There were no assigned parking spaces and I was sick of telling him this, but I'd continued to do so since he was in the habit of ringing my bell to deliberately wake me when I was asleep. I also kept telling him that the low riders didn't belong to me, but he ignored that information too.

"Tell me your name and address. I'll go to the council with you right now and we'll discuss it with them." I shouted into the entry phone.

"Don't blame me if anything happens to your car."

"Tell me your name."

There was no reply. Instead I heard Mr. Bullshit go into his flat, which was beneath mine. Shortly afterwards, I heard his wife screaming. Mr. Bullshit was beating her up, which was what he usually did after I'd refused to move my flatmate's car. I felt sorry for Mrs. Bullshit but she wouldn't speak to me, she just cowered on the stairwell every time I saw her. She always did everything she could to avoid me. If I'd been able to move the car I might have done so to prevent her from being hit, but then I'd never learnt to drive—and even if I had, Swanky would never have given me a spare key for his motor.

The bell rang again.

"Motherfucker!"

It was one of the teenage boys who came onto the estate to take drugs. They all hated me because I regularly destroyed their buzz by asking them to get off the stairwell to my block, and I'd stand there repeating myself until they left—it particularly pissed them off that when I was punched or threatened with knives, I didn't really react and I certainly wasn't intimidated.

"Motherfucker!" the schoolboy repeated since he'd got no response from me so far.

"Bring your mother here and I'll fuck her."

The boy's mates stopped laughing; I wasn't supposed to respond like that.

I could hear more screaming from downstairs. Mr. Bullshit had moved on from his wife, and was now beating up his two elder daughters. The youngest was still in diapers but it seemed almost inevitable that Mr. Bullshit would start hitting her as soon as she learnt to walk.

There was a knock at the door. It was Atima from across the landing. She asked if I could look after her daughter Indira while she went out for a driving lesson. I said that was okay. So Indira came in with a couple of dolls and the keys to her flat, in case she wanted to go in and get something out.

Dance To The Drummer's Beat

Diana had introduced me to Stephen Milligan, and on those occasions when she was unable to get up, I'd drink with him. Increasingly Diana spent whole days in bed. She was a binge drinker, getting blasted for three days, then taking a week or more to recover. Diana was full of self-pity, she was raging and abusive when drunk, full of apologies and self-recrimination when sober. Then there were the nights filled with headaches, stomach upsets and aching limbs, where she'd endlessly ask herself "What's wrong with me?" Milligan, like me, imbibed steadily. There wasn't much else to do at Scapa Loch. We paced ourselves between drunk and dead drunk, avoiding the perils of sobering up that so distressed Diana.

"Have you noticed how most of the people here are English?" the former Tory MP asked me. "That was a deliberate policy of course, get in ordinary English families whose bread winners worked in the oil industry, and they'd act as a cover for the rest of us. However, even the oil workers have gone underground, otherwise they'd never have been persuaded to come here. Mostly they are police informers who've been given a new life and a new identity. They won't ever go back to their friends and extended families, all they've got is the wife and the kids. They can't leave, there are prices on their heads. We're living in the ultimate open prison, that's why you were brought in, to keep us amused."

"But I could leave."

"Yes, you could leave, but you won't because it would drive you mad to tell people what you've seen here and not have anyone believe you."

"I'm a spatially displaced person, I was forced out of London by the spiralling property prices."

"Why don't you leave then? You could go to France or even Jamaica."

"I will do eventually, when I've completed the project here by grabbing all the readies being squandered on cultural flim-flam in Hoy. If I'm lucky I might even pick up some extra cash by selling my story to the papers. You know the sort of thing, *I scammed my living as an artist and my only qualification was my skill at impersonating two bit painters*. It would piss off my alter-ego but once he saw what the publicity was doing for his career he'd get over it. After I've finished here I want to bag myself a job on a government think tank.

I've got this plan to make Scotland and New York part of the Scandinavian Federation, then we could have England join the United States. Cornwall, alongside Wales and a united Ireland would join Scotland and New York as a part of a Viking Union, while London would link in to a revived Hanseatic League stretching from Tallinn in Estonia to Sydney in Australia."

"You can't do that," Milligan objected, "it would undermine English liberties and a democratic system that took centuries to build. Don't you know the Gresham family who founded the London stock exchange were the hammer of the Hansa? You probably think the Euro is a merely a convenience rather than part of a sinister conspiracy, and all because the currency facilitates easy payment if you go and do some artistic odd-jobbing in Finland."

"Finland, my Finland," I replied. "Finland is for me what America is to Jean Baudrillard, a unique combination of both the East and the West, which simultaneously illustrates the ultimate compatibility of all cultures as they are woven together in a global web of planetary humanism."

"Marxist nonsense, but instead of arguing, let's change the subject. I don't know why you won't have it off with Diana, she really fancies you."

"She's a drunk."

"So are you."

"If I shagged her she'd become a pain in the butt. In imagining that she'd allowed me to possess her, she'd hope simultaneously to control me. In her deluded mind, from that point on my life would revolve around her whims and wants, and she'd throw a tantrum every time I failed to act upon them."

"I'd shag her if she fancied me."

"Let's forget about Diana, or we'll end up rowing.

Instead, let's get back to what we were just speaking about. You rant against America for all the wrong reasons. For sections of the avant-garde in the last century, particularly the left-communists who emerged from Berlin Dada, it was a utopian grail. Of course, there was and is economic exploitation, most visibly symbolised by the ghettos, but America is its ghettos as well as its suburbs. America is an inescapable historical reality, it has become something we all must pass through before we can arrive at a truly human future. You have to address the history of racism and slavery before you can move beyond race."

"I'm bored. I don't even know what you're raving about when you talk of America. I need another drink."

"I'll fetch some more beer."

Grab This Thing

I got a job moving furniture. When I say a job, I mean one job, one day's work. I was standing outside the bagel shop in Brick Lane counting through my change to see if I had enough for a family loaf, or whether I was just going to buy a small white. A guy came up and started talking to me.

"Do you want a day's work shifting furniture?"

"Yeah."

"Then meet me here at seven tomorrow morning, we're moving a guy from Wolverhampton down to Dalston."

"Fine."

So the next morning I was outside the bakery and the

guy was buying bagels and tea to have in the van. We exchanged pleasantries as we trundled out of London and up the M1. At some point the conversation turned to family matters.

"How's Kevin?"

"What?"

"How's your older brother Kevin?"

"I don't have an older brother called Kevin."

The guy I was working with really laughed at this.

"I thought you were Kevin's younger brother. You really look like him. When my mate Kevin went back to Dublin, he told me to look out for his younger brother who lived in Bethnal Green. You'll get well paid for an easy job today, and all because you look like my friend."

So I spent half-an-hour loading up the van in Wolverhampton, and even less time unloading it in Dalston. The guy we were moving was house bound, so we had to put him in his wheelchair when we stopped at a service station on the way back to London. He bought us a cooked meal. I spent most of the day sitting on my arse, I wasn't even doing the driving. I got fifty quid cash in hand for nothing much at all, Social Services were paying. I felt like my luck had turned. Unfortunately, there wouldn't be any more removal jobs for me, since I wasn't really family.

So Far Away

I'd started snorting lines of coke with Diana. Financially the cost of this gear was crippling me. Fortunately, I'd copped some insurance money to offset the pecuniary damage of my burgeoning drug habit. The Scapa Loch Community Hall in which the Comparative Vandalism exhibition had been housed, burnt to the ground after it was deliberately set ablaze a few weeks after the show had opened. A note in Diana's hand justifying this action was delivered to my door on the night of the not-so-mysterious fire.

The missive explained that the pyromaniac who'd destroyed the work did so to improve upon my efforts. The vandal had particularly strong objections to a small piece in which I'd montaged the image of a Buddhist monk who'd set himself ablaze onto a photograph of David Mach's *Polaris*. I'd also added the quasi-Baudrillardian commentary: "And Signs? And Signs." The princess claimed this was an exploitation of, rather than an improvement on, the initial act of destruction I'd invoked.

Mach's model of a nuclear submarine made from thousands of used car tyres was set ablaze by James Gore-Graham on 21 August 1983. Gore-Graham poured petrol over Mach's sculpture and then singularly failed to do a runner after setting it alight. The blazing sculpture exploded. Gore-Graham was severely burnt and died a few days later without regaining consciousness. The note from Diana, which was signed "JGG", concluded by saying: "And stop patronising me by insisting that my dialectics would improve if only I'd drink more—after all I've just destroyed your show without killing myself, which is a considerable improvement on my action against Mach."

In an effort to rake in some extra ackers with which to destroy my nose, I'd transformed what had started as a conceptual art piece into a palpable reality. In the beginning, The Orkney & Caithness Wife Swappers Club had consisted of nothing much more than headed paper, a rubber stamp, xeroxed posters and the power of rumour. Whereas traditional artists used canvas as their medium, I was using the media in the form of an outraged local press. Having been denounced as depraved and sinful by several fundamentalist ministers, it was not difficult to turn my non-existent wife swapping club into a living-breathing nexus of compromised human relationships. My right-hand man in all this was a skinny little guy called Richard Edwards, who before he'd faked his own suicide used to pose as a musician with a guitar he couldn't even play. Richie didn't have any discernible talents but a lot of bored housewives on the Scapa Loch Housing Estate found him attractive, so he was the bait with which I attracted willing pussy. Edwards, like Diana, was single, so they'd be paired up as a couple, and when the men's car keys were thrown into my bobble hat, all the guys were hoping Diana would pull out their ring, while all the wives where rooting around for Richie's keys.

We'd have the weekly wife swap meets at my house, and I'd charge an entrance fee. Once the women had pulled their partners from the hat, people could either go home for some private fun, or stay around and get involved in collective sex. I had an agreement with Richie that he'd always hang back, so that I could get some digital video shots of him in action with whoever grabbed his ring. One night Edwards was paired up with a young woman of twenty-two, whose twenty-three year-old husband took off with a housewife of forty-eight. The girl led Edwards into the bathroom, filled the bath with warm water and made him lie in it.

"I'm going to piss in your mouth," she giggled.

I caught that giggle on camera, or rather my camera digitally encoded it both visually and in sound, and it was a giggle that would send cash registers tingling once I had the footage up on my pay-to-view Randy Wife Swappers web site. Fresh piss, I'm told, tastes like nothing else on this earth, and Richie got a hot mouthful of the golden stuff. It was a long leak, the piss just kept coming, I thought it would never end. When the amber nectar finally stopped flowing, and the girl giggled that giggle again, this golden laughter was both a blessing and a curse. As canned happiness it provided me with the readies to buy industrial quantities of cocaine. Charlie wasn't my problem, what caused me hassles was the smack I'd started taking to straighten myself out as I came down from the snow high.

After washing off the piss that had dribbled down the side of Edwards' mouth and under his chin, the girl pulled him up from the bath. She towelled Richie and herself down, before hauling him through to an empty bedroom where they started fucking. I recorded it all as zeroes and ones. Perfect shots right down the line, until Edwards finally came all over the girl's peachy face.

You Should Have Been In The Pub Last Night

"Do you remember?" Tony Cheam enquired.

Cheam had been permanently disadvantaged by his old Islington background, which he'd attempted to escape via the fantasy world of art. Cheam exhibited and reviewed, so his name appeared regularly in the quality art press. That said, his twelve year-old daughter was growing up too fast in a cramped council flat, the rent covered by Cheam's wages as a technician at a central

London school of art. From a purely financial point of view, if Cheam was an art world success, it was difficult to imagine what constituted failure. Money wasn't an issue among the artists I knew. Either their families had it or they didn't. If Cheam's folks had been new Islington, then his daughter could have confronted the demons of adolescence much more comfortably. Since being quick witted is a burden to someone from Cheam's background, he'd have done better scoring an office job and blunting his intellect as quickly as possible. As it was, culture was a succubus draining Tony of energy and life.

"Do you remember?" Cheam repeated.

Remember? Of course I remembered. I could remember so much that day in and day out I wearied myself with the effort of trying to forget. I remembered getting up that morning and making coffee for breakfast. When I say I had coffee for breakfast, I realise a lot of people would call it lunch. I get up at noon. That's when bhangra hell starts. You can set your watch by it. Mr. Inconsiderate who rents the flat above mine works as a waiter. He wakes his kids up around two in the morning, when he comes home with a bunch of his work mates. Mr. Inconsiderate and his chums then proceed to party loudly enough to prevent anyone in our block from sleeping. The screams of Mr. Inconsiderate's young children, who are regularly woken from deep sleep, simply adds to the general cacophony. Mr. Inconsiderate goes to bed at four and gets up at twelve. Midday is when he slaps *Dum Dumk Dumk* by Achanak onto his turntable and plays it repeatedly at high volume for a couple of hours. That's why I always go to bed after four and get up at noon. I was an early riser before I moved to the Stanton Drew Estate in Hoxton.

When I draw the blinds in the morning (I call it morning, even if it is ten past twelve), I usually find Mrs. Inconsiderate has hung her washing over my windows. That morning I went up to flat five and complained about the washing. I even explained that our tenancy agreement with the council banned us from hanging washing from our windows. When making these remonstrations, I always deal with Mr. Inconsiderate. His wife won't answer the door. As usual, Mr. Inconsiderate went apeshit. He ranted about having to wait three days to get his son's trousers back after his wife had accidentally dropped them onto my balcony. He claimed to have called repeatedly at my flat but I was always out. On account of this, he considered me a poor neighbour, so his wife wasn't going to lift their bed sheets just because I wanted to look out of my windows. Abandoning this abortive attempt at rational discussion, I got my breakfast, or should that be my lunch?.

I remembered. I remembered. I remembered saying hello to Mrs. Khartoum from flat two on my way out of the block. I liked Mrs. Khartoum, she was very good at pestering the council about little improvements to our block. She'd spent a year lobbying the local housing office about the lack of a regular cleaning day for our communal stairwell. Thanks to Mrs. Khartoum's efforts, someone now came in every Monday and mopped the stairs down. The place would have looked clean if this had been done twice a day, seven days a week. I remembered taking a 55 bus from Old Street to Oxford Street. I remembered wasting most of the afternoon in Berwick Street. You can forget the market and the clippers, what interested me was music. That said, all I had to show for my efforts were six copies of *The Very Best Of Billy Butler and The Enchanters*

59

put out by Marginal Records of Brussels, and plucked from the bargain basement of Mr. CD. Considering that this reissue contained a bunch of classic Chicago cuts recorded for the legendary Okeh label (including both *My Heart Is Hurtin'* and *Right Track*), at a quid per CD it was a bargain no rare soul fan could resist. My favourite track is actually *Boston Monkey*, although it wasn't a hit. Okay, so the packaging on the reissue was lousy. But then what bothers a fan of sixties soul is the music. The band weren't really The Enchanters as someone (like a record shop assistant) buying the CD blind might imagine, they were the Chanters. The name was shortened early on to avoid confusion with Garnet Mimm's rival group The Enchanters. There were no sleeve notes to explain either this, or the fact that Billy Butler was billed with a group to differentiate him in the public's mind from his older brother Jerry.

I remembered. I remembered. I remembered catching a 55 bus on Oxford Street and getting off at Shoreditch Town Hall. I remembered begrudging the Stagecoach company the round pound I paid for my transportation. The transportation I got from Billy Butler was priceless, and as far as I was concerned public transport should have been free. I remembered, I remembered, I remembered, and like Tony Cheam I was sleepwalking. For years, while my friends were worrying about mortgages, I was pondering bigger questions like the meaning of life. I'd tried to box clever. Setting myself up as a freelance librarian had seemed like a good idea for as long as the government was prepared to pay me forty pounds a week to run my own business. In retrospect this had been a mistake, I should have got myself a proper job. Instead I'd had enough advice to see me through to doomsday in the afternoon, with most of it coming from a bent accountant. I'd paid him to help me set up my own company. I'd allegedly done the smart thing. I was a company director and since my firm made sod all money, I'd been able to sign on the dole while simultaneously working part time for a good few years. That was then, this was now, and welfare payments had become rarer in the British Isles than sightings of red squirrels.

"Do you remember?" Tony Cheam was determined to buttonhole me—he didn't have to work Captain Swanky quite so hard—since the former public school boy was enraptured by the gift of the gab, and he viewed this as a birthright of us lucky horny handed sons of toil, "Do you remember how back in the seventies everyone did their own thing at all nighters? I was watching some old footage of the Wigan Casino the other day, and the sheer range of dancing was phenomenal. But when I went to a northern soul night at the Orange Bar last week, the dancing was incredibly stylised. Everyone did their back flips and spins in exactly the same way."

"It goes with the territory," I observed laconically. "That's what critics never seem to understand about pop music. They wrongly imagine that there are stand out tracks but a really good record for fans of any particular genre is one that follows the template of that form to the letter. What marks a classic song as special is its lack of originality. The musicians are honing the sound down to perfection as they knock out fresh tunes day after day. All you need are a couple of chords. Pop music is a process of boiling things down to the bare essentials. The stylised dancing of northern soul revivalists matches this phenomenon."

"Another round?" Captain Swanky put in as a way of covering his embarrassment at being unable to contribute to the conversation.

The Captain was even further out of his depth at the bar. We were in The Macbeth on Hoxton Street, just around the corner from the flat I was unfortunate enough to share with Captain Swanky. In theory, The Captain shouldn't have been the joint tenant of a council property. Apart from anything else, he owned a holiday home on the south coast and had inherited several houses and a hotel up north. Swanky, of course, down-played the value of his extensive property holdings. The hotel was nothing special, at most it would realise a million pounds if he sold it on as a going concern. As for the houses up north, well most of them were let to students at peppercorn rents. Admittedly, his five bedroom holiday house in Brighton was part of an exclusive sea front redevelopment—but then a man needed rest as well as recreation. The fact of the matter was that when I'd worked out that the only way I'd get a pad from the council was by applying (in triplicate) with a joint tenant and a cock-and-bull story about being homeless, Swanky had offered to help me out. Once the tenancy was signed, rather than dropping away discreetly as promised, The Captain decided the credibility of occupying public housing in Hoxton would greatly enhance his image as a streetwise DJ working at the cutting edge of seventies revivalist culture. That's how my almost fictional co-tenant unexpectedly metamorphosed into an inescapable physical presence. Swanky's Brighton base became a holiday home, and he joined the Hoxton crowd.

The Macbeth was schizophrenic in every sense of the word, and most especially if you take the term to mean being blessed with a split-personality. It was a typical instance of old Hoxton being eaten alive by new Hoxton. Dinner music for cannibals with Raymond Scott on the juke box. The smell of blood wafting up from under the floorboards, and all the perfumes of Arabia wouldn't have sweetened the acrid air. Hell too is murky and the decor in The Macbeth was something else, being evenly split between neo-classical and rococo. I'd accustomed myself to the effect over time—but the greatest improvement was achieved by distance. Once the beers I'd been drinking kicked in with dull, soothing consequences, I felt more comfortable in these surroundings. Difficult to say then whether the decor attracted the drinkers or if the drinkers were simply an extension of the decor. The resident boozers were an army of clones and collaborators, whose fatal strategy was to take on the destiny of objects. I wanted to scrawl "those about to die, we salute you" across the pseudo-classical frescoes behind me. Instead I talked agreeably about Billy Butler. I had half-a-dozen CDs weighting down my bag and I wanted to off-load this ballast at a tenner a piece. That said, this desirable reissue would have cost at least fifteen knicker on the internet, that is if you'd been able to source it.

There was a mirror ball towards the back of The Macbeth, and a cornucopia of knick-knacks had been spread around the premises for the aesthetic delectation of drinkers. The clientele was less judiciously mixed. Trendies seeking the real (but finding only its double) were swarming to The Macbeth because it was more "authentic" than the Bricklayers Arms or the Electricity Showroom. The Macbeth wasn't as crowded as its fashionable rivals, at least not just yet, but fresh air was still at a premium and like most pubs, it reeked of stale cigarettes. Some artists had persuaded the pub management to let them put on a show of their work and this, so the owners hoped, was just the thin end of a lot of wedge. Eighty percent of the drinkers were new Hoxton. They were scattered on sofas like so many pin cushions impervious to pricks. Those who were dressed down in the strictest accord to current fashion codes monopolised the pool table. Sporting its best weekend finery, Old Hoxton hugged the bar for protection against the encroachments of high culture and high finance. On stage a middle-aged man in a suit called Val Rogers was crooning his way through a series of standards. No one paid him much attention. I was waiting for the better looking of the barmaids to get up and do her turn. It was the tastier barmaid who served Captain Swanky, and I knew he wasn't interested in her. He liked girls of twenty, he couldn't get excited by a woman of forty-five.

"Cheers!" I said as The Captain returned with Guinness.

Tony Cheam downed his beer swiftly, then disappeared. It was time to move on.

At The Woodchoppers Ball

A decision had been taken by Retro-Americana (Suburban) Homes that the Scapa Loch Community Hall would not be rebuilt. Instead the local council were prevailed upon to construct a children's play park on its former site. Although it had previously been earmarked for demolition, The Ship Inn was now to be renovated and converted into a new community hall, which was a considerably cheaper and quicker option than building something from scratch. While I was waiting for my new base of operations to be made ready, I decided to stage a series of historical re-enactments at Scapa Loch. The first of these was the assassination of John

F. Kennedy. This took place on John F. Kennedy Drive, with Richard Edwards acting the part of the president, and Diana standing in for Jackie.

We mustered a crowd of about fifty people for the event, three of whom agreed to stand in for the tramps on the grassy knoll. James Rushbridger played the part of the driver and I was the bodyguard in the car. I'd decided to "historically improve" the hit by having Jackie killed instead of her husband, so Diana bit on a blood capsule and slumped in the car at the crucial moment. This really annoyed the small crowd we'd attracted, and there were boos before a slow hand clap started up. I leapt from the speeding soft top in which we'd been travelling and as the motorcade sped on, ran up the embankment to where the tramps had been lifting their hats. I grabbed a loudhailer that I'd hidden in some bushes earlier in the day. Through this amplification I denounced terrorism as a sign of revolutionary immaturity, since it assumed consciousness could be brought to our class from outside the workers' ranks, and it was thus deformed by all the usual idealist and vanguardist pretensions that typified anarcho-Bolshevik politics. This speech did not go down very well, and I was pelted with stones by a group of youths who persisted in their anti-social antics until I'd clambered off the grassy knoll.

"What was that all about then?" a middle-age bloke demanded angrily as he approached me.

"You can't blow up a social relation," I explained.

"Aren't you that artist-in-residence weirdo, the one who used to go to The Whipping Club and who also runs the wife swapping parties. You're a bit wacky when it comes to that male sex doll you've got. Still, if you don't like girls and there are young ones who've hit on you, you could pass them my way."

"I'm Tony Cheam," I lied as I held out my hand, "and if it's seventeen year-old girls you're after, they are a bit of a rarity at my car key parties. But you're still welcome to come along, the next session is at my place on Friday, the weekend starts there!"

"I'm Fred West," the man said cheerfully, "I live next door to Steve Smith, and he told me loads of seventeen year-old girls are after you despite the fact that you're a poofter. Steve tells me all the teenage girls go nuts for artists. Now you just send those young runaways to me and I'll show them a bit of my carpentry. If you send me a particularly tasty bit, I'll put a young boy your way in return."

"How's Rose?" I asked.

"Rose, what do I care about Rose? She thinks I'm dead, she never realised I was playing a game of double bluff with the Russians. I've got a new wife now, common law of course, and she likes a bit of three way between me and a young girl."

"Doesn't everybody?"

"Now Mr. Cheam, you're being sarcastic, let's leave the press out of this."

"Last night?"

"We only knocked the tramp about a bit, she loves it, she's a confirmed alcoholic and a semi-convinced masochist."

"I wasn't talking about Diana, I was talking about the music I can hear, it sounds like the Mar-Kays. It's coming from one of the houses across the street."

"I wouldn't know about that, but if you come across any seventeen year-olds who are gagging for it, and who you can't satisfy because of your inclinations, then send them my way."

And with a wave of his hand Fred was off.

"You lured me here under false pretences!" someone

else was complaining. "I wanted to see the greenie offed, and after that I was going to show him what's what by getting Jackie Onassis in my pants."

"No chance," I spat and the next thing I knew I'd been punched in the face.

I woke up in hospital on the Orkney Mainland. Apparently, I'd been kicked unconscious by hostile members of the crowd.

Mysterious Vibes

I'd been working The Hole. The Hole was a secondhand book emporium owned by two prickly Trotskyists who were my employers. They gave me £2 an hour, well below the minimum wage. For that I sat in a basement all day without any sunlight. I sat there alone from ten in the morning until six at night, with no lunch break. There wasn't much to do between ten and half twelve, so I'd read and listen to tapes. I read a lot, including about thirty volumes of the *Deathlands* series by James Axler. There was a lunch time rush of office workers, so I'd be working the till and while I got to listen to a lot of soul music, I didn't get to read much in the middle of my work day. What sold was mainly non-fiction, history and new age stuff. My employers didn't have a clue about novels, so their fiction stock was unbelievably duff and never moved. After two, things quietened down again until five, when the clerical workers got out from their office jobs. The last hour was always manic, and I'd inevitably be throwing people out at six, they didn't want to go and I didn't want to hang around since I wasn't being paid for my time if The Hole stayed open late.

One day, as a tube train rattled beneath me, one of the owners came down the stairs. The Sailor looked, as he always did, harassed.

"Bad news?" I asked.

"Bad news," he said.

"Am I out of a job?"

"Not necessarily," he said.

"Not necessarily?"

"Well, you've seen how it is, this place covers your wages but it doesn't make money. We'll let you buy us out for two grand, plus fifty percent on our stock as you sell it."

"I haven't got two grand, if I had two grand I wouldn't be working here."

"I realise that. We wouldn't expect the two grand up front. You could work it off as you went along. I've been through the figures and we reckon you can cover the rent, pay us off and make a bit more than you're already earning."

"But you just said it only covered my wages."

"Yeah, but that was a figure of speech, I meant it covered your wages, expenses and a bit more."

"I know how things stand with this shop, and I'm not interested."

"What do you mean you're not interested? We'd be doing you a favour letting you have it for two grand plus the stock at half price."

"I'm not interested."

"Get out you ungrateful bastard!"

So that was it for me as far as shop work went.

Everybody's Going To A Love In

I was sitting on a terrace in James Rushbridger's back garden, he was drinking Talisker and I was stoned out of my mind on junk. I was quite happy to let Rushbridger talk as I stared at a nail in the fence at the bottom of his garden. The nail hadn't been hammered all the way home. It wasn't quite straight, it must have bent as it was knocked in.

"I used to travel up from Cornwall to London all the time," Rushbridger reminisced. "There was a pub in Marble Arch where I'd meet guys who shared my sexual interests. There were some really strange blokes who went to this place. Some were pretty sad, like Dog who was a pop musician obsessed by the Nazis. He seemed to believe that he was a direct descendent of the last King of Atlantis, who Dog claimed had been in Europe on a state visit when the continent disappeared beneath the sea."

I nodded. I was nodding off. The nail seemed to be moving imperceptibly. I was having trouble focusing my eyes.

"Anyway, another of Dog's fixations was William Hope Hodgson's *The House On The Borderland* and when he found out I wrote for money, he wanted me to write a sequel which was an impossible task because the book ends with the death of the cosmos and swine creatures pattering up the stairs. Dog wasn't actually offering to pay me to write the sequel, he thought he'd given me this fantastic commercial proposition that I could take to a publisher and make a lot of money from. I foolishly gave him my home number, and he'd call up and get into this whole fantasy thing where he wanted me to wear my gas mask when we spoke on the phone. He'd be droning on and on about Hodgson, or how he was dressed up in this really rare Nazi cam-ouflage gear. I just couldn't convince him that nobody cared about Hodgson, that the project was dismal and there wasn't a commercial publisher in the world who would touch it."

The nail I was gazing at seemed to be splitting in two, or rather, where there had been one nail, I could now see two.

"The weird thing about this guy Dog was that he really had a lot of money. I mean, you'd never have heard of him, it wasn't like he sold a lot of records. He was doing his own merchandising and I guess there was money in that, and it was obvious he wasn't paying tax, he didn't keep any records about financial transactions. I often wondered if there was a far-Right sugar daddy somewhere in the background."

I'm sure I fell asleep at this point. I don't think Rushbridger noticed and when I awoke he was no longer talking about Dog or Hodgson, he'd moved on to another British horror writer.

"As for Arthur Machen, he grew up in south Wales but lived in obscurity in London for years writing hack journalism and conjuring up Grail fantasies. He was haunted by the landscapes of his memory. So in his fic-tion there's a continual crossover between London and the Welsh borderlands, which function as a metaphor for the borders between life and death. Machen is one of those people that don't seem to have had a fully earthed existence. There is no Arthur Machen because he was actually Arthur Lllewellyn Jones, whose clergy-man father went bankrupt. He was part Scottish and part Welsh. He took his mother's name and adopted a shadowy existence in London."

My concentration and focus were going again, and

where there'd been one nail, there were again two, or at least a visual illusion of two nails.

"There is a particularly fine Machen book, *The London Adventure: The Art Of Wandering*, which some sassy publisher ought to reissue as a work of psychogeography. It features endless roaming across the London landscape and houses with dark histories that may or may not really exist. Then there is his classic story *The Great God Pan*, about an operation that takes place on a young girl and people who vanish into the borderland landscape. One of the characters is called Helen Vaughn. J. G. Ballard reused the name in *Crash* for his demonic character. Machen, of course, took it straight from the twins Henry and Thomas Vaughn, one an alchemist and the other a poet."

I couldn't see the nails any more, I couldn't see beyond the end of my nose. The world didn't exist, I was looking at my nostrils.

"It is interesting that Machen's most successful book was about these angels appearing during a battle in the First World War, and nobody could decide whether it was truth or fiction. Machen wrote endlessly about walking from Caerleon, which is a Roman legionary town where he grew up. His fiction is all about setting off into hills or woods and during the course of the walk these become something else, shining pyramids or creatures from another dimension. As a writer he's quite close to Hodgson, but he was more caught up in the ambience of The Golden Dawn. He was a friend of A. E. Waite. Mysticism was important to him. He joined The Golden Dawn and he peddled books on tobacco, wrote pornography and did translations, all the grubby stuff most writers do to survive. Machen never really made any money, he never reached a popular audience. There are deluxe small press editions of his work, and paperbacks with lurid covers, but beyond a few collectors and teenage horror fans with criminally indiscriminate tastes, no one is interested."

I can recall no more beyond falling sound asleep.

A Quiet Place

It was the fifth of November. Some tosser had put a leaflet through my door ranting on about William Of Orange landing in England on 5 November 1688, and freeing the country from "the Papist tyranny and Jesuitical scheming of James II and his advisers". The reactionary leaflet contained a list of important facts to remember on 5 November, including "the attempt of the Catholic gunpowder plotters to blow up Protestant democracy in 1605". Beyond offending people, it was difficult to see what the leafleteers hoped to achieve. The residents of The Stanton Drew Estate were predominantly Muslim, with a good chunk of the remainder—like me—having Irish Catholic family backgrounds. Captain Swanky was the only person I knew on the scheme who'd grown up attending Protestant church services.

A bonfire had just been lit on the green immediately outside my flat by various boys ranging in age from seven to fourteen. I'd dismantled two bonfires the previous day and one the previous night. The kids were stealing planks from a nearby building site, so no matter how many bonfires I dismantled, they'd always be able to put another one together. To stoke the fire that was now burning brightly, they'd also hacked down a couple of trees, and thrown an old motorcycle on top. I just hoped there wasn't any petrol in the motorcycle's tank. Acrid fumes wafted into my flat. This had happened every year since I'd moved onto the estate. The boys were holding repeater fireworks in their fists and aiming them at each other, as well as the windows of flats on the estate. I didn't bother calling the council's emergency line. They had one bloke working on dismantling illegal bonfires, and since there were always dozens in dangerous places across the borough on 5 November, he wouldn't bother dealing with this one. It would take too long because it had already been lit. The anti-bonfire man concentrated on dismantling unlit fires, a fairly pointless exercise, since they were always quickly rebuilt.

I put my coat on and packed a small overnight bag. I wouldn't be able to stay in the flat that night, I always got smoked out on bonfire night. I could either go to an all night club, or ask a friend to put me up. As I exited the block, several boys were throwing fireworks at a six month old baby, who was being pushed home in a buggy by her distraught mother. Fortunately, the fireworks missed their target, so the baby wasn't as upset as her mum. However, there was usually at least one fatality in the borough from this sort of behaviour on 5 November—more often than not, a teenage boy who'd been involved in a fireworks fight.

"Batty man! Batty man! Boom bang-a-bang batty man! We're going to kill you. It is sick to get your arse fucked!"

The boys had spotted me and were hurling fireworks in my direction. They didn't like the fact that I lived with Captain Swanky, and the only explanation they could find for this fact was that we were, to use their favoured term of homophobic abuse, "batty men." They'd leave me alone if there were only three or four of them, but whenever there was a large group together, like the thirty who were running towards me at that moment, it was par for the course to be attacked. I'd been kicked, jostled, punched, spat on, had lighters flicked on and off in my face, and threatened with knives. Someone ran into my back, I staggered but stayed upright and continued walking in my chosen direction.

"Go on, hit me!"

"I don't hit little boys!"

"I'm not a little boy."

"You are a little boy and I don't hit little boys!"

"I'm the leader!"

"You're just a little boy."

"Don't call me a little boy, I'm fourteen."

"Like I said, you're a little boy of fourteen."

By this point I was off the estate, and well away from the bonfire. The kids didn't want to leave the fire, so after lobbing a few more fireworks at me, they turned around and sloped back onto the Stanton Drew Estate.

Karate Boogaloo

I'd pretty much given up on cocaine. Rather than using skag just to come down, I was using it all the time. I saved a lot of money sticking with the smack, and it was easier to score than charlie. A lot of guys working in the fishing industry were users and their boats passed through the islands all the time. I felt like I was reliving the fifties, but with syringe instead of a pipe. The gear I was using was taking its toll on my scamming talents, but since my house and pay cheque depended on my doing something, I decided a re-enactment of the mass suicide at Jonestown would be an eminently suitable art work for the Scapa Loch Housing Estate. The seventies revival was an ongoing phenomenon, and the idea went down well with the young.

Stephen Milligan suggested I lace the pop I handed out in plastic cups with real cyanide. The former Tory MP seemed to hate the young, but he would have been horrified if he'd known I'd dropped acid into their drinks. I didn't tell anybody what I'd done, I just waited to see what went down. After everyone had been given LSD enhanced lemonade, I got up onto a podium I'd constructed and mimed along to a recording of Jim Jones' final speech to his followers. The event had been recorded by the CIA and endlessly bootlegged, I had a copy in my record collection that I'd listened to once, and then filed away. The platter had been boring the first time I'd played it, and hearing this disk again didn't alter my initial impression of tedium.

"How very much I've tried my best to give you a good life. In spite of all that I've tried, a handful of people with their lies have made our lives impossible. There's no way to distract ourselves from what's happened today."

"Not only do we have a compound situation, not only are there those who have left it to me, the betrayal of the century, some have stolen children from mothers and are in pursuit right now to kill them, because they stole their children. I mean we are sitting here waiting on a powder-keg and I don't think that is what we want to do with our babies, I don't think that is what we have in mind to do with our babies."

And so on, ad nauseam, with endless references to The Bible. By the time I'd played both sides of the album, the teenage audience I'd attracted was no longer acting like a crowd, people were getting very absorbed in their own little worlds, and there was no communication going on between them. The acid was hitting. If I'd dropped my pants and taken a shit on the podium, no one would have noticed. I switched a microphone on and mechanically read through a speech I'd prepared months earlier.

"The reason I say we're living in America is because this estate is an American suburb, it isn't a simulacrum. It was built for US Naval Intelligence not as a replication but rather as an extension of the social system the military hoped its personnel would never leave behind. However, what is interesting about it is that when the Americans were here, it was integrated, which is a perfectly normal situation—but not in racist Amerikkka. The ghetto and the suburb produce and mediate each other, but we have to move beyond such false separations. I want to collapse them into each other and move elsewhere. You can't live in the ghetto because of poverty, overcrowding and noise. You can't live in the suburbs because they are so boring, and aren't even tolerable with the sounds of Eddie Harris and Sun Ra to help keep you amused. What I'm after is the realisation of our species being on a planetary scale. That's my project, and it goes beyond art because it entails a recognition of the fact that the supersession of all specialist roles is an urgent and practical necessity."

"As the people of the Grail, the Celts are not a 'race' but proof, as if it were needed, that miscegenation is the creative principle at work in evolution. Noble Drew Ali allowed Celts to join his Black Muslim religion in the twenties because he considered them to be Africans. As recently as 1992 this idea formed the thesis of the book *The Black Celts: An Ancient African*

Civilization In Ireland And Britain by Ahmed Ali and Ibrahim Ali, who state quite explicitly that this culture became completely mixed with that of a later wave of Indo-European settlers. The discovery of Europe by the North American Iroquois Indians, whose landings in Iceland and Eire prompted various Viking chiefs to sail West, led to the highly developed tri-racial culture of the ancient Celts. Thus for us, the terms Celt and African describe exactly the same thing, a rejection of the bourgeois-centred subject in favour of a constantly changing identity, or to use philosophical jargon, a state of continuous becoming."

"We intend to transform our currently banal everyday lives into an Afro-Celtic carnival, a party that never ends. To do this, it is necessary to dissolve the identities and organising principals of Babylon. Two of our most immediate targets in this war against oppression are those twin phantoms known as the avant-garde and the occult. While occultists spend a great deal of time faking the antiquity of the activities in which they are engaged, the avant-garde's insistence on the element of innovation within its creations leads to a spurious denial of its historic roots. In this sense, the avant-garde and the occult are two sides of the same coin, they are the positive and negative poles which generate that multifarious enigma known as contemporary society."

"Since the avant-garde makes itself visible through manifestos, it must be banished. Correspondingly, the occult as a collection of hidden doctrines, must be realised (i.e. manifested) if it is to be simultaneously suppressed. Since the avant-garde is undesirable, we will vanquish it by uniting it with its polar opposite. By bringing together the avant-garde and the occult (in its Celtic-Druidic form) under the rubric of the avant-bard, we will dissolve both these phenomena, and simultaneously destroy the false community engendered by capitalist social relations, a 'social' form predicated on the spectacular opposition of these twin modes of occultural invocation."

"It doesn't matter what you look like, being a honkie is a mental disease, it's time for all of us to realise our common humanity as Afro-Americans. The reason I say we're living in America is because this estate is an American suburb, it isn't a simulacrum. It was built for US Naval Intelligence not as a replication but rather as an extension of the social system the military hoped its personnel would never leave behind."

I wasn't stoned, I was repeating myself quite consciously in an effort to conjure up a calculated rhetorical effect. I was straight and nothing was thrown at me. I wasn't even heckled. People were drifting off, or else they simply paid no attention to what was going on around them. The teenage cosmonauts of inner space who'd been drawn to the spectacle of a Jim Jones re-enactment were only interested in dredging the depths of their own psyches. I was bored. I slapped *Jewels Of Thought* by Pharaoh Sanders onto the deck which had earlier relayed the last Jim Jones speech. Half my audience had wandered off, so I went home and shot up. Before long I'd crashed out. I dreamt about Hegel's *Phenomenology Of Mind* and the night in which all cows are black.

Got Myself A Good Man

I couldn't stay away from Whitecross Street. With no job and no money, I had to drool at the bargain CDs, but there was always the chance that I'd run into June Gregory.

Sometimes I went into The Trader and chatted with Captain Swanky, who'd feel obliged to buy me a couple of drinks. When the market closed I'd head down Silk Street to the Barbican Library, where I'd read the papers. One day I did meet June Gregory and my heart nearly stopped. I wasn't sure if she'd talk to me, so I just smiled.

"Hello," June said, 'how's things?"

"Oh, fine, except I've no job and no money, and I never see you."

"I'm engaged," June said.

"Who's the lucky man?"

"You remember Gavin the dispatch rider who'd come to Dreadnought in white leathers? "

"Vaguely," I lied.

"We were going to buy a house, but now we're going to live at his mother's place, at least until I find a new job."

"Tell me why?"

"Dreadnought is closing down. You remember all Mr. Martin's talk about using Crowley-style magick to win the lottery? Well, Mr. Martin kept claiming to have had decent wins, not the jackpot but good amounts. He bought new cars, went on flash holidays, he even took me out for some expensive meals, although his wife hit the roof when she found out about it. Anyway, it turns out that what Mr. Martin was actually doing was embezzling money from the firm. So Dreadnought has gone bankrupt and once all the investigations into its financial affairs are over next month, I'll be out of a job. I'd found a dream home but now I won't be moving into it with Gavin because we can't get the mortgage we need. I feel I've let Gavin down, but he still says he wants to marry me."

Think About The Good Times

I was round at Diana's place and I'd been shooting up. Diana hadn't got into smack the way I had. She'd even cut back on the amount of coke she'd been snorting because she was worried she was going to destroy her nose. Diana was still drinking, but then wrecking her liver wasn't a matter of much concern, since this organ wasn't something that could be seen externally. I was dreaming of perfection, or rather I was dreaming of how perfection was completely unfulfilling in and to itself, and so perfection broke its own bonds, unfolding itself into the states of perfection and imperfection before combining them into a higher unity.

"Get up you lousy junkie!" Diana screamed as she kicked me in the ribs. "Get up, get up, get up!"

"What?" I mumbled as I rolled over. Diana continued to kick me, so eventually I stood on my feet and said: "What is it?"

"I need some help."

"Help?"

"Yes, help."

"What sort of help?"

"Help shifting the furniture around."

"Why do you want to move the furniture?"

"I've just been reading about Feng Shui and everything in this house is wrong."

"Feng Shui is just a bunch of bullshit, don't worry about it."

"Don't worry about it? My life is a disaster. I don't know what's wrong with me. This Feng Shui business is my last chance to sort it out."

"It's a complete and utter waste of time, I want to go back to sleep."

"I want you to move my bed to the south-west corner of my bedroom."

"You want me to do it? Aren't you going to help me?"

"I'm a fucking princess, I can't go shifting furniture around!"

I couldn't be bothered to argue. I went upstairs and lay down on the bed. The next thing I knew I was asleep. I'm not sure how long I slept, but Diana made a mistake when she tried to wake me by breaking a vase over my head. All she succeeded in doing was knocking me unconscious. I don't know why she was so mad, she might have been a princess but I was a junkie, so it wasn't realistic to expect me to do anything very much, even when I'd just promised to go and do it.

Rhythm Is Rhythm

At 9.40 a.m. on Sunday I was woken from my sleep by a disturbance outside the block. When I got up and looked out of the window, Mr. Bullshit was sitting in his car screaming abuse at a BT telephone engineer who'd parked his van in front of our block. After swearing angrily for some time, Mr. Bullshit sat in his car until the BT engineer had driven off. He then parked in the space that had been vacated by the BT van. At this point, a woman came out of a neighbouring block and asked Mr. Bullshit if he was the man who'd left an obnoxious note on her car when she'd last parked it in the space he'd just taken.

"This is my space!" Mr. Bullshit thundered. "I pay one pound seventy a week for this space. I pay my hard earned money for this space."

"Show me some proof."

"What do you mean proof?"

"If you pay for this space, then you must have a letter from the council, or a rent book for it, or something."

"No, no, you ask the council, they'll tell you this is my space."

"No they won't, I've already asked them. They've said I can park in this space if I want to."

"Don't be stupid, you haven't lived in Hoxton for very long."

"So what?"

"This isn't Brixton, we'll have none of your riots and bad behaviour here!"

"I'm not from Brixton, I was born in Morocco and I've lived in east London ever since I came to England fifteen years ago."

"But I've got a street parking permit from the local council, and I pay one pound seventy a week for it."

"Yes and I've got one too, and I pay one pound seventy a week for it. It entitles me to park on the streets in this borough without using meters, but you don't need a street parking permit to park on this estate. The service roads on this estate aren't public highways."

"But I've got a radio worth three hundred pounds in my car that might be stolen."

"And I've got a child seat in my car that might be stolen."

"There is an agreement between me and other car owners on this estate not to park in each other's spaces."

"Well, if you made the agreement without consulting me it is meaningless, if I'm not included in it I don't have to abide by it."

"You come to the council with me, they'll tell you it is my space."

"Okay, tomorrow at ten sharp."

"I'll come if I'm free."

"When are you free?"

"Not during the day, I work at night, I'm just going in now to go to bed."

So Mr. Bullshit went into his flat, and a few minutes later I heard his wife screaming. He was beating her up.

Ain't It Funky

I was, I realised, a court jester. Theoretically as sham artist-in-residence at Scapa Loch I was supposed to edify everyone, in reality there was a core audience to be amused—and beyond this elite, it mattered little what anyone else felt or thought about me and my scam. I could understand why my presence was resented by many of those around me. I could feed their children LSD and this was applauded as a side-splitting prank. I was a pied-piper, since handing out free drugs got the kids on my side too. Just as annoyingly, I seemed to embody an endless unfolding and sensuous realisation of the self, which was something missing from the lives of ordinary workers. This was, of course, an illusion—like everyone else, I reproduced the conditions of my own alienation. I had to keep producing art to justify the free housing and monthly salary I enjoyed.

I sometimes fantasised about giving up impersonating a barely professional artist and turning to crime, but I was too stuck in my junk rut to make any changes to my life without being pushed into them by external forces. Besides, all of anarchism could be found in the idea that it was possible to live differently in this world, and I understood well enough the difference between proletarian and bourgeois individuality.

The conversion of the Ship Inn had been completed and I was required to put up a new exhibition. Tony Cheam had sent up a number of paintings I didn't much care for and so I'd stored them in the community hall without ever putting them on display . They'd been ruined alongside everything else in the fire. I'd run through most of my ideas and all the worthwhile artistic conceits I'd been instructed to see through by Cheam. Indeed, I'd supposedly been working from a script provided by my alter-ego in London, and hadn't bargained on the one exhibition I was required to stage being burnt down—so there was no contingency plan. I wanted to remake the destroyed work, but my employers wouldn't hear of this, since my ability to redo the pieces would jeopardise the full insurance payment we'd received for their loss. I wasn't sure what move to make next, until I recalled a Charles Willeford novel I'd once read *called The Burnt Orange Heresy*. The book was about an artist called Jacques Debierue who never painted anything. His first piece was a frame he'd placed over a crack in a wall in his framing studio. This created a lot of critical excitement, then—nothing! Critics had to invent the work Debierue had failed to make in order to justify their own position in the capitalist cultural hierarchy. Debierue swanned around the world with his unused paints and blank canvases being chased by cultural commentators desperate to review his throughput. He never allowed anyone to see anything he'd done, since he was loath to admit there was nothing to show. Ambitious critics filled this void with their own fantasies.

I decided to formally realise Debierue's fictive "anti-work", and provided the following explanation for the blank and unprimed canvases I exhibited: "The opposition between manual and intellectual, between nature and culture, used to be indispensable. Separation between the artist who painted and the critic who judged was for centuries the motor by which art history moved forward. Since art no longer contests anything, this division has become a hindrance to the autonomous unfolding of sensuous human activity. We must end the division between artists who make, and critics who think. The senses themselves must become theoreticians. Critics who not only criticise over dinner, but engage in manual work in the morning and make love in the afternoon, are no longer merely critical critics, they are creators of real human community. When the critics do my work, and I do the work of the critics, then we will have abolished the difference between mine and thine."

"This is all very well," James Rushbridger told me over a glass of red wine at the private view, "but I think you've fallen short of your own premises. The titles you've given the blank canvases are too restrictive—*The African Quest For Freedom & Identity, Impossible Individuality, From Romanticism To Critical Theory, Refiguring The Real*—surely the meanings of these phrases are too specific to allow any real critical freedom."

"They're just book titles," I assured him, "I got them by doing some quick searches with ridiculous key words on the Amazon web site."

"Darling," Diana said coming up to me and kissing me on the cheek, 'you are interested in women after all! The piece entitled *Fuck You*, a simple frame over a hole you've knocked into the gallery wall, is undoubtedly the best thing you've ever done. It is exquisite and divine! The shape you've hacked out of the plaster is clearly intended as a representation of female genitalia. We've finally uncovered your real desires, they were just very deeply repressed. I'm now certain that you've always wanted to make love to me, until now you've just been unable to admit it."

Do The Dog

I got myself a job selling fresh chicken door to door. I was on a commission and after three days I quit because I hadn't made any money. I didn't know it, but the good residents of Haringey had been forewarned by the local council that the meat I was hawking was condemned as unfit for human consumption. The bloke I was working with drove the van, we both knocked on doors and after three days I was heartily sick of no sales but plenty of verbal abuse.

"Would you like some fresh chicken?"

"What d'ya think I am, a chicken hawk?"

"No, you don't look like a bird of prey to me."

"A chicken hawk is a pervert who likes young boys you moron!"

Then the door was slammed shut in my face. I guess it could have been worse, the geezer might have punched out my lights.

INTERLUDE

On the Misery of Literary Life

I too was once young, and having reached middle-age, I can see that I've learnt much more from my own mistakes than any guidance I was offered by my elders. This, of course, had as much to do with my extravagantly stubborn refusal to listen, as the rather obvious flaws in the counsels I received. Among the things that particularly irked me as I grew up were threats, wrapped in flattery, that were endlessly dispensed as if I was being offered sagacious advice. Throughout my teenage years, the constant refrain directed at me by stucco authority figures was that since I was obviously intelligent, if I'd just knuckle under I'd get on in life. In the minds of these sawdust Caesars, intelligence was the ability to understand that those who didn't bow down before the Great God of Authority, drew a short straw in the "adult" world. I grew up in a time and a place where there was pretty much full employment, and the fact that by the age of seventeen I was happily claiming welfare became, for my former teachers, a shocking illustration of the fate of those who refuse to do what they are told. Thoroughly perplexed by the tedium of their own dull lives, these buffoons vainly imagined they could condemn me for lacking their humble ambitions, and for having no wish to hold down a regular job. I was interested in rather more grandiose projects, such as overthrowing capitalism and thereby transforming life on this planet into something that was actually worth living.

As a result of these teenage experiences, I'm not inclined to tell the young what to do. I have no advice to give, and instead simply offer stories from my life as parables, in the hope that they will at least raise the odd belly laugh. Of course, my teachers' claims that my innate intellectual abilities would enable me to get on in the capitalist economy were patently untrue—when I entered the employment market, I did so with the handicap of having attended a sink school. The ability to conform and having the "right" social background were much more easily assessed and rewarded than something as nebulous as "intelligence". Fortunately, I was able to turn this to my own advantage. The exams I'd passed at school without making any particular effort to do so, meant I was over-qualified for factory work. I did try labouring immediately after leaving school, since such employment was readily available to me if I played down my modest academic successes, but after a few months I concluded that breaking my back six days a week was too much like hard work.

To be entitled to welfare payments, I had to actively seek employment. My local Job Centre would secure me interviews for low-grade clerical work, and I'd go along to these parlays smartly dressed in a black suit and white socks. When potential employers asked about my hobbies, I'd say I liked to read German philosophy and French literature. I'd blatantly lie about my ability to pursue these interests in the original languages. What I'd actually read were translations and these amounted to little more than a few dozen novels by the likes of Sartre and Robbe-Grillet, which I'd rounded out with some meagre scraps of Marx (at that time I hadn't even started on Hegel). I always made sure I did very well in interviews, so that potential employers would think

I'd leave them the moment something more lucrative came up. Needless to say, while I was not surprised by my inability to secure a position, the welfare officers assigned to me were inordinately perplexed by my predicament.

I claimed welfare on and off for many years, and while doing this knocked out the odd book. Right from the start, I was aware of the misery of literary life, and I was simultaneously developing a critique of the notion of characterisation within literature that demonstrated how it was inextricably linked to the thoroughly ossified and ideological chimera of "national character". I was interested in world culture and continuous becoming, and despised literature, since literature was always and already "national literature". As a consequence, I saw those men and wimmin who made up the British literary establishment as a legitimate target for the odd prank that contested the hegemony of their views. My hoaxing of the camp that developed around Salman Rushdie in the wake of the Fatwa against the author of The Satanic Verses was considered to be among the more obnoxious of my japes. Rushdie had written a book that was considered blasphemous by certain Muslims, and the death threats that a small number of those he'd offended made as a consequence of his shenanigans became an international news story. In early 1994 I mailed the following fake press release to various literary critics as a way of addressing issues raised by the Rushdie affair:

THE CONSORTIUM PRESENT SMASH THE FATWA, BURN THE KORAN!

At a secret location in London, 14 February 1994.

Salman Rushdie has teamed up with conceptual

artist John Latham to create a protest piece on the fifth anniversary of the death sentence issued against him by the Iranian government.

Latham will be recreating one of his famous SKOOB towers of the 1960s, using copies of the Bible and the Koran. Like its predecessors, this tower will be spectacularly burnt, reducing the books to ashes. Skoob is, of course, books spelt backwards.

Salman Rushdie says this collaboration demonstrates his commitment to artistic experimentation and opposition to censorship. 'Since going into hiding, I've been studying middle eastern history and now realise that the workers are the only people in a position to defy intransigent Islam,' the author explained. 'In 1958 when Qasim and the free officers seized power in Iraq, the workers killed the monarch and burnt the Koran. This is the kind of activity my collaboration with John Latham is designed to encourage.'

Journalists wishing to attend this unique artistic event are asked to ring Brian on 071 351 7561 by 10 February, so that they can be vetted prior to being issued with details of the redirection point.

The telephone number was that of Brian Stone, one of Rushdie's literary agents. This hoax caused a huge security flap costing thousands of pounds and for several days, the Rushdie camp were left wondering whether my mailing was part of an international plot being orchestrated against the author of *The Satanic Verses*.

All good pranks are done for a purpose, and I wanted to protest against a situation in which one was either supposed to be for Rushdie and free speech, or else one was allegedly a Muslim fundamentalist. I found the British press coverage of the Rushdie affair quite extraordinary, it treated Islam as if it was monolithic, whereas if Christianity had been presented in this way there would have been an outcry, since the differences between Catholic, Protestant and Orthodox positions are readily apparent to white European journalists. By ignoring the very different forms Islam takes—for example in its Shiite, Sunni and Sufi guises—much of the British press coverage of the Fatwa was unconsciously racist. This is something I'd hoped Rushdie would speak out against, since it is inconceivable that he hadn't grasped the ways in which his plight highlighted how art and culture—much more than pseudo-scientific justifications of bigotry—were the chief conduits of racism and ethnic absolutism towards the end of the twentieth-century. I deliberately gave Rushdie political views to the left of those he actually held in the statement I made up from him, since this was what I'd have hoped he'd use the situation he found himself in to say. I wanted to demonstrate there were other positions to those being expounded in the British press.

When a Big Issue journalist put two and two together, and fingered me as the man responsible for the Rushdie hoax, I was threatened with legal action and told I'd be shunned by the publishing industry. Apart from a story in The Big Issue (#65, 8-14 February 1994), at the time I played this prank, it went unreported in both the British and the international press. Due to government cuts that made it increasingly difficult to claim unemployment benefits, I came off welfare shortly after I pulled the Rushdie prank, and I've made a living from my writing ever since. Contrary to various people's expectations, and not least my own, the literary

91

establishment has embraced rather than shunned me. This does not, of course, prevent me from criticising it—and exploring the ramifications of this and similar examples of repressive desublimation as I do so.

I was surprised when in June 2001 I won an Arts Council of England Writers' Award and Salman Rushdie, who was presenting the prizes, gave me mine without so much as addressing a single word to me about my prank, since he knows who I am and what I've done. Prior to Rushdie handing out the prizes, he'd made a speech. At the end of his pep talk about the importance of writing, the microphone was appropriated by an MC, so there was no opportunity for me or any of the other prize winners to make use of it to raise political and cultural issues. I went along to the ceremony hoping to question Rushdie about the cultural racism that had been mobilised around opposition to the Fatwa against him, but the event was orchestrated in such a way that I was unable to talk to him about why—to the best of my knowledge—he'd never publicly challenged the bigotry of some of his supporters. The fact that I consider Rushdie to be a mediocre novelist does not necessarily mean that I must also hold a low opinion of him as a person, but I have to confess that I was unimpressed by the fact that while he was prepared to shake my hand, he said nothing to me whatsoever—not even "congratulations". Those who make half a (counter-)revolution only dig their own graves.

PART 2
SUBURBAN HELL

Never Love A Robin

My wife swapping parties had given way to slumber parties. After I'd turned most of the wife swappers onto junk, they lost interest in sex. I wasn't much bothered by this, since I was able to make just as much money from drug deals amongst this fraternity as I ever had from shagging. Besides, there was plenty of hot action up on my pay-to-view wife-swappers web site, so I was still raking in the ackers from that. Now, instead of coming around to my place and pairing off with a new sexual partner, people would shoot up and spend hours staring at their shoe. When Fred West finally put in an appearance at one of my little happenings, he was less than happy about this state of affairs.

"I thought this was supposed to be a den of iniquity!" the serial killer thundered. "I was expecting sexual perversion and almost inhuman depravities! You're all so stoned not a single one of you could manage an erection!"

"Chill out man," someone mumbled, "I'm trying to sleep."

"Chill? Chill? I'm more likely to kill!"

West took a jacket that was hanging on a wire hanger from the coat stand. He dumped the garment on the ground and straightened out the hanger. Then he started looking around for a young girl. This proved to be frustrating for him, since everyone at my slumber party was aged twenty-five or upwards. Eventually. West picked out a woman in her mid-twenties and began to beat her with the hanger he'd straightened out. We all ignored his behaviour, even the girl who was being beaten. She'd been unconscious prior to West launching his attack.

"What's the matter with you?" West bellowed. "Come on bitch, scream!"

"Give it a rest, man," someone put in, "she's dead to the world, unconscious, she can't feel a thing. If you get off on inflicting pain, then you're just wasting your time with her."

"In that case, I'll beat you."

"I won't feel a thing, no one here will feel a thing, we're all too high to experience pain."

"I'm gonna call the police!" West exploded. "Fucking degenerate junkie scum! You don't deserve to live, and you certainly don't deserve to die!"

West tore around the room, eventually locating a mobile in the pocket of a discarded jacket.

"Hello, is that the police," West belched into the phone once he'd grabbed it, "I'd like to report a heroin slumber party. Yes, that's right, I'm calling from the Scapa Loch Housing Estate. What, you're not interested? But this is completely illegal, there are people lying around doing absolutely nothing because they are smacked out of their minds. I started to beat one of them with a coat hanger and nobody batted an eyelid. This could be a huge drugs bust, I'm sure it would win you a promotion. What, you won't come over here? So much for British justice."

West threw the phone against a wall and stormed out of the house. A few days later, he left the Scapa Loch Housing Estate for a safe haven somewhere on the mainland, where he wouldn't be taunted by junkies.

Love For Sale

Captain Swanky was trying to develop some kind of relationship with Mrs. Minker, a single mother who lived in one of the blocks opposite ours. Mrs. Minker did a bit of prostitution to supplement her benefits, and since what Swanky basically wanted was a shag, his best bet would have been to part with a score. Being an incorrigible romantic, The Captain didn't want to pay for sex. Instead, he figured that if he offered to look after Mrs. Minker's baby Pearl every now and then, Mrs. Minker would give him the odd freebie. I was trying to sleep when Swanky rang up on the entry phone and demanded my help with the infant. I got dressed and went down to his car.

"I can't get the seat belt to work on the baby!" Swanky complained.

"Hardly surprising," I told him, "you need a child seat."

"What do you mean I need a child seat? Are you saying there is something wrong with the seats in my car?"

"The seats in your car are designed for adults, there isn't a car seat in the world that is suitable for infants and adults."

"Well, what am I supposed to do if I haven't got a child seat?"

"The best thing is to get someone to go as a passenger, so that they can take the baby on their lap."

"Okay, you'll have to come with me."

"Where are we heading?" I asked Swanky as I got into the car and he handed me the baby.

"Weavers Fields."

"Why Weavers Fields? Why not Coram's Fields? That's a much nicer park, and not that much further west than Weavers is east."

"You don't understand do you?" The Captain said as he slid into the drivers seat and turned the keys in the ignition.

"What don't I understand?"

"Well, you don't get schoolgirls hanging out in Coram's Fields do you? A baby is a babe magnet, young girls who want a baby of their own will ask if they can get a shot of Pearl. If they're wanting a baby, then they've got to be up for a shag."

"What if they are underage?" I demanded.

"I'm not going to shag a girl in a school uniform without asking her age first. You do get sixteen year old schoolgirls you know. It's the law that kids have to stay in school until they are at least sixteen, and conveniently sixteen is also the age of consent."

"Well, what if a girl lies to you and says she's sixteen when she isn't?"

"It wouldn't be my fault if she lied, I'd have shown I was responsible by asking her age."

"It's well known a lot of people lie about their age."

"Yes," The Captain shot back, "and women tend to claim they are a few years younger than they really are!"

"What about my internet music marketing plan?" Swanky's babe magnet bullshit was winding me up, and since I could never get him to see sense, I figured the best thing to do was change the subject and keep a close eye on him once we got to the park.

"What music marketing plan?"

"That we do a site whereby over a year subscribers build up a sophisticated CD collection by buying two recommended albums a week from us by mail order."

"Sounds like too much of a boy's thing, I can't see girls going for it."

Swanky parked his car in Vallance Road and used this

as an excuse for talking about the Kray twins, who'd grown up in the street. We walked through Weavers Fields to the play area. Swanky was excited as there were a couple of really good looking Asian girls on the swings. He was probably the oldest male excited by the girls, but he certainly wasn't the only one. A group of Bangladeshi boys were working up the courage to go and talk to the girls. Eventually one of them left the safety of the bench they were huddled on, and made his way across to the girls.

"Hi," the teenager said, "I don't think I've seen you here before."

"We're not Bengali, you know," one of the girls spat.

The boy slunk back to his friends, who were already disappearing south towards Three Colts Lane. Captain Swanky seized his opportunity.

"Hello girls, would either of you care to hold my baby?"

"Why would we want to do that grandpa?" the bolder girl cried. "I'm not falling for your tricks. If I took the baby, you'd probably put your hand up my skirt and there wouldn't be a lot I could do about it. Sod off, sailor. I don't like dirty old men."

"Are you Pakistani?" Swanky countered.

"No, I'm Bengali."

"So why did you just tell those boys you weren't Bengali?"

"Because I don't like being hassled by men."

The Captain had more than met his match.

I Can't Stand It

Diana was off on one of her "let's get ourselves sorted out" trips. She hadn't touched a drop of alcohol for at least three days. She wanted me to go to a rehabilitation centre with her, where she'd get off the booze and I'd lay off the smack. We could hold hands and do twelve step together in blissful union. I could imagine Diana caught up in the phoney religious euphoria of a detox clinic, where she'd suddenly rediscover her belief in God. The whole thing was bound to end in tears, since I wasn't prepared to offer myself as a sacrifice to a non-existent higher power. Then there was cold turkey to consider. I'd be locked in a room until all my most immediate cravings for skag had passed. This would, of course, take several days. All in all, drug rehabilitation wasn't an alluring prospect.

"Once we're both cleaned up, I can marry you and have your babies," Diana announced chirpily.

"Peter Blake," I said doing my best to ignore this provocation, "emerged from the first wave of British pop art, a group of painters whose work was so quickly assimilated by the establishment that it is difficult to understand why their output appeared so exciting in the fifties. Blake claimed pop art was rooted in nostalgia for old popular things, and this belief is reflected in his use of imagery drawn from fairgrounds, wrestling matches and strip-tease. Major works by Blake, including *On The Balcony* and *Toy Shop*, are said to have influenced the iconography of the burgeoning mod movement through their depiction of practice targets and union jacks. Despite this, Blake's pictures are every bit as sentimental as those of the Pre-Raphaelites."

"I'd like a really big garden and we could go out in

it together to direct the gardeners as they weeded the flower beds, and mowed the lawns."

"It is over thirty-five years since the appearance of Blake's best known work, the cover design for *Sgt. Pepper*, the Beatles album regarded by many as the peak of the group's creativity. *Sgt. Pepper* saw the Fab Four at their most loved-up and at the time Blake's baroque cover crowded with famous faces appeared to be the perfect visual compliment to the music. The impact of Blake's work for the Beatles was reinforced by the way it clashed with the stark minimalism of the later White Album, considered alone it has aged badly."

"We could home educate the children, or at least we could have tutors in to do it for us."

"However, Blake's Beatles artwork hasn't attracted the mass of folklore that developed around *Abbey Road*. To give just one example, the Secular Order Of Druids insist the *Abbey Road* cover mimics a photo of a druid procession at Tower Hill and that John Lennon was dressed in white because he was leading the group into the realm of legend. The *Sgt. Pepper* sleeve is a psychedelic period piece which only works today because of the tensions inherent in its relationship to other Beatles records. Blake's more recent commercial work, covers for Paul Weller's *Stanley Road* and various terrible charity records, are at best forgettable. He lives on his reputation."

"The first born would be named Dylan, and we'd call his younger sister Gwendoline."

Delirium

I got a job washing dishes. It was hot in the kitchen and I had to stand with my hands immersed in dirty water at the sink. The proprietor had Radio Two blaring constantly as he fried up orders like double egg and chips; eggs, beans and chips; or, egg, sausage, beans and chips. The proprietor's wife took the orders, served the food and worked the till. She didn't think I washed dishes as well as her son, who as she never tired of telling me, had gone to night school and now had a job as an accountant. She sacked me after two weeks.

Soul Superman

I wanted to blow up the Old Man of Hoy—a one hundred and thirty seven metre stack of fissured and layered red sandstone. The Old Man was a ubiquitous tourist image because the battering this bit of rock had suffered from the Atlantic left it looking like a larger-than-life human figure. I felt that by attacking this icon, I could really move forward with my dialectic of vandalism, since it should go without saying that the urge to destroy is also a creative urge. Unfortunately I made the mistake of mentioning my plans to Stephen Milligan.

"You can't do that!" the former Tory MP flounced. "The Old Man of Hoy is a national monument."

"What do I care about that?"

"Oh, I was forgetting you are a Marxist."

"I'm not a Marxist," I corrected, "I'm a communist. I'm against the cult of the personality, and although

Marx made a significant contribution to the workers' movement, I'm not about to name my politics after him. To do so would be both a tactical and a strategic error."

"Very well, but I always despised communist states like the Soviet Union."

"I could never see any substantial difference between the USSR and other capitalist regimes in terms of economic organisation. Okay, so in England a significant percentage of agricultural workers were transformed into factory workers unconsciously and bloodily, while in the Soviet Union, Stalin consciously and bloodily transformed a lot of agricultural workers into factory workers. Both were and are brutal capitalist states, even if one was a democracy and the other a dictatorship. If we use ten percent or less of the population working in agriculture as a bench mark of when any particular nation was transformed into a capitalist state, then it becomes obvious that Russia entered the modern world considerably later in the scheme of things than England and America. Likewise, it would be a mistake to characterise the former Soviet Union as an example of state capitalism, since states are always ruled in the interests of a class and not by a mode of production."

"What are you on about."

"The crucial factors that distinguish my analysis, or rather Bordiga's analysis, from that of the ultra-left—which at the end of the day, is deformed by the pre-history of its late break with Trotskyism..."

"I thought you wanted to blow up The Old Man of Hoy."

"I do."

"Well you can't do that."

"Why not."

"Because it would be too visible a statement about

what is going on here. You're employed on this estate to amuse us, not to draw attention to the fact that many supposedly dead and disappeared individuals are living here under new identities."

"Well I know very well who you are."

"Yes, but officially I'm now Peter Peterson."

"So why worry about me blowing up The Old Man."

"Because hundreds of tourists pass it by boat every day, and someone is bound to notice."

"You can't stop me blowing it up."

"I don't need to, the British state has its army and police to prevent you doing anything as anti-social as destroying a national monument."

"You'd grass me up?"

"I'll have you hung, drawn and quartered if you so much as mention this silly idea again."

Quite obviously there were strict limits to my role as scam artist-in-residence, and evidently I'd suffer dire consequences if I was anything less than subtle in the ways I transgressed them.

Wade In The Water

I'd been listening to Ramsey Lewis. I'd consumed a pot of tea. It was about 11 pm and I decided to take a leak before choosing a fresh record. Water was seeping in through the toilet ceiling. I went through to the bathroom, water was dribbling in through the ceiling there too. I got buckets from under the kitchen sink to catch the drips but a lot of water had already fallen, and some was coming straight down the wall, so I had to put down towels to soak those parts of the spillage I was unable to catch before it reached the floor. I could hear someone moving about in the flat above mine, so I went up to speak to them. I knocked quietly—the Inconsiderates had young children and I did not want to wake them—but got no answer. I went back down to my own flat only to find the water flow getting worse. I located the council's out of hours emergency repairs number but concluded there was little point in phoning it unless I could get the occupants of flat 5 to agree to let somebody into their home to deal with the problem.

Since I was unable to get an answer by knocking lightly on the door, I resolved to listen and watch out for Mr. Inconsiderate who always comes in from his work as a waiter after midnight. When Mr. Inconsiderate entered the block with several of his friends at 12.30 am, I stopped him on the stairwell and after telling him there was water coming into my bathroom from his flat, asked if he would allow emergency repairs into his home if I phoned them. Mr. Inconsiderate said he would deal with the matter, and shut his door in my face after I followed him up the stairs. I went back into my flat, but since I could hear no evidence of Mr. Inconsiderate doing anything other than partying with his friends (I can hear him using his phone in my flat) and the water seepage was worsening, I went back up and knocked on the door.

After I shouted at Mr. Inconsiderate through his closed door that I wanted him to do something about the flooding, he opened the door and told me that he had called the emergency repair service but they were busy and nobody could come until the morning. So I asked Mr. Inconsiderate if the water was coming from his flat or the flat above. He showed me his bathroom which was flooded, and said the water was coming from the toilet cistern. His flat was laid out like Atima and Idira's flat, with a bath, basin and toilet suite in a single room. In my flat, there was a separate bathroom and toilet. I asked Mr. Inconsiderate to turn his water off at the mains, and he said he didn't know where the stopcock was. On my way out of the flat I glanced through the open door of the flat's smaller bedroom, and saw that it contained a broken chair and a lot of tools. It appeared Mr.

Inconsiderate and his family all slept in the master bedroom. He seemed to be using the second bedroom as some kind of workshop, which no doubt explained the hammering that would often disturb me all afternoon.

Once I'd been back in my flat for about fifteen minutes, Mr. Inconsiderate came down and knocked on my door. When I answered he asked for the emergency repairs number, which I gave him. Assuming Mr. Inconsiderate had decided to sort out the problem, I listened to some rare soul albums on my headphones. The headphones enabled me to hear my music despite the bhangra blaring above me, and meant that I wasn't adding to the disturbance already being caused in the block. I listened to rare groove until Captain Swanky came in with Jasmine.

"Get that shit off the recorder deck!" Swanky screamed after he'd unplugged my headphones. "You know Jasmine and I hate soul music."

"You're weird!" Jasmine announced. "You sit around all night listening to records on your own. That is really creepy. You ought to move out. The Captain needs this place for himself. You're wrecking his life and mine by cluttering up this pad with your freaky behaviour."

"I can't afford to leave this flat, I don't earn enough

money to pay a commercial sector rent. If the Captain doesn't like sharing this place with me, then he could get somewhere else. He's got plenty of money."

By the time I'd finished speaking, the Captain was making up G&Ts in the kitchen. Jasmine was chanting the word creep at me, so I decided to head for bed. The next thing I knew it was 7.45 am, and Jasmine was shaking me awake.

"The bathroom and toilet are flooded! There's water pouring in through the ceiling! Do something about it."

I got up and dressed. It transpired that Jasmine and The Captain had been out boozing all night, and after a couple more drinks they'd fallen asleep in the living room without ever stepping out of their glad rags. I decided to go upstairs and ask the Inconsiderates what they had done to sort out the flooding. However, although I could hear movement in the flat, nobody answered the door when I knocked.

I phoned the emergency repairs number at 8.10 am and was told I'd have to wait and phone the local housing office because there was no emergency cover for the hour between 8 am and 9 am. I phoned the local housing office immediately and left a message on their answering machine asking them to call me back and let me know what was being done to halt the flooding we were suffering. Since I'd heard nothing by 9.15 am, I rang again and was greeted by the same answering machine message I'd heard an hour and five minutes earlier. I called again at 9.30 am and was told I would be called back. However, no one called back, so I called again at 11 am and was told that an emergency repair order had been issued and the problem would be sorted out in due course. By 10 pm the flow of water had slowed, but not stopped. By then I'd emptied too many buckets to count and run through all my towels. The Captain, of course, had gone out. This wasn't such a bad situation, since at least it meant that I didn't have to put up with Jasmine, who'd left with him.

Burn Baby Burn

The estate was deserted. A body had been dredged from the harbour at Lyness and a convey of cars had set out from Scapa Loch to view the corpse. Stephen Milligan was barely recognisable. He was bloated and white, and his face was covered with bruises and scars. According to a doctor who mysteriously appeared on the island, there was nothing suspicious about all this, since the injuries might have been sustained after Milligan had fallen into the sea. As for the fact that his hands were tied behind his back, it was well known that the former Tory MP indulged in dangerous auto-sexual acts. The restraint was elasticated, so it was quite possible that Milligan had leashed himself up. All in all, the doctor concluded, it was a tragic accident and a terrible waste of a life. He concluded that Milligan had been getting his jollies by immersing his head in salt water with his hands bound behind his back, when bending too far forwards, he tumbled into the sea.

The doctor was all for tossing the corpse back in the waves, since officially Milligan was already dead and buried. I wanted to give him a proper send off, so we loaded the body into the back of a Land Rover and headed for Scapa Loch. By the time we'd built a pyre on the site of the former Community Hall, and had placed Milligan and most of his worldly possessions on top, it was getting dark. I threw a liberal amount of petrol over this construction and then passed bottles of beer around. I stood next to the funeral pyre with a flaming torch in my right hand, and a bottle of Stella in the left. I raised the booze into the air, then scattered half of it on the ground as a libation. I put the bottle to my lips and drank the remaining beer in a single gulp.

"Friends!" I announced. "We are gathered here today not to bury Stephen Milligan, but to burn him. The perfection of suicide lies in ambiguity. Indeed, many of the most spectacular suicides of our benighted era were in reality political murders carried out by the secret state. As you will no doubt be aware, Milligan was a right-wing mystical cretin whose every pronouncement exuded the rotten egg smell of the idea of God. Stephen always insisted that some of his best friends lived in South America. Drowning is an occupational hazard of those who eat plankton. Let us remember Milligan as the man he really was, a bully and a coward. Only last week, this conservative worm was threatening to grass me up to the police. So as we watch Stephen's mortal remains burn, let us not forget that he was directly responsible for making the world we inhabit a living hell. Although Milligan died today, it is not in the least bit paradoxical to say that he never really lived."

With that—and amid cheering, hand claps, whistles and the stamping of feet—I threw my torch onto the pyre causing it to erupt into flames. Free jazz blared from a beat box, and with our hands on the hips of the person in front of us, everyone present did a snake dance around the fire, and then across the entire estate. When the dancing stopped, we broke up into little drinking groups with our world illuminated by the flickering flames of the funeral pyre.

"It's a shame the Ship Inn has been converted into a

community hall," someone said, "because if it was still a pub, we could loot it for booze."

"There must be some hooch, or something else worth looting in the community hall," someone else put in.

"Let's just do it," a third voice announced decisively.

This was no sooner said than it was done. The door to the community hall was kicked in, and moments later various items—including tables and chairs—where being hurled out through its shattered windows. Shortly afterwards, bottles of wine were being passed through the door and circulated among the increasingly excited crowd. Flaming embers were soon removed from the pyre and thrown into the community hall, which a number of individuals were still stripping of its contents. Someone pointed out that Milligan's car was parked outside his house, so a crew went off to set it alight. Once this had been accomplished, it was inevitable that a blaze should destroy not just the dead man's house, but also those of his immediate neighbours. By this time, the former Ship Inn was also a smouldering ruin.

"It's just like Paris in May Sixty-Eight!" a pallid figure cried.

There was another shout, a ghostly echo and I couldn't make out whether what was being said was "Watts" or "What?" I decided to leave the festivities behind. I needed a shot and some sleep.

Two Stupid Feet

I saw the sign on the door of a printer's as I walked down Redchurch Street: "Courier wanted for weekend job." I went in. It was a bank holiday and the firm had to get a box of leaflets to Manchester by Monday morning. It was Friday and the work wouldn't be finished until eight o'clock. It was cheaper to buy a train ticket to Manchester and pay someone thirty quid to take it up than stump up for the holiday rates of regular courier firm. I picked the tickets and the box up on Friday night. It was heavy but I could carry it, so I walked back to my flat with it. On Saturday morning I took a bus to King's X. I sat on a train for three hours, then got off and after a short walk, which had been marked out on a map for me, I was relieved of my burden. I took a brisk stroll around the city. I didn't find anything to do, so I took the next train home. On Monday morning I went back to the printers. They phoned their client, and once it was confirmed I'd successfully delivered the leaflets, I was handed three ten pound notes. That was it, that was the job.

"Got any more work?"

"Not really, you were just lucky we screwed up our scheduling on the run up to a bank holiday weekend. Most of the time it's cheaper to use a regular courier."

Our Love Will Grow

I received a rather stern warning from my employers about the funeral festivities. In the aftermath of the debacle surrounding the burning of Stephen Milligan's corpse (part Viking festival, part posthumous lynching), I discovered there was a governor in charge of the entire Scapa Loch Housing Estate. Jim Fletcher, the estate manager, was only a front man. The governor called me to his office, which was in one of the show homes. He sat in a high backed chair with his right hand poised above a pile of papers, a fountain pen held tightly between the thumb and index finger. He looked at me sternly, indicated that I should sit down, removed his glasses and proceeded to speak.

"This estate," the governor explained, "is an experiment, an invisible open prison that the inmates mistakenly perceive as their home. They can even leave Scapa Loch, but not the islands of Hoy and Flotta. That was Stephen Milligan's big mistake, he tried to board a ship to the Orkney mainland. He'd worked out what was going on and imagined that by joining a car ferry as a foot passenger he could fool us. My men were onto him before he'd left his house. For people to be happy here, they must believe they have come as a matter of their own free will and made this prison camp their home. We are offering fugitives from criminal gangs and the mass media protection from the outside world. You are supposed to entertain these voluntary prisoners, and as an artist-in-residence your ultimate interests are identical with those of the prison officers who have been disguised as an estate management team. The guys who mow the lawns and do general maintenance are, to use the dehumanising language of the criminal, screws."

"Fine," I said, "but I didn't know this was a prison, I might have behaved differently if I'd known that earlier."

"You are an artist, and it wasn't considered necessary to inform you of exactly what we where doing here.

However, as a result of your foolishness, I've not only had various buildings burnt down, I've also suffered a riot in my open prison. If I was dealing with Category A prisoners, a riot wouldn't be a very big deal, but in an invisible prison it is a real blemish on my work record."

"So what are you going to do about it?"

"I'm going to vent my feelings of powerlessness, frustration and anger on you."

"And how do you propose to do that?"

"Easy," the governor replied, "it is well known to me and my staff that you, like a number of the inmates, have a hard drug problem. I'm going to make you clean up your act, and then set you back to work."

"You can't make me do anything like that, there's nothing in my contract that says I can't take drugs."

"I don't give a fuck about your contract."

"I'll sue for constructive dismissal."

"No you won't, not if you can't contact a lawyer. You're not going anywhere, you can't leave Hoy without my agreeing to it first."

"But that's a suspension of habeas corpus."

"You can forget about your herbaceous borders, drug addiction is an emergency situation."

"On a relative scale, being a junkie hardly compares with the suspension of the due process of law."

"I wouldn't know about that, what I do know is that I'm going to lock you in a room and make you do cold turkey. Once you're clean I'm going to make you paint pictures, because that's what artists are supposed to do."

Voices Inside (Everything Is Everything)

The communal windows in our block had been smashed by the gang of teenage speed freaks who descended on our estate the minute school was out. Water was dripping from leaking pipes. It dripped day and night, I'd phoned the estate office every day for the past five weeks to complain about the dripping water. It stopped me going to sleep at night, and if I did get to sleep then every time I woke up it sounded as if it was pissing with rain, even when the sun was shining. The situation was more than just depressing, it was out of control. I was low on funds and would shop carefully, only to come home and find that The Captain had eaten all my grub, so then I'd have to skip meals. The local housing office had branded me a trouble maker, and I was dragged from my bed on more than one occasion when Andrea Curwain, the estate officer, knocked on my door.

"I've just received another of your letters," Curwain complained. "It isn't my fault if the people who work under me can't spell or write grammatically correct sentences. When my assistant said the communal windows weren't being repaired because they were subjects of vandalism, I can assure you he meant they were subject to vandalism. The council would not install self-vandalising windows, and we are not going to repair them because they've been broken too many times in the past. I've never had another tenant like you on this estate. I don't know what you're doing here. You've got clerical skills that would enable you to earn good money, so I don't understand why you don't just go and buy your own home."

Andrea reminded me of someone; she wasn't the only woman who went on and on about how I should move off the Stanton Drew Estate. That was Jasmine's constant refrain. All I was trying to do was stick up for myself, but being assertive got me branded as an obnoxious trouble maker. I wasn't sure how much more I could take.

Bok To Bach

Conveying the horrors of cold turkey to someone who has never suffered it is a task on a par to writing a ten thousand word essay about the inside of a ping-pong ball. In other words, it is something that is only ever attempted by the foolish or the brave. I am neither foolish, nor am I brave, but I was locked in a whitewashed room, with a bed and bars on the window. There was a sink to wash at, and a pot to piss in. After being left alone in the room, I paced from the bed to the window, and from the window to the bed. Sitting on the bed and looking out through the window, I could see the tops of trees and a pallid blue sky above them. Standing at the window I could see lawns and flower beds, as well as trees and the sky. The sky was pale blue, and partially obscured by thin white clouds. The clouds seemed to hang motionlessly in the air, although I'm certain they must have been moving, even if their motion was imperceptible to me.

The single bed had a battered wooden headboard and battered wooded legs. The initials "F.N." had been carved into the headboard, and it was covered with scratches and ink stains. The white sheets were worn, the blanket that was thrown over them had suffered a two and a half centimetre tear just off its central point, three centimetres in from the edge at the bottom of the bed. The pillow case had yellowed in the middle, but was still white at the edges. The blanket was light green, a lighter green than the lawn outside. The white-washed walls, or rather two of the four whitewashed walls, were stained with a light brown damp patch in the corner above the sink. This stain also blemished the whitewashed ceiling in the same corner. A spider had spun a web on the outside of the window, and a gnat was trapped in this snare. The white paint on the window frame was peeling.

I walked from the window to the bed, sat down on the bed, got up again and walked back to the window. The boards beneath the worn brown carpet weren't laid evenly, and they creaked as I moved over them. I looked out across the lawns, and saw flower beds, with trees and the sky behind them. A ginger cat stalked over a lawn and disappeared from my field of vision. I turned and walked from the window to the bed. I sat down on the edge of the bed, then allowed myself to fall back onto the mattress. I swung my legs up onto the bed and pulled the pillow under my head. Several springs in the centre of the mattress had given way, and I had to shift to the edge of the bed in order to feel comfortable. I took a dozen deep breaths and listened to myself inhaling and exhaling air. From somewhere in the building I could hear the sound of an extractor fan. Footsteps echoed on stairs. I felt dizzy, and had I not been lying down, I may well have collapsed.

Bird song from beyond the windows became a pneumatic hammering in my head. I forced myself up, pushed my feet down towards the floor. The floorboards creaked beneath me as I placed first my left leg in front of my right leg, and then my right leg in front of my left leg. Eventually I reached the window and with considerable effort, forced it open. The fresh air made me feel sick. The bars across the window prevented me from sticking my head out and puking into the garden. I staggered across to the sink and emptied my guts. I fell to my knees, crawled back to the bed, but unable to haul myself onto it, I lay on the floor.

Someone came in and took out the pot I'd been left with, replacing it with a clean one. I don't even know if I'd filled the pot that was replaced. Whoever took the pot out helped me onto the bed. When I awoke I felt sick, and when I slept I felt sick. Sometimes I was stretched out, at others clenched up into a foetal ball. The sheets were soaked with my urine, and they were also soaked with my sweat. I huddled under the blanket. I'd never felt so cold in my life. I cried and I cursed. I cursed and I cried. I slept without sleeping and woke without waking. The blackness of night was a terror, and the brightness of day a crippling pain. I slept with my eyes open, and kept them screwed tightly shut when I was awake. The bed was a bed of nails. The world was smoke, fire and flames.

Sham Time

I tried the Job Centre again.

"You want to go for this job?"

"Yes, I want that job."

"I'm not phoning up and asking if you can have an interview for that job."

"Why not?"

"Well, didn't you tell me you had A-levels?"

"Yes, I've got A-levels."

"You're over-qualified for the job."

"If I'm over-qualified, that means I'm competent to do the job."

"You might be able to do it, but that doesn't mean you'd stick it. Besides, you'd be taking the job away from someone who didn't have as good an education as you."

"What about if I told you I was lying and I didn't have any A-levels?"

"Well, if you lied, that means you're unreliable and I can't send you for the job."

Heavy Bopper

I chilled out at home for a couple of days after getting back from the clinic on the other side of the Scapa Loch Housing Estate. Three days after my return, I went across to see Diana. She'd had a fake banana plantation installed in her back garden. The plastic trees were arranged in neat rows. Leaving aside for the moment the fact that the trees weren't very life-like, the area covered was also way too small for the folly to pass as a convincing banana plantation. This didn't prevent me from imagining that I was an anti-character in Alain Robbe-Grillet's nouveau roman *Jealousy*. We were sitting on white plastic chairs under a veranda. On the white plastic table that was positioned between us stood tall thin glasses filled with gin, ice, lemon and tonic. Diana had a green plastic straw in her glass. I'd taken the straw out of my glass and laid it on the table beside my drink. The straws had a ridged section two thirds of the way up, so that they could be bent. I'd straightened my straw out. The top end of Diana's straw stuck out over the lip of her glass, at a right-angle to its stem, which descended to the bottom of her gin-filled chalice.

Towards the centre of the table, slightly closer to Diana than to me, was an ash tray. I fixed my gaze on Diana's nicotine stained fingers as she stubbed out a dog-end. I tried to work out how Robbe-Grillet would have described the yellowed digits. I couldn't get my mind to focus, idealism was beyond me, it was years since I'd last read Robbe-Grillet, or Robert Pinget, or Nathalie Sarraute, or William Burroughs, or J.G. Ballard, or even Michael Moorcock. Robbe-Grillet would have focused on Diana's nails which were well manicured and decorated with red polish. The mysterious objects of desire in his books were rarely blemished by their entanglements with commodity culture. A sado-masochistic attraction to the allure of commodity fetishism was readily evident in Robbe-Grillet's work, and given this textual orientation, he was sexually incapable of denouncing a system that turned people into things for the sake of profit.

"A lot happened while you were away," Diana announced tensely.

"Such as?"

"Police raids. There were a lot of drug raids. The cops apparently decided things had gone too far and that a bubbling undercurrent of anti-social activity was threatening to engulf Hoy."

"Who got nicked?"

"Who didn't?"

"Okay, if you won't tell me who got lifted, tell me who didn't."

"I wasn't raided."

"And?"

"Please tell me I'm not really a princess, I'm just a look-a-like, an ordinary woman with a passion for kitsch."

"What are you talking about?"

"While you were away, the police came to see me, and they told me that some of the junkies on the estate were so out of it that they believed I'm really Princess Diana, that she didn't die in a car crash in Paris, and that I'm her."

"So? What did they want to do? Kiss your hand?"

"No, no, much worse than that! They wanted to slip me a hot shot—that's when you deliberately give someone an overdose of heroin to kill them. Then when I was dead, they were going to charge people hundreds of pounds to have sex with my corpse. They were convinced they could make a fortune."

"That's ridiculous!"

"But it's true, the police told me it's true."

"How do they know?"

"The police know everything."

"No they don't."

"Tell me I'm not really a princess."

"You're not really a princess."

"You're just humouring me."

"Who cares?"

"You think I'm really Princess Di too, don't you?"

"What does it matter what I think?"

"I don't get it, if you really think I'm Princess Di, why won't you sleep with me?"

"Leave it out, I'm going home."

"Don't."

I got up from my chair.

"Don't go."

"I'm going."

"Why?"

"I'm sick of this conversation."
I finished my gin and left.

Home Is Where The Hate Is

I didn't have any money and Captain Swanky was at a loose end too. So we went out to The White Hart on Whitechapel High Street and Swanky bought me Adnams. I ended up in The White Hart more often than the pub merited, mainly on account of my weakness for Adnams Suffolk Ales, which weren't that widely available in London. The White Hart didn't get too crowded, unless there'd been an opening on at the nearby Whitechapel Gallery. The drinkers were usually a mix of city types and locals who didn't quite gel together. That was what it was like when I went in with Swanky. The clientele was almost exclusively blokes, and most of them were watching an unbelievably dull international soccer match on a wide screen TV.

"The way I see it," I told Swanky, "is that there are a lot of people out there who'd love to buy some decent music if they just knew where to get it. Record sales are in steep decline because most people are sick of the corporates punting out crap."

"Look at that!" the Captain exclaimed pointing at a woman who'd just come in wearing a skirt with a slit in it that went all the way up to her waist.

"So I figure we could go for a whole mix of quality music, some soul, some contemporary classical, Glenn Gould and Cornelius Cardew, maybe even some Luigi Nono..."

Swanky wasn't paying me a blind bit of notice, his

eyes were following the woman in the slit skirt as she moved around the room. She was going up to most of the customers and kissing them. She even came up to Swanky and kissed him. I pushed her away when she approached me. Someone gave her a drink, so she jumped up on a table and started to dance.

"I'm going to have her," The Captain hissed, "so why don't you blow?"

"She looks like a professional, so you'll either get nowhere or end up paying."

"I'm not paying, I'm just going to have her."

So I left Swanky to it. It wasn't a long walk home, twenty minutes at a clip. I cut up Commercial Street past a slew of prostitutes. Swanky came home several hours later, a hang-dog expression on his face. He didn't tell me what had happened. He didn't need too. It was all too obvious he hadn't got off with the chick.

What About The Music

For Sale signs were mushrooming on the front lawns of houses at Scapa Loch. The demographic make-up of the estate was being transformed. The prisoners who'd made up the bulk of the initial post-US military population were being transferred to new locations, the screws and prison administration were disappearing too. Replacing the English population were cheerful Scots drawn almost exclusively from the skilled working class. Simultaneously, Calvinism was destroying the open plan layout of the scheme. Fences were springing up to mark out spatial territories, neighbour was divided from neighbour in an unabashed frenzy of possessive individualism. The estate was deserted for most of the day, families would disappear to Kirkwall and beyond, not returning home until school had finished. Breadwinners still tended to work in the oil industry, but now there were more of them. And they were allowed to travel unescorted beyond the oil terminal on the neighbouring island of Flotta.

For some time, The Governor was still a presence and still on my back. This cretin was forcing me to produce what he called proper drawings; in other words, tiresome representations of things that he could identify from his everyday life. Since my skills as a draughtsman were at best rudimentary, I enlisted the aid of technology to help me do the work. The Governor would have blown a gasket if he'd known I was taking photographs and tracing their main outlines onto paper. My patron liked this hack work so much, he got me to frame some of it so that it might hang in his office. Several weeks down the line The Governor said my rehabilitation was coming along very nicely. Then one day he was gone, and I was left to my own devices. I roamed the empty streets wondering what to do. All around me was desolation. I'd been pretending to be an artist for so long I'd become one by default. I stretched some unprimed canvases and slashed them with single strokes from a cut-throat razor, producing secondhand modernism for a secondhand world. Copies without originals. Replications. It would have been naff to show this work in my own house. The old show homes had been emptied of furniture, so I broke into one of them and renamed it Gallery Zero, using it as a venue to put on a show. The Retro-Americana (Suburban) Homes press officer, who'd dealt with mailing lists and publicity for my earlier artistic impostures on Hoy, had decamped for pastures new. No one turned up for my private view, and the next morning there were no visitors to the show. I left the gallery door on the latch, so that if anyone wanted to see my work, they could let themselves in. I went to see Diana. Her front door was open, and her possessions were being loaded into a removal van. Diana was sobbing in the kitchen, a half empty bottle of gin standing on a fitted work top.

"What's wrong?" I asked.

"I don't have any ice," Diana had difficulty getting the words out, "I defrosted the fridge last night, and it has already been loaded into the van."

"You've got the remains of a bottle of tonic." I coaxed.

"Yes, but I don't have a glass in which to mix it with the gin, all my dry goods are packed up. I don't have lemons either."

"Where are you going?"

"Far away."

"Where far away?"

"Somewhere you'll never find me."

"Why would I want to find you?"

"You're heartless."

"I'll go."

"You'll come with me?"

"No, I'll go home."

"Stay, I don't want to leave if you won't go with me."

"So why move?"

"What choice do I have?"

"Can't you stay here?"

"No, the Russian mafia knows where I am and they're planning to kidnap me."

"Who told you that?"

"The police."

"And you believed them?"

"Of course I believed them, they're the police, it's their job to protect me."

"So where are you going?"

"I don't know, somewhere I'll be safe, the police have organised it all, what does it matter?"

"Well, you know my address, you can always write to me if you feel like it."

"No, never, I'm not allowed to contact you, the intelligence services tell me that you're in on the plot. You sold the information about my whereabouts to the Russian mafia for fifty grand, and when they discover I'm not here, they'll probably kill you."

Spear For The Moondog

I didn't go to the Job Centre. In fact, I didn't even get up until after it was dark. When I did get up, I sat in the kitchen and went from my chair to the cupboard, and from the cupboard to my chair. I don't believe in the unconscious but I know psychologists would call what I was doing comfort eating. Back and forth I went. Up and down. On and off my chair. I'd find something in the cupboard, heat it or eat it cold, then I'd go back to the cupboard and see what else I might consume. I'd started on baked beans. Followed by a can of tomato soup. Then I'd had a can of rice pudding that I couldn't be bothered to heat. Now I was onto noodles, and since there weren't any vegetables in the flat to make a sauce, after boiling this staple I'd simply dressed it with ketchup. The idea was classical simplicity, the result was slop. I'd also been going back and forth between the kettle and my chair and the fridge. I guess this is a minimal retelling, since before I could put a tea bag in my cup, I had to fetch one from the cupboard. It was only after I'd done this that I added the boiling water. So back and forth I went between my chair and the cupboard and the kettle and the fridge. Once the tea had stewed, I'd add some milk and every time I did this, I returned the pint bottle to the fridge. On and on I went, up and down, back and forth, from the cupboard to the chair, from the kettle to the fridge. I'd heard that fat people were supposed to be jolly, and I wasn't sure whether I wanted to be jolly or if I'd simply enjoy becoming fat. Then I started to worry that all my motion and movement might be burning off the calories I wanted to pile on. After that I sat on my chair and when I did move, I moved slowly and with great deliberation. I left the milk on the table. I emptied the cupboard and laid everything I might eat in front of me. I positioned myself so that I could reach the kettle from my chair. I couldn't reach the cold water tap from my chair at the table, and that is something else that until now I've left out of this minimal retelling, my movements back and forth from the sink. Eventually, I just sat and wondered and worried about whether I should fill a jug with water and place it by the kettle. I wanted to conserve my energy rather than waste it, but I wasn't sure of the best way to signify heaviness and immobility without effort. I wanted to embody the heaviness and immobility that Kierkegaard claimed was so characteristic of the English.

Sunshine Of Your Love

Washington propagandists were describing the Middle East as being in a state of anarchy. There had been another incident involving a US spy plane over Chinese coastal waters. American relations with Russia were unravelling, and there were rumours of a second Bay Of Pigs invasion. The so called War On Terrorism was back in the headlines. The residents of the Scapa Loch Housing Estate felt this called for celebration, so a street party was organised. Trestle tables festooned with St. Andrew's flags and studded with cans of beer and sausages on sticks sprouted along the pavements. Fiddle music was blaring from beat boxes and adults sunned themselves in deck chairs while simultaneously getting blind drunk. Children were running around screaming, or stuffing themselves with finger foods until they puked. The last time I'd seen behaviour this crazed, it was to celebrate the royal wedding of Charles and Diana, and way back then

I was living in London.

"Can I have a Pringle?" I asked my new neighbours as I was surveying their contribution to the festivities.

"Take them all," a man replied jovially, "we do nae care, we're gang to be rich."

"Aye," someone else put in, "I'm gang to buy a hoose in Edinburgh, and I will nae need a mortgage!"

"We've just got tae hold oot til the Americans become a wee bitty more desperate," the first speaker added sagely, "they've offered twice what I paid for ma hoose not more than a month ago, but if we hold oot they'll at least double that agin."

I was beginning to feel sick, and decided to give the Pringles a miss. I didn't own my house, I didn't even rent it, my pad was tied to somebody else's job.

The previous day I'd phoned up my bank to check my account balance, only to find my monthly wages hadn't gone in. Of course, the account wasn't in my own name because I'd long ago learnt I could only get what I wanted by using an alias. When I'd belled Tony Cheam's employers to complain about the non-payment of my wages, they'd claimed I'd failed to meet the terms of their contract, and that my position as artist-in-residence was under review. The woman I'd spoken with wasn't concerned about the fact that I might starve while waiting to hear whether or not my contract had been terminated. In fact, she'd only semi-humorously suggested this might suit Retro-Americana (Suburban) Homes, since my death would prevent me attempting to sue on the grounds that I'd suffered a constructive dismissal. Further, I was told I should consider myself lucky I still had a roof over my head, but that this situation wasn't going to carry on indefinitely, since my rent-free housing situation would come to an end as soon as I'd received formal notification that I'd lost my job.

I wandered down to the perimeter fence that separated the housing estate from the listening base, and wasn't much surprised to see that it was being patrolled by military policemen with dogs. I turned around, and stood with my back against the wire mesh, taking in what—thanks to a sudden deterioration in relations between the US and various other regimes—had just become a prime piece of real estate. I could see what was going to happen to me, I'd be made homeless again, and there didn't appear to be anything I could do about it. I had no plan, I had no money, I had nowhere to go. I was a spatially displaced person and no one was concerned about my fate. What happened to me didn't even enter the calculations of the planners. I would simply disappear, and the world would trundle on as if I'd never existed.

"Back off!" someone was shouting. "Back off! Move away from the fence!"

"What?" I said as I turned around, once I'd realised this order was being directed at me.

"Back off from the fence. That fence is US military property, and we don't want a dweeb like you interfering with it."

I wanted to protest but I couldn't think of a witty response to this insult. Besides, the military policeman had drawn a gun, and I didn't view getting shot as a laughing matter. I didn't want to go home, I didn't really have a home, just a temporary shelter. I walked off the estate, into the heather and hills of Hoy.

Unreal City

I couldn't sleep. All I could hear was Jasmine ranting on about her crap housing situation. It didn't seem so bad to me. She had a room in a house owned by a housing co-op, she had a room in a hostel for people who found it hard to cope, and she stayed at our place five nights a week. She liked the flat I shared with Swanky, what she didn't like, what she was complaining about, was me. I had to go. She was also whinging about spending the odd night in the hostel. She hated it, but had to show her face occasionally to make it look like she actually lived there. If she could stick it out for a year, she'd be entitled to a housing association flat. She considered that an indignity when her family could afford to buy her a pad. She was working on them, but then the reason her dad was so stinking rich was his reluctance to part with his money.

Jasmine had been ranting on about these matters for several hours, and I wasn't getting any sleep. I got up to make a cup of tea. The tea bags had been hidden, they must have been hidden because I'd opened a new packet the previous evening. There didn't seem to be any milk either, which was odd because there were two pints in the fridge when I went to bed. It was all part of a war of attrition. The Captain and Jasmine had taken to hiding and throwing out food in a bid to force me out of the flat. I was hanging on in there, I needed the place a lot more than they did. I didn't have anywhere to go other than back to my mother's in South London, whereas Swanky had his property holdings, and Jasmine had at least two rooms—not to mention her parents mansion in Hampstead.

I searched through various coat and trouser pockets and eventually scraped together the price of a cup of tea. There were two bagel shops on Brick Lane, a twenty-four hour café on Bishopsgate—indeed there was quite a choice of places within walking distance to get a cuppa in the small hours. Stepping out into the night, my thin jacket unzipped, the city itself a cocoon against inclement weather, I felt all at sea. Hoxton and Shoreditch were the new Soho, Camden, Notting Hill. But walking down Shoreditch High Street and Norton Folgate, the transition from a clubbing and high fashion area to one of high finance made the illusion of youth autonomy hard to maintain. There was more than one unreal city unsettling me here. There was a doubling which brought about two further doublings and so on, ad infinitum and ad nauseam. That first doubling/coupling consisted of an unreal city of finance generated from and mediated by an unreal city of cool. London was supposed to swing but finance was attracted by fashion, and fashion couldn't exist without finance. I was supposed to buy into the fantasy through novels, clothes, clubs, even the food I ate in restaurants. But I was excluded too. London was great if you were young or rich, preferably both, but I was neither young nor rich. I was just a poor fool.

I'm not sure when the idea of London started becoming a problem for me, when I started to doubt that the city existed. I can look back and see the process unfolding, but it is impossible to put a date on it. Reading too many London novels may have had something to do with it, indeed, I think I could explain it in these terms without anybody challenging what I had to say. Iain Sinclair caused me as many problems as Michael Bracewell. For a long time I was young and single and I loved to mingle. I'd travel beyond the bounds of the city without even realising it. I thought the Thames ran through my veins. The river was my constant point of reference. The Thames twists and turns, but I'd imagine it as a straight line and navigate my way around town by taking it as an east/west axis. I'd walk from Dulwich to Hackney, cycle from Stoke Newington to Reading, ride the tube from Richmond to Upminster, the entire length of the district line. When I lived in Kennington and I'd spent the day on Hampstead Heath, I might take the Northern line back south of the river, but instead of getting off at my stop I'd ride on to Morden. I'd get off, walk to Merton. Jump on a bus, get off and catch a train. I could please myself, I was claiming social security and had few responsibilities.

For too long I wandered the city, not really aware of how lucky I was to have been born in London in the sixties. I did well, and looking back on it, the only way I might have done better out of the welfare state was to have been born ten years earlier. I knew how to live cheaply, how to scavenge food, there were free fruit and vegetables to be had at New Covent Garden Market. Plenty of scavengers went there for the end of trading, to pick through what was unsold. I could get free wine at art openings and a little later I started turning up early for the launches of Verso Books, because I liked expensive finger foods from Marks and Spencers, but didn't have the readies to pay for them. I'd spend my money on records, and that is where—if I was to be disingenuous—I might claim my troubles began. Unfortunately, as the twentieth-century reached its end, I spent increasingly long stretches of time working—or more often than not, looking for work and dreaming up unfeasible get rich quick schemes, Welfare benefits became harder and harder to claim, and when I wasn't cooped up in an office, I was too drained by my surroundings (council housing that was being quite deliberately run down) to enjoy living in London. Life had become a pain in the arse and I wasn't enjoying doing what I was doing. Given the social system I was living under, money was the only thing that could cure my ills. I needed to become an owner/occupier in a plush pad with a West London address. I needed to get my dot.com music merchandising scam up and running. That night I didn't even get as far as purchasing a cup of tea. As dawn broke I found myself sitting in Finsbury Circus, with my head in my hands.

Right Track

My mornings and my nights were endlessly disturbed by the reactivation of the listening base. New buildings were being erected, a few of the old ones torn down, and I can only assume that the most up-to-date equipment was being installed. The sound of construction work was a constant irritant to anyone living on the Scapa Loch Housing Estate. Several residents who were holding out for a better price for their home told me sonic weapons were being deployed against them. There was endless whinging about the dirty tricks being used to acquire houses at a fraction of their real value, but in the end everybody went and in doing so, realised at least four times what they'd paid for their home. Rather than sonic weapons, the ultimate ace up the sleeve of the military establishment was compulsory purchase orders. But then, since we all knew the American government—like any other government—was made of paper money (and if they didn't have enough, then they could always print more), too much could never be enough, and the houses on the estate were destined to fall short of the former owner's estimation of their true financial value.

I guess James Rushbridger just couldn't stay away from trouble. He was found dead in the old listening base after the refurbishment began. There was much speculation about this in the local press (a D-notice was sent to the nationals, so they couldn't touch the story). Rushbridger had specialised in writing on spookery, and there were rumours that he might have been working for the Chinese or the Russians. No one believed he'd actually suffered a second auto-sexual death, despite the official story being he'd been found naked under a gas mask and an oil skin, a segment of orange in his mouth and a rope around his neck. I stayed away from the listening base, I barely went out of the house. The streets were filling with American children, the houses with US military intelligence personnel, all of whom were under strict instructions to have nothing to do with me.

The fences on the estate had been torn down, the layout was open plan once again. Kitchens and bathrooms had been refitted. New central heating systems had been installed. Much of what had been pulled out of the houses was piled up on the streets, and a not insubstantial part of it was to be found in my front garden. I would sneak out at night and pile this junk up on the pavement, hoping the dustmen would collect it. However, whenever I gave up my night vigils, or else fell asleep on them, I'd always wake to find my garden piled high with refuse. Exactly who was throwing it there, I was never able to ascertain. It just appeared, or rather reappeared, whenever I wasn't looking. It was also at night that I scavenged food from the dustbins of neighbouring houses. It was amazing what people threw away, especially when they had kids who'd demand huge meals but couldn't be bothered to eat them, so rather than starving, I was putting on weight.

My electricity had been cut off, so I was unable to play records. The phone had been cut off too, I was unable to contact the outside world. I rarely got any mail, and what I did receive was inevitably bills or demands for council tax. I'm sure if I'd sent a letter to my mother, the missive would have been intercepted by the security services. When I wasn't peeking out from between the curtains, I'd reread one of the few books I kept in the house. I had several theoretical works by Baudrillard, and a copy of *Black Boy* by Richard Wright. I read slowly, stopping to explore the associative possibilities of every word. It would take me all morning to read a paragraph, all day to absorb a page. I'd been conditioned by my education to read texts quickly, but now I was really taking my time, and my understanding of the books I worked through was completely transformed.

So Many Rivers To Cross

Three ten year old Asian boys were larking about on the fenced green outside our block. The sound of kids playing never bothered me. It was a better accompaniment to making tea and toast than any music station I could find. It was certainly better than talking to Captain Swanky, who was sitting at the kitchen table, depressed at the inability of The Purple Haze club to make money. I didn't give a damn, I was banned. I looked out of the window and a couple of younger white kids were approaching the green. The gate to the green was slammed shut.

"Let us in."

"No dogs!"

"Let us in."

"Read that sign, it says no dogs."

"Let us in."

"No dogs, especially no bulldogs."

"Let us in."

"This is a play area, the sign says no dogs."

"Let us in."

"No, this is for Pakistanis only."

"What, you're not Bengali?"

Then the two other Asian boys began hitting the one who'd spoken first.

"Bengal, Bengal!" they screamed as the beat him.

The two white kids drifted off.

"I hate racists and I really don't understand this anti-Pakistan thing among Bangladeshis." The Captain announced as if he was saying something profound.

"A lot of people object to racism,' I put in, "but what's important is attacking the dominant and institutionalised white racism head on. It is white racism that results in the Bangladeshi community around here suffering the worst housing and the worst unemployment in the whole of London. Doing something about that must be the best way of improving all community relations."

"Cobblers!" the Captain spat. "The Bangladeshi kids out there are racist, and until people are prepared to admit that we'll never sort out these problems."

I continued to put my point of view across to The Captain, but in retrospect I was just wasting my breath. It was people like him who'd been moving into the area who'd really exacerbated the problems it faced. The poor couldn't afford to move, but those with skilled jobs or badly paid clerical work could, and they were getting out to places where their money went further. The gap between rich and poor in the area was becoming starker. There was more resentment, communities were smashed up. Kids turned to heroin and crack, and hard drugs turned them onto crime. While it was the poor who got branded criminals, it was flash money moving into Hoxton that created these social problems. Money destroyed truly human relationships.

A Quitter Never Wins

I was woken by a knock at the door. At first I ignored the sound, but as it endlessly echoed and repeated itself, I was forced to conclude that the caller wasn't going to go away just because I didn't want to deal with them. I got up from the chair I'd been sleeping in and went to the door. I'd fallen asleep in my clothes, so there was no need to pull anything on in order to make myself decent. I put the chain on the door before opening it. There was an attractive woman of thirty on my doorstep. She was smartly dressed in a black jacket and skirt, white blouse, black stockings and sensible flat black shoes. Her shoulder length blonde hair was tied back in a pony-tail, and she had a black brief case in her left hand.

"Mr. Cheam?' the woman said.

"Yes." I lied.

"You look rough."

"I've just woken up."

"Can I come in?"

"Who are you?"

"I'm Sandra Smith, I've come to discuss the termination of your contract as artist-in-residence at Scapa Loch. I've travelled all the way from London. It would have been much easier if you'd answered my letters."

"What letters?"

"You didn't get my letters?"

"Evidently not."

"Can I come in?"

"Do you need to?"

"Well, it would be more comfortable than discussing these matters on your doorstep. It would probably be to your advantage not to have your neighbours overhearing what I'm about to say to you."

"Okay," I said relenting, and simultaneously unchaining the door, "Come in."

I drew the curtains in the lounge, then I opened the windows. It was a little musty in that way rooms get when you've been sleeping in them, and you haven't washed for days or even weeks.

"Is anything wrong?" Sandra enquired.

"The water is cut off, the phone is cut off, the electricity is cut off, you've stopped paying my wages—but apart from that, no nothing is wrong."

"Does the water being cut off mean you can't offer me a cup of tea?"

"It does. It also means I can't take a bath or do the cleaning, which is why the house stinks."

"I won't take it personally. I can't get through the day without my tea, so I'm not surprised you're looking a bit rough."

"About the contract?"

"It's been terminated."

"On what grounds?"

"There is no evidence whatsoever of you doing any work as an artist-in-residence for the past month."

"I haven't been paid for the past month either."

"That, I'm afraid, is no concern of mine. Not getting paid is something you'd have to take up with wages. I'm from personnel, it's my job to hire and fire, and since you haven't kept up with your work, you've effectively dismissed yourself."

"This is ridiculous. The entire estate, barring this house, has been sold back to the Americans, and you say I haven't done my work."

"You're supposed to be an artist-in-residence, which means you have to do artistic things to edify the local community. And you mentioning it reminds me the house is something else I need to talk to you about.

Can you vacate today? We've had an offer we can't refuse from the US military and we want you out as soon as possible. You've no right to be here now your contract has been terminated, so if you could just hand me the keys and blow, that would probably be the best thing for everybody concerned."

"What about a severance payment?"

"You'd have been entitled to severance money if you'd stayed on top of your work. Since you broke the terms of your contract, you're not entitled to a bean."

"Where am I supposed to go?"

"I don't know. I thought you came up from London, surely you've kept a place on down there?"

"I got evicted from my flat in Hoxton before I came up here."

"That's your problem."

"So where am I supposed to go?"

"You must have some relatives. Why don't you go and stay with your mother or something?"

"Moving back home would be an unacceptable admission of complete and utter defeat. I'm not going anywhere, I'm staying here."

"You won't stay here. I'll start legal proceedings today and have you out in a week. I'll go now. I'm desperate for a brew. Could you tell me the nearest place where I'd get a good cup of tea?"

"Yes but no."

"You're taking this far too personally. Surely you understand that I'm only doing my job. I'm not to blame for your problems, and taking out your frustrations on me isn't going to resolve any of them." And with that Sandra Smith left.

Skin I'm In

I found a dozen collectable punk singles in a charity shop. I paid one pound twenty for them, and sold them for three hundred quid. I made the money in Berwick Street and half of it stayed there, because I spent it on rare groove. It was a potlatch, deliberate waste, what, after Bataille, I might call solar economics if I didn't find this theorist's attraction to the sublime aesthetics of tragedy and sacrifice so unpalatable. It wasn't as if I'd actually listen to the original vinyl pressings I'd bought. I didn't need to, since I already possessed what I'd purchased on cheap CD reissues. Besides, playing the records might well reduce their value. Certainly overplaying them, so that they ended up scratched and worn, would lessen their financial worth. Analogue and digital are two quite different things. A vinyl record wears away: every time you listen to it, you never hear quite the same thing. Flaws are gradually introduced and these increase with repeated plays. Whereas a CD either works or it doesn't. If a CD plays you always hear the same thing. With CDs change is absolute. A damaged CD is useless and worthless. What I coveted was obsolescence as the ultimate luxury product, so my distaste for ruined CDs is not quite as odd as it may at first appear. Vinyl records possessed me and the only way I could undo this hoodoo voodoo was to purchase the items by which I was enchanted. It was a fatal strategy. The revenge of the object became the object of my revenge. A dialectic of metaphysics with Jean Baudrillard and Rudy Ray Moore battling it out at an all night blues party saturated with gut-bucket funk. It could have been worse, since unlike some people I know, I'm not into the eight track cartridge—a fetish that greatly restricts the choice of music available to you.

Actually, what I've just said isn't quite right, because although I returned home from Berwick Street with vinyl and a small wad of cash, I'd also spent money on other things. I sat in a café with a coffee in front of me. Then I sat with a coffee and one dirty cup in front of me. Then when I'd finished my second coffee both cups were cleared away and I sat with a third cup of coffee and a croissant before me. Well, at first—or rather latterly—I sat with a third cup of coffee and a croissant before me, but I gradually consumed the croissant and coffee, so that eventually I sat with an empty and dirty coffee cup and a plate littered with crumbs and smears of butter in front of me. After the best part of an hour, I got up, paid for my fare and left. I also forgot to mention that while I sat at the table, I examined my vinyl purchases to make sure I hadn't missed any flaws when I'd gone over them in the Berwick Street record shops.

Hold To My Baby

I spent the next few days laying in supplies. This turned out to be ridiculously easy. Nuclear fall-out shelters had been dug into the back gardens of most of the homes on the estate, and these had been well stocked with tins of baked bins and other essentials by the US military. I systematically broke into the fall-out shelters, and carried the food back to my place. I used ripped out kitchen units to barricade the ground floor of my house, and painted a thin layer of white paint over all the windows, to obscure my movements within the building. While I was doing this, I also daubed the following slogan over my front door: "SMASH THE

SPECTACULAR COMMODITY ECONOMY!" Then underneath, in much smaller letters and what I hoped looked like a different hand, I added: "DON'T PISS DOWN MY BACK AND TELL ME IT'S RAINING." I forlornly hoped this would fool any bailiffs into believing a commune of violent anarchist nutters had squatted the property.

Before long the post office was attempting to deliver an eviction notice to my house. Fortunately, I'd nailed up the letter box. Eventually, the court order was sealed in a jam jar and left just outside my front door. I considered this to be a legally questionable tactic. Nevertheless, a few days later six burly bailiffs were stomping down my garden path. I'd spent the night drinking my way through several bottles of 100 Pipers and was in a jolly mood when the heavy mob arrived.

"Open up!" the enforcers screamed as they hammered on the door.

"There's ain't nobody here but us chickens," I cackled back at them.

"Who are you if there's nobody in?" the bailiffs demanded in unison.

"Who am I?" I repeated. "Surely such a question lost any meaning it may have possessed once modernism went into decline. Who am I? Tell me that and you've solved the riddle of the sphinx. I am that I am. I am a man. And as for me, I've no interest in issues and debates that revolve around completely arbitrary notions of identity. As a proletarian post-modernist I'm engaged in continuous becoming, and I've no time for nonsense about centred subjects."

"We've got a right nutter here," one of the bailiffs muttered, 'but it isn't anything to worry about. I've yet to meet a theory obsessed malcontent who was any good in a scrap."

"If you don't open up," a different bailiff shouted, "we're gonna kick your door down."

Within seconds, the bailiffs were battering my rather flimsy defences. I decided discretion was the better part of valour, and bolted out the back. So much for protecting my record collection with my last breath, but the fresh air smelt good and I was glad to be out of the house after spending so long cooped up inside it. I walked to North Hoy where I caught the tiny foot passenger ferry at Moaness. The old bill were waiting for me when I got off in Stromness, and I found myself arrested—not as a fugitive, but for failing to pay my fare on the ferry. When I explained that I was financially embarrassed, and having searched me to verify the truth of this claim, the cop who'd arrested me said he'd reimburse the skipper and see that all charges were laid aside, if I'd dig up his mother's garden. So I spent the rest of that day, and all of the next, clearing an overgrown yard in preparation for a new lawn being sown.

Drop The Bomb

It hadn't been a good weekend. I should have been at the 333, or down The Blue Note, except that the latter club had been closed by the council for noise violation. Instead, I paid one of my periodic visits to my dad. I performed this duty roughly once a year. My dad was happy enough with this arrangement, but being obsessed by appearances, he was permanently pissed off that my visits didn't coincide with Christmas. My dad is the kind of bloke who thought it was perfectly respectable to get pissed seven nights a week, as long as he changed out of his mechanic's overalls, and put on a suit before he went down the pub. He also considered it perfectly reasonable to go home pissed and beat up his nearest and dearest, which was the main reason my mum had filed for divorce.

A weekend in New Addington with my dad, his most recent wife Jean and her ten year old son Christopher, was enough to send me into deep depression. Christopher was obsessed with computer games and the fact that his old man had been stabbed to death in a street drug deal that had gone horribly wrong. Jean was obsessed with soap operas, which she watched wall to wall on satellite. And my dad, well, he thought I owed him something because without his sperm I wouldn't have been here, there and every-fucking-where. The fact that my mum had brought me up alone was not something he liked to discuss. Or rather, he was happy to discuss it with anyone—like Jean—who accepted that his ex was a stupid bitch, who'd driven him out of his own home because she didn't understand that a man needed a little relaxation after work. One of the many problems my dad had with me was that I didn't share his views on this matter. Knowing the violent reaction it brought on, I avoided any mention of the brief spell I'd spent in care when my mum was hospitalised—or the visits my dad had received from social services and the police. In fact, it wasn't really my dad I was going to visit at all, but my half-brother Michael, whose own mother had the misfortune to die in the crash that cost my dad his driving licence. When breathalysed dad had been well over the limit. I was trying to encourage Michael to move out, maybe move up to The Smoke—and get a life.

You can imagine my surprise when I got home on

Sunday night and my flat had been emptied of most of its contents. There was a note from Captain Swanky on the floor saying he'd moved out. He'd bought a pad in Stepney, although he failed to provide me with the address. I went to make a cup of tea. Swanky had taken the kettle and all the food from the cupboards. The fridge had gone, as had the cooker and all the shelving in the flat, which I'd bought and put up. Swanky had left the carpet and curtains in my bedroom, and my bed. He'd taken virtually everything else, my hi-fi, a pair of sixties Levi's sta-prest that he'd long coveted, as well as my best tonic suit. Fortunately he didn't like soul music, so while a few items had been swiped, my record collection was largely intact. However, he had removed all the bulbs from the light fittings, and taken the shades too.

I was too depressed to go out and walk the streets, or find a club where I could dance my blues away. Instead I lay down on my bed. The next thing I knew it was Monday morning and someone was hammering on my front door. I ignored the noise, but then I heard the door open and someone come into the flat, so I got up. I was confronted by my estate officer Andrea Curwain.

"What are you doing here?" Curwain boomed.

"Well, aside from anything else and as you well know, I rent this gaff off the council."

"Oh no you don't!" Curwain broke into a laugh. "Your co-tenant cancelled the tenancy."

"Well he can do what the hell he likes, but I didn't agree to it."

"You didn't have too."

"I know I don't have too, and I won't, this is my home, I live here."

"Not any more!"

143

"What do you mean not any more?"

"It only takes one tenant on a co-tenancy agreement to cancel a tenancy. The legislation was introduced years ago, largely so that abused wives could rid themselves of their husbands. The wife can cancel the tenancy and then once the husband is out, we'll immediately re-house her and any kids back in her own flat, with a new tenancy agreement solely in her own name. However, the legislation has other uses. I'd noticed that you and your flat mate weren't getting along. He was very interested when I told him about the subsidised mortgages available to people vacating council properties, so he cancelled your tenancy agreement and got himself a very nice place in Stepney."

"That's unbelievable."

"No, it's life. We've got to get this flat ready for the new tenant, but I'm a generous woman, so I'll give you until first thing tomorrow morning to clear your stuff out. I'll be glad to see the back of you, you've caused me nothing but grief."

Have You Ever Had The Blues

I spent the next few days bumming loose change from tourists and sleeping in garden sheds. Eventually, I persuaded a German couple to convey me onto a ferry in their camper. They were getting the Aberdeen boat from Kirkwall, which suited me fine. Hitching from Scrabster on the north coast down into the first belt of heavy population would have taken as long as the boat trip to the Granite City. The ferry took all night to arrive at its destination. I slept in the camper van below deck. Nobody knew I was there, and I'd have been in real trouble if the ship had sunk, but it didn't and I arrived in Aberdeen well rested. The German couple then drove me south to Edinburgh, where they planned to stay for a few days, before catching a boat home from Newcastle. I wandered Princess Street asking tourists for loose change. I wanted to get back to London, and hitching there could have taken days. I hoped to ponce the price of a train ticket, but by the time darkness fell I only had enough money for the overnight bus. That was, of course, a lot better than walking.

The guy sitting next to me on the bus drank steadily. He looked like a squaddie, and when he started talking, it quickly became apparent that he was a man wedded to his uniform. The boy was institutionalised, and once he left the forces, there was a good chance he'd end up on the streets. When you've spent your working life with accommodation laid on, having to fend for yourself in the capitalist housing market is a tough job. Squaddies were often their own worst enemies, and they rarely understood why they were widely disliked. The army ruined working class boys, and my unwanted companion was a perfect example of this.

"I love it in the services," the man announced, "I've seen the world, and now I know there is nowhere like the British Isles. Germany was a laugh, but it doesn't compare to Belfast. We were always allowed to do whatever we wanted in Northern Ireland. We didn't take any lip. If any Proddy gave us gyp, we'd tie the bugger up and dump them in a Catholic area. Green whingers got the same treatment but in reverse. It was fucking great. We'd take the cunts down back allies and beat the living daylights out of 'em. Best days of my life, I loved Belfast."

I was counting the motorway lights we passed

beneath, I wanted to sleep. Carlisle, Manchester, Birmingham, for me they were all just cities of dreams. I was heading back to my personal omphalos, the city in which I'd been born. As the rosy fingers of dawn broke across the horizon we weren't yet in London, but I knew we'd be there soon, so very soon. My heart leapt as we trundled off the M1 and onto the North Circular, then down through Swiss Cottage and across Oxford Street to Victoria. I stumbled into the morning air, feeling truly happy for the first time in weeks. I was home, or almost home, all I needed was a place to kip.

Quick Change Artist

Tony Cheam borrowed a van and we took my records and clothes around the corner to his place. Tony was more than happy to look after my vinyl and CDs, I had plenty of rarities he'd enjoy spinning while my collection was in his care. We decided to leave the bed, Tony didn't have anywhere to put it, and it had seen better days. Cheam was on a high, he'd copped off with a posh girl called Claire who worked as a psychotherapist. Once we'd moved my gear, he suggested we pop around to the University of Cripplegate to give Captain Swanky a mouthful. I knew it was pointless, it was late afternoon by the time we reached Whitecross Street, and Swanky would be down the boozer. We went up and got a frosty reception from the secretaries, who told us The Captain was on holiday. We checked out The Trader but he wasn't to be found there. We moved on to The Masque Haunt, and I insisted we get a drink while we were there. I'd just got back to our table with pints of Directors when Tony's mobile went off.

"I'm embarrassed to tell you where I am. Okay, I'm in The Masque Haunt in Old Street, you know, one of those chain pubs. It wasn't my idea, we were trying to find someone. Okay, its just up from the roundabout, opposite the Somerfield supermarket. I'll try and wait here, but this is the sort of place that is ruining traditional drinking culture. They get the punters in by undercutting everybody else, but you just don't have the range of beer that a good independent stocks. If you don't find me here it's because I couldn't stand it any longer, so just give me a buzz on the mobile, and I'll tell you where we are. We won't go that far, there are plenty of pubs nearby that I do like."

"What's wrong with this place? I demanded.

"Everything!" Cheam shot back.

"I like it," I replied. "You would too if you just gave it a chance. Have you eaten?"

"No."

"Well, why not settle your stomach with a Wether Burger?"

"You must be joking."

"They're good value, it will fill you up."

"Everything in here is good value, but there's no atmosphere. It's soulless."

"It's great."

"I hate it."

"It has everything I want. It's cheap. It's quiet. There is no music, not that I object to music, I just object to the bad music that is always played in pubs. I don't want to go out and have to listen to trash like Abba, The Clash and The Sex Pistols. You can always have a conversation in here without shouting. If you come in after eight in the evening, a lot of the city workers who patronise the place have pushed off home, so getting a table isn't a problem. The food isn't top range, but it is reasonably priced and fills you up if you're hungry. There is a huge no smoking area, so I'm not left gasping for breath after a night out."

"What use is a no smoking area to me? I smoke, don't forget I smoke, what am I doing right now?"

"Okay, I'm sitting in the smoking area so that you can smoke, but I've always got the option of going into the non-smoking area."

"You might as well drink in an aircraft hanger."

"I've got nothing against aircraft hangers."

And so we went on until Claire Grogan arrived.

"Tony darling!" They kissed. "And you must be John, the guy Tony was telling me about who lost his job, and has now lost his home. Has Tony talked to you about his little problem and how by helping him you could sort yourself out?"

"No, we've just been arguing about whether or not this is a good pub."

"Boys, boys, these silly conflicts get you nowhere, we must address the emotional conflicts that underlie these petty disputes."

"You're right Claire," Tony concurred, "but I've accommodated John's tastes in drinking holes, so now he should show some respect for mine. Let me and John drink up, then we'll walk over to the Wenlock Arms so I can get you something."

"You want me to wait for my gin?"

"Patience comes to those who wait."

"Tony, you are changing so much, I can see those therapy sessions I've been sending you to with my friend Christabell have been doing you a world of good."

So we sauntered to The Wenlock Arms on the corner

of Wenlock and Stuart Street. It was a longer walk than either Grogan or I expected, but Tony cajoled us to keep moving with promises of it's just around the corner, alongside much excited chatter about the joys of authentic London drinking culture. When we got there, The Wenlock turned out to be a beatnik joint with a wide selection of real ales. There were three guys crammed into a corner playing trad, and whenever they stopped they got a lot of applause from the fifty-somethings in dark clothes and dark glasses who patronised the place. Tony ordered some beer, and we stood near the bar because there weren't any seats.

"Tony," Claire explained, 'is a very great artist, but his problem like so many of those whose talents take time to be recognised, is that he is suffering from stalled career syndrome."

"Isn't that what I've got?" I put in. "After all, I've just lost my job."

"No, no, no!" Grogan exclaimed. "Stalled career syndrome is not something that troubles ordinary men and women, it is a curse of the genius."

"But I can tell you," I insisted, 'being out of work is a serious drag, especially when you've got no savings and the welfare people say it is your own fault you lost your job."

"There are two sides to every conflict," Claire rejoined, "you mustn't blame your inability to get social security on those who turn you down for it."

"I don't, I blame government welfare cuts!"

"Politicians are humans too you know!" Grogan continued. Her privileged background seemed to make her completely oblivious to the plight of people like me. "You should try and see things from a politician's point of view. They have to try and make sure the entire economy runs smoothly. That is a difficult job."

"Yes, I guess it must be really tough shouldering all that responsibility."

"That's more like it!" Claire clearly hadn't realised I was being sarcastic. "Anyway, let's get back to Tony's problem. He met me shortly after applying for a job as artist-in-residence at the Scapa Loch Housing Estate. Now I've got Tony in analysis and my impression that he is suffering from stalled career syndrome has been confirmed, I've told him he needs to spend time gently recuperating with me in London. However, having got the job as artists-in-residence at Scapa Loch, it would look unprofessional if Tony didn't take it up. There is a simple solution, you could go in his place and pretend to be Tony."

"But I don't know anything about being an artist-in-residence."

"No problem," Grogan assured me, "Tony had to provide a detailed outline of what he'd be doing during the residency as part of his application, he'll give you this and you just follow it as thought it was an instruction manual."

"Well, where the hell is Scapa Loch?"

"On the beautiful island of Hoy in Orkney, just a stone's throw off the north coast of Scotland, with easy access by ferry to the thriving town of Thurso and the groovy Dounreay Nuclear Power station. The housing was built for US military intelligence and since the abutting listening station has been closed down, it is being sold off as a private redevelopment. It is a wonderful opportunity for retired people to buy quality housing at a knock down price, and might also suit young families whose breadwinners do extended shifts in the oil and nuclear industries."

"But surely people would realise I wasn't Tony? We don't look in the least bit similar."

"Tony wasn't interviewed by anyone who'll be on site. It will be fine, if you turn up and say you're Tony Cheam, people will take you at your word. After all, Tony isn't going to show, so no one will have any reason to be suspicious."

"I don't know, it seems like quite a difficult thing to pull off."

"You can do it!" Claire encouraged me. "It will provide you with a house and a job, and since you don't have either right now, it will see you out of a tight corner."

The Beat Goes On

I'd arranged to meet Tony Cheam in the Bricklayers Arms. I'd phoned him and suggested a lunch time drink in the hope he'd also put me up for at least one night. Shoreditch had changed. There were more trendies than ever, and the pub wasn't my scene any more, even during the day. There had been a time when I thought the Bricklayers was fine place to drink daytime or night, then the evening clientele grew increasingly youthful. When I'd left London, the Bricklayers had still been acceptable to me as a lunch time drinking den, but it wasn't any more. I bought a pint and when a couple moved on, I grabbed their table. Tony was late, and when he came in he went straight to the bar and bought himself a beer without offering to get me one. Usually he was a friendly bloke, so this was very out of character.

"You fucked up!" Tony hissed as he sat down.

"I fucked up?"

"Yes, you fucked up."

"How?"

"Don't ask me how you did it, you're the one who fucked up. The whole deal was straightforward enough. I told you what you were to do at Scapa Loch, and all you had to do was go along and pretend to be me. It was simple, but then you arbitrarily decided that you were an artist in your own right, that you'd go ahead and make things without consulting me. I gave you a break. You got a house when you were homeless, and a job when you were unemployed, and all this just by covering for me. Now word has gone around that Scapa Loch was an unmitigated disaster, my name has been dragged through the mud and I'll be lucky if I ever land an artist-in-residence job in this country again."

"What does it matter? Claire is loaded, she doesn't want you doing crummy residencies, she'll support you and you'll get to concentrate on prestige exhibitions."

"I've split up with Claire."

"When?"

"Last fucking night."

"Why?"

"Because she thought I was spending too much time on my art and not enough with her. She gave me an ultimatum, I either had to give up art or get out of her life. I've devoted myself to my art, so the choice was simple. The trouble is, if I can't get a residency somewhere, then I'm financially fucked. I'll probably have to humiliate myself by applying for the kind of low-grade clerical work you used to do. Somehow I allowed Claire to persuade me to give up my job at the art school. My peers will be laughing behind my back, if they ever find out."

"Let's just forget about it," I suggested generously. "I'm out of cash, can you get me another beer?"

"I'm not sure I can even bear talking to you!" Tony spat. "Look, here's a tenner, get us both fresh drinks. You can keep the change, but when you come back I want you to sit down and tell me what actually happened at Scapa Loch."

So I got more beers and proceeded to tell Cheam of the adventures that had befallen me since I'd last seen him. He went pale and then green, but he stoutly refrained from interrupting my narrative. When I'd finished Tony made his way over to the gents. He emerged again about five minutes later and told me he'd just thrown up. I knew there wasn't any point in asking if I could stay at his pad. I left Cheam contemplating beer puddles on our table. I looked for solace in the fact that as I made my way out of the pub, a little more change was jangling in my pockets than when I'd gone in. I desperately needed a place to stay, and I didn't have enough cash to pay for a room in a hostel. I decided to make a few phone calls. The only person I was able to rouse from a pay phone was my mother who lived way down south. I decided to wander about the hood to see if anything turned up. If I drew a blank, I'd still have the option of stopping with my mum. Walking around I sank into a depression, because it quickly became apparent that even if I'd had the wherewithal to cover an inflated rent, the place where I'd hoped to live didn't exist any longer. The Shoreditch and Hoxton I'd once loved had receded into the mists of history. Money trampled everything before it, and in the case of this and other recently gentrified neighbourhoods, what got destroyed were the very things that had attracted these fatal attentions in the first place. I was the last of London, and now London was the end of me.

The Infernal Return

On Norton Folgate I stopped and turned around. I took one last look at the purple haze of Shoreditch. The polluted air shimmered in the sunlight. I wanted to leave my dreams behind in the miasma. Traffic thundered down Shoreditch High Street. I followed an army of HGVs as they headed south towards London Bridge. I could have picked up a Northern Line tube at Moorgate or Old Street but I wanted to walk to the other side of the river. I'd catch a train to Morden from London Bridge station. I hadn't seen my mother for the best part of a year. Living alone in her two up two down she was excited by the prospect of me coming home, even if it was only because I had nowhere else to go. Well, there was another option, my dad lived in New Addington but I preferred purgatory to hell itself. When I'd phoned my mum to confirm I'd stay with her, she'd said she'd speak to Mr. Smith across the road about getting some work in his grocery shop. He'd been very pleased with my diligence when I'd done a Saturday shift for him in my last two years at school. My mum knew he had a vacancy and she was certain he'd give me the job. She thought it would save me the bother of commuting up to the city. I didn't have the heart to tell her not to bother Mr. Smith. I wasn't intending to hang around. It would only be a matter of a few weeks before I sorted something else out. Maybe I'd go abroad. I'd left home fifteen years previously and I didn't intend to return on a permanent basis. I'd suffered a temporary set back, but would win the war to make my own way in life.

THE BRIDGE

FUNKIER THAN A MOSQUITA'S TWEETER: Stewart Home Interviewed by New Laddism

Stewart Home needs no introduction to his hardcore cult following, and yet he remains an enigma to many of his fans. Home looks every bit the master of the house as he lounges in a study sipping chilled wine and playing with his eight cats as they wander in and out of the room. On the wall are original Wain and Spare paintings, while rare first editions are neatly arranged on various bookshelves. Home has come a long way since his early days writing pulp-splatter novels and signing on the dole, he's dropped out of the sights of the anarchist movement who viewed him as Satan incarnate, with the majority of those purchasing Home's books now perceiving him as a profoundly moral author. A bright spring morning is in the process of being eclipsed by an afternoon of torrential rain as I press the record button on my Walkman.

Laddism: Okay Mr. Home, I'd like you to tell me about your belief in Christ. Do you see Christ as the Son of God or do you see him as a master who has been reincarnated?

Home: Dealing with the issues raised by the question of the impact of personal computers on the production of commercial fiction means doing more than just looking at technology, you also have to grasp the nature of the relationship between technology and society. There are obviously a lot of very different positions on this—one being that technology isn't neutral and that rather than controlling technology, wo/man is controlled by it. I feel this is a little too pat, and while I wouldn't unreservedly endorse everything Walter Benjamin had to say on the subject, I feel his thinking in this area is useful. To dialectically transform and paraphrase Benjamin, in an alienated capitalist society technology produces catastrophes. However, in a communist society technology can assume a useful role in the development of real human community. Unfortunately it is probably necessary for me to avoid misunderstandings about this by stating the USSR was about as far removed from communism as it is possible to get. Stalinist rule being an example of state capitalism developed along principles of organisation first systematised by the anarchist reactionary Michael Bakunin.

I actually think we are living through a period of cultural decline albeit a temporary one, but I wouldn't put this down to technology. During the revolutionary upswings of the sixties and early seventies, it became easier to innovate and produce culture socially and collectively. If the social conditions in which culture is produced have worsened (due to the last revolutionary wave receding), then rather than being to blame for this, technology can at times provide a counterbalance (although not a corrective, which is a matter of human action). However, the relationship between social conditions and culture is complex. To say capital is temporarily ascendant doesn't mean that it isn't worth making cultural interventions. Out of the horrors of slavery and the black holocaust came the Black Atlantic culture that is the basis of almost all worthwhile music and literature today. Moving on, it is also difficult to get a really accurate picture of what is being produced culturally right now, obviously you can miss a lot of what is going on and either its existence or its relevance may only be apparent in years to come. That said, I do think there has been a general decline in the quality of fiction recently but I would put this down mainly to social conditions and the publishing industry clinging to the exhausted form of the traditional novel. While I know you are into a stream-of-consciousness style of writing, and I think this is fine for a first draft of a text, personally I like to rewrite and computer technology has made this easier. Every book I've done has been written on a computer, with the first draft typed in since I am able to type faster than I can hand write. I like computers and for the time being I think I'll continue to use them.

Laddism: How would you relate that to Free Spirit heresies, the belief that if God is everywhere, then we are all part of God and in fact, must be God ourselves?

Home: Yes, I was mentioned by Will Self in his *Independent* obituary of the literary critic Elizabeth Young; some of my friends considered this fairly gracious of him, others noted that he misspelled my name (Liz was always frustrated by the fact that we don't get along). Liz was described as championing me before I was famous in *The Times* obituary. This led to some extended email discussions over whether I could sue *The Times* for libelling me as famous. In the end I thought it best to avoid court action, since if anything was going to make me famous (something I'd prefer to avoid), a libel case was the thing to do it. It would, however, have been very curious to witness the effects of suing a newspaper for describing me as famous! Liz did champion me where she could, but this was usually behind the scenes because despite her requests, very often her literary editors wouldn't let her review my books (the problem being a mixture of me being considered obnoxious, Liz having a much more sophisticated understanding of what I did than her editors, and the fact that I was perceived as a cult writer who wasn't of much interest to broadsheet newspaper readers with a liking for literature rather than a taste for its negation).

I first met Liz when she came to the launch of my novel *Pure Mania* at the now defunct Compendium bookshop in Camden Town in 1989. We got along well, and I started to visit Liz quite often. However, the thing that will always stay with me about Liz is the long late night phone conversations we'd have about books. There were certain authors we were both very interested in—particularly Lynne Tillman and Dennis Cooper—and when they had a new book out, we'd both read it and then talk at length about it. I rarely spoke to Liz on the phone before ten in the evening, but conversation about a new book by someone like Lynne Tillman could easily go on till three or four in the morning. Liz was a great person to discuss books with, she was incredibly well read and very fast and perceptive. I got an awful lot from those long late night phone conversations, they'll always stay with me. Liz was always very generous about other people's books, but she found it difficult to discuss her own fiction, she should have been a lot more confident about that than she was. Reading the obituaries was sad and strange. *The Guardian* obituary in particular stressed how she scared people and was an incarnation of the counterculture. I never saw her like that, to me from the first time I met her she was always very approachable, but I can see how other people might get that impression if they weren't familiar with the things that engaged her—even if over time they came to be a part of her quite deliberately restricted circle of friends.

Laddism: I think Christianity is a syncretic religion, what are your views on this?

Home: I've found over the years that the audience for what I do is surprisingly diverse. Since the initial flush of support for my fiction came from the London music and style press (and yes, back in the mid-nineties *i-D* even sent current art mega-star Wolfgang Tillmans to take my photo when they were running a feature about me), I think people assume I must be appealing to the "kids". However, when I do readings I find the audiences are pretty mixed age wise, and very often mainly in their twenties and thirties. Obviously, the crowds for my readings do not exactly match the demographics of the audiences for my books, so it would be wrong to make too many assumptions based on my impressions of my gigs. Also, the audiences at readings are noticeably younger when I tour in places like Finland than the crowd I attract in London. That said, I don't really feel I'm just pitching for the attention of the "kids" or that I have to compete with computer games. Besides, a "kid" might want to play computer games in the morning, read one of my books at lunch time, engage in debates about fiction in the afternoon, and fuck their boyfriend/girlfriend to the rhythms of the psychedelic soul jazz guitar sounds of Boogaloo Joe Jones all night. Most "kids" generally do more than just play computer games. Likewise, historically individual books have generally had fairly small circulations (although there are obvious exceptions like The Bible—which has proved popular as a particularly "violent" and self-consciously "extreme" anthology of prose fiction), and sales of fiction only really went mega with the rise of paperback original publishing in the mid-twentieth century, and this phenomenon isn't really something that has lasted. And again, books can often find their readers over time, so I really don't need to compete with computer games.

Laddism: That's very much a Protestant view, within Catholicism there's a tradition of praying to Mary or various Saints rather than directly to God.

Home: Intergenerational relationships are far more complex than the model you invoke suggests, and since I've never really been famous (despite *The Times* libelling me as such) most twenty-somethings who come across me can feel quite comfortable with anything I've done if they are at all interested by it or in sympathy with it. I think the subversion of what I do has gone on much more with people of my own age. So you have someone like Tracy Emin making her *Bed* after she'd exhibited one of her T-shirts opposite my *Art Strike Bed* in the Charlotte Street *Yerself Is Steam* group exhibition in 1995. The idea with the *Art Strike Bed* was that a different bed would be used every time it was shown. I wanted to do something radically inauthentic because there is no authenticity under capitalism. Emin's bed is about trauma (she wet the bed) and thus authenticity. So while my bed(s) and Emin's bed might superficially appear to be similar, they are actually very different. Emin's bed is an attempt at recuperating my (in)activities. People like Emin, Damien Hirst and Rolf Harris are very, very worried that what I do is going to undermine their position in the cultural hierarchy, which is why they want to recuperate my interventions.

Laddism: In practice most Catholics tend to pray to Mary or one of the Saints, and some people would say that was the influence of pagan Goddess worship on Catholicism.

Home: This rather reminds me of my fascination with Jennifer Lopez (or J-Lo as she was renamed by disappointed former "fans" after much of her bottom mysteriously disappeared), who is at the root of my fixation with amateur police women. After seeing Lopez in *Out Of Sight*, I started thinking about doing Japanese-style bondage stuff on women in their twenties and thirties who I'd partially dressed/undressed in American police uniforms. However, I eventually realised I was simply inverting rather than challenging the values of the dominant society with this bondage kick, and this despite the fact that I knew more than a dozen women who were very turned-on by it. I then decided I needed to get back into bread doll fetishism, and also that I wanted to act out a father and son procreation and rebirthing routine with two amateur mid-wives who would be partially dressed in freshly starched nurses' uniforms (if any of your readers are interested in helping me with this, perhaps they could mail me some recent rude Polaroids, and at least one pair of their dirty knickers wrapped for "freshness" in a Safeway carrier). Moving on, I don't agree with this ironic Radio 2-style thing. An Abba record is a bad record whether or not the DJ thinks they are being ironic when they play it. And by the way, the only thing I ever liked about Abba was the fact that both the female singers had large backsides (but I could never really make up my mind whether I preferred the blonde or the redhead, which I guess rather lets the cat out of the bag—and it is a tom cat—about how I first got into fantasies about three-way fucking). I think the problem with the music zines you're describing is that too many of them are into boring, reactionary and uninspired rock music, and what they need to do is get into northern soul, or jazz funk, or something else that is at least half-way decent. I'd particularly recommend late Atlantic period Eddie Harris or the Super Breaks series of albums that Ace are putting out.

Laddism: I'm interested in this idea that I find in some of your work that Christ has reincarnated and walks amongst us again, although perhaps reincarnation isn't really the right turn of phrase.

Home: Well, I have quite a turnover of books, most of the stuff I have is to work with, and when I'm not likely to need something any more, I tend to get rid of it. There is a limit to what you can get from public libraries and sometimes I need something for longer than I could realistically borrow it from an institution (and there is also stuff that just isn't available in that way). I borrow from friends too, of course, but sometimes it is just easier to possess a book (despite my awareness of the danger that this can lead to being possessed by books; the book was the first perfected capitalist commodity and bibliomania is one of the great diseases that characterises our epoch). My "library" these days is actually much smaller than it used to be (less than a fifth of the size it was ten years ago). I always liked the story put about by some far-Right twit who went to visit Oswald Spengler (a self-styled "revolutionary conservative"—i.e. a German fascist who looked down on the Nazi party as too plebeian for his "aristocratic" tastes). After hearing endless boasts about how great his host's library was, it transpired that the spineless windbag who concocted *The Decline Of The West* and a whole slew of other bilge only had one shelf of pornography. Spengler's great library was a fiction, and as fiction it was roughly on a par with his ossified "thought" (I use the term thought quite deliberately here, since it can be taken as implying the past tense, and thus carries quite different connotations to thinking, which is far more dynamic).

Given that most books these days are printed on acid saturated paper and as a result will auto-destruct within fifty years of being manufactured, there isn't even a possibility of building a durable library of modern works. Besides, private libraries are seen by very few people. Over the course of my life a lot more people have seen my love truncheon than my library, thus it is my books even more than my pettifogger that function as an occult memory system. Books must be shuffled around on their shelves to create new meanings and new associations. I hate seeing books filed alphabetically. I group books according to use and uses change over time. Books die and become redundant, which is when they get passed on (when they die for me, I take the notion of their passing on quite literally). There is no truth to the rumour that if I consider a text seminal then I acquire as many copies as possible to wank over before surreptitiously sliding them into other people's book collections. You can track at least some of what I've read by what I've written and what I've said. Like me, Marx used the British Library and like all communists he was suspicious of private libraries and the bourgeois subjects they conjure up (incidentally, there is some great footage of me in the British Library included in the Bookmarks documentary about Richard Allen). That said, I think my real vanity is my collection of my own books, but then I do sometimes refer to them, just to reassure myself I'm no longer the person (or illusion) I used to be. I have many translations of my books too, and perhaps that is just a fetish since I always refer to my stuff in the English original rather than blindly trying to work from, say, German translations (it might be interesting to do that, since I'd have to reinvent the text pretty much wholesale unless I learnt to read German).

I don't have a record deck any longer, mine finally stopped working a few months ago and I threw it away, indeed it hadn't functioned properly for several years. So I still have a little vinyl, but mainly I'd switched to tapes and CDs. I'm rather more fond of my CD collection than my books (discounting, of course, both my own books and my own CDs). My tastes mutate over time but my relationship with music is a lot more subjective than my rather self-conscious manipulation of texts. I'm more attached to music, finding it simultaneously both more abstract and concrete (and I would stress here that I am not using concrete in its Hegelian sense). I don't think Michael Landy understands any of this, indeed he appears incapable of making a coherent critique of commodity fetishism. Rather than moving forward to a communist praxis, he is a throwback to the earliest bourgeois type, a man (and I use the term "man" here quite self-consciously) who wishes to assert in absolute terms "his" ownership of what he views as "his" possessions. Landy is a kind of latter-day Daniel Defoe stripped of both intelligence and historical context. I find Landy's art (ha ha) mind-numbingly dull. In short, he isn't even worth talking about unless one wishes to illustrate the complete impoverishment of bourgeois culture under late-capitalism. If Landy took on board the notion of social production and social consumption, then he might actually get somewhere—which would simultaneously mean moving away from the possessive individualism that animates his facile nihilism. It is social relationships rather than possessions that define us, and this is why creating truly human relationships is such an urgent necessity.

Laddism: The notion you have of Hitler as Kalki, that the Nazis were demonically possessed and that the Satanic forces animating the Third Reich had previously assailed humanity under the leadership of Genghis Khan, how does that relate to your belief that Christ has returned?

Home: Hard to remember what the reactions to *Cunt* were now, as well as what I felt about them. That book came out two years ago and was written a year and a half before that. In the sixties you'd have had much more outrage from the liberal press about censorship, but these days everybody expects it. In a lot of ways we seem to be living a rerun of McCarthyism, but with most of the population doing large amounts of gear (much of which is promoted in the media as mind expanding, but clearly isn't). Rock music is just another component of overpowering conformism. U2 and Salman Rushdie deserve each other. Real life lies elsewhere.

Laddism: Is it true that you are planning to write a devotional book inspired by your mother's struggle against heroin addiction and her search for Grace in this very personal battle against drugs?

Home: Ongoing whispers about a revival of eighties laddism are more credible than the average chart band, less credible than the idea that mortgages are the new rock and roll. By the way, have you noticed that you can get reissued Incredible Bongo Band albums for around six quid in Berwick Street now that they've been sampled to death?

Laddism: Given your interest in religion, I find it curious that you don't utilise Islam in your work, particularly Sufism, although I can see that you might have problems with the crucial Islamic assertion that "there is no god but God, and His name is Allah."

Home: I don't watch TV and I don't have a TV. I stopped watching TV more than twenty years ago because I found it boring. As Gil Scott-Heron almost said way back when: "the television will not be revolutionised..." However, I'd like to make it clear I'm not against TV per se, since—for example—in this society it can create opportunities for single parents to put their feet up and have a cup of tea.

Laddism: A lot of your use of religious imagery appears very personal to you.

Home: Janet Street-Porter got my number from a mutual friend, then phoned me up and said she wanted to do a book with me because she loved my novel *Slow Death*. Janet is a curious character, and I figured us being a team was a bit like the KLF working with Tammy Wynette. The idea was always that we'd produce a book that would be credited to both of us. We did a fair amount of work on a novel provisionally entitled *Moist: The Channel Men Prefer*, but then Janet got the job editing the *Independent On Sunday*. Street-Porter is adept at reinventing herself and against the predictions of the pundits, she halted the slide in sales of the *Sindy*, which considering the way they were falling off was quite an achievement. However, Janet being the editor of a national newspaper meant that *Moist* was put on hold, since it wasn't right for her new image. Current rumour on the London media circuit is that now Janet has sorted out the *Sindy*, the management want to get rid of her and put in someone more conventional. If this happens she may want to reinvent herself again, and *Moist* might go back on the front burner. All I know is that I've done a fair amount of work and to date haven't seen any money from it. Janet wasn't proposing that I ghost write, but I might well be available to do that if I need the money and the price is right. All of anarchism can be found in the belief that one can live differently in this world. I'm not only human, and not only do I need to eat, my humanity is actually something I value (and when I talk about human community this is something quite different from the arid abstractions of humanism).

Laddism: You don't appear interested in imposing a single response to your work among your audience.

Home: Compulsory state education is there to give parents somewhere to send their kids while they go out to work, and to train the kids up for wage labour, amongst other things. Which reminds me, why is it impossible to find old Chuck Brown & The Soul Searchers albums reissued on CD in London at the moment? Chuck Brown used to fill the Astoria in Charing X Road in the late eighties. I saw him there a couple of times and he was great. A fine Trouble Funk double CD compilation came out not so long ago (a triple if you got one of the early copies with the bonus live tracks), and you can find the original Trouble Funk albums around on CD too if you look, so why not Chuck Brown?

Laddism: I want to move on to your use of childhood imagery, Louis Wain cats and Noddy, and your blending of this with very apocalyptic religious imagery. Is there any theory behind this synthesis, or is it just something that occurs?

Home: I'm on the prowl for lactating women so that they can squirt their breast milk in my face as we make hot and tender—not to mention wild and wet—love (don't know if any of your readers can help me with this). Oh, yeah, and I'm also working on a new novel called *Memphis Underground* in which I'm looking at how the ghetto and the suburbs produce each other. I've also got a novel called *69 Things To Do With A Dead Princess* out on Rebel Inc./Canongate later this year. Richardson Magazine ran an extract last year and three printers refused to print that publication because of the headline at the top of my piece. So as was the case with *Cunt*, once again I've got a book title that is causing problems. Then there is my plan to produce an intellectual biography that conclusively proves Kant only wrote his third critique because he was trying to impress his house keeper, who he wanted to seduce. Kant's problem was that he suffered from inadequate bladder control, and his fear of pissing himself (not to mention his partner) during sex meant that he was unable to engage in normal human relationships, which is why he would molest animals. If only Kant had realised that there are people who get off on being peed on, then it might have been possible to avoid more than two centuries of worthless aesthetic debate (conspiracy researchers should note that I am kidding when I say this, and that I do not subscribe to "great man" theories of history, which is why I parody them—and I can also say pretty much the same thing about the bourgeois subject that conventional media interviews and profiles are predicated on conjuring up. Likewise, I know that it was actually Rousseau who suffered from incontinence, but whenever I hear the word Rousseau I reach for my copy of Derrida's *Of Grammatology* and all I find is negative shelf space—since I was forced to sell this tome when I was in urgent need of readies to buy a bottle of Four Roses). Those of your readers who use computers might like to check out www. stewarthomesociety.org (which contains stuff that will greatly interest anyone with a bread doll fetish), and they could also get "horny" ordering my books from Amazon. Bored housewives can send interesting Polaroids and pairs of their dirty knickers (wrapped in Safeway carriers for "freshness" please, and don't forget to include your contact details) to Stewart Home, BM Senior, London WC1N 3XX.

PART 3
COMIN' HOME BABY

Let's Murder The Moonlight (Again, Like We Did Last Summer)

The less said about the exhibition at the Stromness Arts Centre the better, it should be enough to state I didn't like it. Orkney had been fun, but my ostensible reason for travelling there is best forgotten. I caught the night boat back to Aberdeen, from where there was a 10 am train to London. I read on the train, and I corrected some of my writing. There were the usual non-stop announcements about the buffet, the snack trolley and the restaurant. These were a distraction, but the journey was still an opportunity to get some work done. I had my laptop with me. When I arrived at King's X seven hours after leaving Aberdeen, I walked along the Euston Road to Marylebone. Sophie McNeil opened the door after I'd buzzed up. Her mother Nuccia had laid on a light meal in the kitchen. I slipped out of my suit and into Levi jeans. Then I sat down to green salad, potato salad and crusty white bread. Pudding was a mixture of blueberries and strawberries with cream. Sophie had snacked when she'd got in from work at four, so she sat with me but didn't eat. When I'd finished, we went through to the living room where I sprawled on the sofa and talked art with Sophie, and politics with her mother.

I left the McNeil's at eight-thirty, walked down Oxford Street to a 55 bus stop. I was in Stamford Hill half an hour later. George and Melinda were engrossed in a TV programme called Big Brother. A bunch of people who didn't know each other were stuck in a house and filmed twenty-four seven. It was voyeurism a-go-go, the participants were voted off the show and the last one left got a bunch of money. Melinda made tea, and I admired George's rather battered collection of J. G. Ballard first editions, mainly ex-library copies that had been heavily stamped. It was curious looking at the over-stylised seventies covers, and seeing from the endorsements that Ballard had always been considered a literary novelist. The sixties and seventies had been something else: if Ballard had been starting out as a novelist at the beginning of the twenty-first century, he'd have been a prime candidate for paperback original publication. George pulled out his first edition of *Naked Lunch* by William Burroughs, with its Brion Gysin dust wrapper still intact. This was considerably more impressive as a collectors item than his Ballards. After much talk of grants and auction prices, George and Melinda retired to the bedroom and I crashed out on the sofa.

I was up shortly before Melinda left for work at nine in the morning. I ate muesli, drank coffee and talked to George. He was spinning Incredible String Band albums. I split around ten, taking my time walking through Dalston and down to Brick Lane. I met Ben Seymour outside the Beigel Bake, and he ushered me into a car. We sped into Hackney, where I was interviewed about the many years I'd spent living in social housing in the East End. There was a great deal to say, and I'd been thinking about the subject a lot because I was using these experiences as background material for the book I was writing—and which you're reading—called *Memphis Underground*. Perhaps I should explain that *Memphis*

Underground isn't really a novel. I've produced several texts that have been published as novels but are really something else. After Joyce, post-*Finnegans Wake*, there really isn't any point in writing novels—literature is dead. The only literature that interests me is more anti-writing than writing. Running from Beckett and Trocchi, there's a direct line to what I'm doing. *Cain's Book* was very much in my mind as I embarked on *Memphis Underground*. Moving on, or moving off the subject, I certainly understood the *nouveau roman* as a kind of anti-writing with its autistic descriptions of furniture, rooms, the play of light through bottles and glasses. I too was able, as a purely technical exercise, to take information from maps and diagrams and render it as prose. This is real anti-writing and it produces interesting effects. Take a map and then translate it into prose, so that it becomes harder and takes longer to grasp the information that can so effortlessly be absorbed from a diagram. The end result is an ineffective way of communicating factual information, and thus focuses attention on the act of declaration, rather than the material conveyed. In all of this there are deeply poetic effects. Many of those with a lingering nostalgia for literature privilege poetics over critique, whereas I want to amalgamate these two forms and adulterate them with a third—popular story telling. I looked up at the shelf behind my laptop after I wrote the previous sentence and saw novels by Gil Scott-Heron, Charles Bukowski and Clarence Cooper Jr.—but much more telling is the fact that right now I have the 1971 James Brown album *Hot Pants* on my hi-fi, and as I began the second part of this sentence, the part that comes after the first dash, the track Escape-ism (Part 1) kicked in. Perhaps I should add that at this point, as I'm attending to the corrections I've marked by hand on the print out I made of the first draft of *Memphis Underground*, I'm listening to *Nonesuch Busted Me Bet* by The Mellotones—a vintage Lee Perry production. Before too many misunderstandings are provoked, I will also add that I dislike many of the books that pass through my hands. I find one of the three authors brought up at this point in my first draft—or rather, that point just above, since I'm adding some lines here—unrelentingly mediocre, the other two I enjoy despite the rather patchy quality of their output.

Returning to the day I've been writing about, roughly six weeks before the first draft of what you're reading was written, I'd been thinking about Debord and Burroughs. The latter had murdered his wife, the former was falsely accused by the press of killing his patron. These biographical details had greatly contributed to Burroughs and Debord's celebrity status and aided the sales of their books. The reason I'd been thinking about Debord was because I was in the process of reviewing Andrew Hussey's biography of him for *Art Monthly*. I found the whole phenomenon of biography curious. Debord, like Burroughs, was the subject of three different biographies published in English. Debord had been an alcoholic, Burroughs a junkie. The culture industry pitched Debord at those whose tastes were too refined for them to wholeheartedly embrace Burroughs. Trocchi, as far as I knew, had never murdered anyone. You might have a different take on Trocchi to me. You may consider him to have murdered his father in his prose. You could have been reading *A Man Asleep* instead of this. But from my perspective, or rather from my perspective on the day in question, that is to say on 12 June 2001, Trocchi couldn't even murder the novel, that had already been done by his mentor's mentor. There had been a laying on of hands, from Joyce to Beckett to

Trocchi, so Trocchi was affiliated to the murderer but he hadn't even gone as far as manslaughter—he'd stopped short at pimping his wife. Trocchi was a murderer by proxy. Is it a crime to kick a corpse? The Italian left-communist Amadeo Bordiga talked about the murder of the dead, but by this he meant the destruction of dead labour so that living labour might be used to turn new profits. There are two biographies of Trocchi that might answer my question, but *Cain's Book* is the spoiler for anyone wanting to make a serious study of Trocchi's life. *Cain's Book* is autobiography written by a writer intelligent enough to understand that this meant it was also fiction. Trocchi played with the thin dividing line between fact and fiction, and this was what was on my mind when I fictionalised my own experiences of living death in the East End of London. What I wrote was barely fictionalised because it was always and already fiction. I was both a golem master and a bread doll fancier. So I was working through all of this when I talked to Seymour, but it only formed a background to what I said on camera, none of it was explicitly stated.

Ben was making a film about gentrification. I talked for too long. When I say I talked for too long, I mean I talked for too long from my point of view, Ben was quite happy since the more footage that was taken, the more he had to work with. I was running late for my next appointment, so I got a lift down to Spitalfields market from one of Ben's collaborators. Pauline van Mourik Broekman spotted me as I ran through the stalls searching for her. She laughed about the way my white afro bounced as I sped along. We both bought falafel with humus salad in pitta bread and sat at a table. Pauline had just been at some arts conference and a lot of people there had been talking about how rising property prices were making it impossible for them to pursue their cultural practice in London. A lot of artists were pondering moving to Berlin, where there was at that time a lot of low rent housing. Pauline was sorted in London, she'd owned a flat in Chelsea for years and years, so inflated property prices didn't really have much effect on her. Pauline was the editor of *Mute*, an arts magazine to which I contributed. We talked about what I was doing for upcoming issues, and among other things agreed that I would do the following short review (which was written a week or so later):

A Cavalier History Of Surrealism by Raoul Vaneigem as 'J-F Dupuis' translated by Donald Nicholson-Smith (AK Press, £7.95).

After Guy Debord, Raoul Vaneigem is one of the more celebrated situationist theorists. This short sketch of a forerunner to the group of which he was once a leading light, says more about Vaneigem's theoretical weaknesses than it does about his ostensible subject. Vaneigem usefully stresses the specificity of surrealism, concentrating on its differences to dada. Unfortunately, he rather mechanically expands on the situationist dictum that the dadaists wanted to suppress art without realising it, while the surrealists wanted to realise art without suppressing it. Part and parcel of Vaneigem's reductive treatment of this subject are his blinkered Eurocentric and Francophone perspectives. His more general pronouncements emerge very clearly from his immersion in European high culture, and indicate an inadequate knowledge of other social and cultural forms. Vaneigem's grasp of history

is every bit as defective as his attempts at dialectic. He writes of books being transformed into
commodities by the market, when as perhaps the
first perfected capitalist commodity, the book
actually played a key role in the development of
capitalist markets (there is a dialectical relationship between books and the market, Vaneigem's
treatment is one-sided). However, while this is a
bad book, it is also a very instructive one. The
attraction of situationism for many of its fans is
the air of extremism that emerges from the very
weaknesses that are displayed so extravagantly
here. The text is well worth reading, not as a
critical primer on surrealism, but rather as an
unconscious exposition of the flaws underlying
situationist ideology.

Before locating the file containing this review, I changed
the CD on my hi-fi. So now I'm listening to *Pharoah's
First* by Pharoah Sanders on the ESP label. I enjoy
silence when I write—or should that be type, since
everything I do is typed straight into computers—but
music is good too, I can tap away to the rhythm and
pleasant sounds are a convenient way of covering up
less agreeable noises. Returning to the thread of my
anti-narrative, Pauline and I exited Spitalfields market
together, but we parted company once we'd crossed
Commercial Street. I headed east along Hanbury Street,
and then up Brick Lane. Pauline veered south to her
office on Wentworth Street. From Brick Lane I turned
right, then took a left up Turin Street. The terrain was
familiar, I'd rented a flat on Turin Street for more than
five years, and had only moved out of it a few months
earlier because I was sickened by the trendification of
the area (and the fact that in many ways this made it

unaffordable to me). If *Memphis Underground*—the book I'm working on, not to murder the moonlight, but partly to explore how long news of the (un)timely death of the novel takes to spread—was not fiction, or at least didn't quite self-consciously deal with the ways in which autobiography is a fictional genre, then much of it might have been set on Turin Street rather than in Hoxton. At a clip, one could walk from this book's "real" to its "fictional" setting in five minutes. Or rather, one could walk from one of its "real" to one of its "fictional" settings in five minutes. While certain sections of the book reflect my experience of living on the Avebury Estate in Bethnal Green, others are drawn from the nine years during which I rented a council flat on the Teviot Estate in Poplar. Housing and gentrification have been dominant themes within my fiction from the mid-eighties onwards, so the issues I am addressing here are in no way a departure from my previous concerns. I wanted to explore the domestic, a favoured theme of many feminist writers, while like any feminist theorist worth her or his salt, insisting that the domestic is not something that can be treated in isolation.

I cut across Gosset Street and into Wellington Row. My friend Paul Tickell had just got married, in fact I'd attended his marriage celebrations at Chelsea Physic Garden a few weeks before. I knocked on the door, Paul answered and ushered me into a living room. Paul's house had been valued the day before I visited him and he couldn't believe what it was worth—not as much, of course, as his wife's flat in Notting Hill, but its value was rising faster than properties in west London. I'd just written pieces for three different magazines about Paul's recently completed second feature *Christie Malry's Own Double Entry*. *Sleazenation* hadn't run the puff I'd done for them, despite the fact that they'd sponsored Paul's first feature *Crush Proof* on its appearance at the Raindance film festival. Bizarre ran what I wrote about Tickell in the issue that appeared the month after the meeting I'm now describing. In June 2001, in other words at the time I'm writing about or approximately six weeks ago now, the piece I did for *Mute* on *Malry* hadn't appeared—but it ran as follows:

Christie Malry's Own Double Entry directed by Paul Tickell. A star vehicle for Nick Moran of *Lock, Stock & Two Smoking Barrels* fame with a script by ultra-hip playwright Simon Bent (*Goldhawk Road, Shelter* etc.) based on a cult novel of the same name by B. S. Johnson. The plot involves urban terrorism, perverse sex and the malign influence of the Italian renaissance on life in contemporary London. *Malry* has all the ingredients of a blockbuster, as well as a nifty line in art house tricks that add resonance and depth. Unfortunately, a national release date has yet to be set because the industry is dominated by people who lack the vision and bottle to make a killing from the first great film of the twenty-first century. Since abandoning his training for the Jesuit priesthood, the career of director Paul Tickell has been dogged by controversy. His hard hitting 1995 television mini-series *Zinky Boys Go Underground* about Afghan army veterans and drug running in Moscow is the only BAFTA award winning drama never to be repeated by the BBC. Tickell's first feature *Crush Proof* wowed critics back in 1999, but his uncompromising portrayal of Dublin kids doing their own thing was still considered unsuitable for UK national release. This despite *Crush Proof* doing brisk business in Europe and resurfacing recently on the Sky movie channel. Likewise, Tickell's Arena documentary *Punk & The Pistols* didn't enthral the BBC hierarchy, but Julian Temple was sufficiently impressed to rip it off wholesale in *The Filth & The Fury*. Fortunately there are other industry insiders who believe Tickell deserves more than backhanded compliments. Virgin have released Luke Haines' stunning soundtrack for *Malry*, and with the help of PR firm Savage & Savidge they've been involved in organising private screenings at Soho House, as well as public ones at places like the ICA. Catch this if you can!"

I spoke with Paul about the costs of making prints of films for cinematic release. He made coffee, and supplied various nuts as a snack. We looked through some press coverage for *Malry*, and also for Luke Haines. Luke, who'd I'd introduced to Paul, was busy promoting a Pop Strike, which he cheerfully admitted was influenced by the rather different Art Strikes proposed by Gustav Metzger and me. After a while, I walked out with Paul to the Bethnal Green Road Post Office, and then the Tower Hamlets Parking Shop, where my friend purchased visitor parking tickets. I strolled with Paul back to Turin Street, then he went home and I headed over to the Bookworks headquarters in Holywell Row, on the far side of Norton Folgate. At Bookworks, I chatted with Craig Martin who was nearing the end of his tenure there as an editor. I left with copies of an art publication that Craig had commissioned and to which I'd contributed, *Material: Public Works—The Bridge*

2000, Thomas Hirschhorn. Next, I perambulated to the offices of Creation Books in Leather Lane. There I saw Miranda and Laurie, got an early copy of my royalty statement, and was told I'd be sent the cheque on Friday. I doubled back across Farringdon Road and the next hour or so of my life is covered in yet another piece I wrote for *Mute*:

BaudriR charts the live reproduction in internet chat rooms of the Jean Baudrillard book *In The Shadow Of Silent Majorities*. According to Baudrillard, the strength of the masses lies in their silence and their ability to neutralise critique. Accepting Baudrillard on his own terms, cyber-artist Annabel Frearson has typed Baudrillard out word for word into chat rooms where the fragmented structure of the on-line "interactions" precludes coherent expression and juxtaposes Baudrillard's high-flown "anti-theory" with clichés and inanities, producing truly hyperreal effects. Baudrillard is largely ignored as the conversation ranges across politics and religion, but still manages to hinge largely on sex. Frearson's *BaudriR* project very cleverly reveals the limits of Baudrillard's theoretical work, and as such it undermines him in ways that are unimaginable to those—such as Christopher Norris—who have launched frontal attacks on post-modernism. I was intrigued, and arranged to meet Frearson in Messrs C, a coffee shop opposite Farringdon tube station. I'd jotted down a few questions in a note book, and began with the most obvious of them.

"How did you get the idea for this project?" I asked after purchasing a cappuccino.

"I wanted to learn more about Baudrillard."

"So why did you chose to work with *In The Shadow Of Silent Majorities?*"

"It was the only book I'd read by Baudrillard, I read it when I was at college, and I had a copy at home."

"What are your opinions about Baudrillard's claims to have broken with Marxism in works such as *The Mirror Of Production?*" I enquired.

"Your question seems to imply Baudrillard used to be a Marxist. I really know very little about him and have never heard of *The Mirror Of Production*. Tell me about his involvement in Marxism?"

"Baudrillard was Henri Lefebvre's assistant for a time."

"Who is Henri Lefebvre?"

"He was a leading Parisian communist intellectual, well known for his sociological interest in everyday life. As well as working with Lefebvre, Baudrillard also had a flirtation with Maoism. Despite his claims that he has broken with Marxism, what Baudrillard actually does is invert the communist critique of commodity fetishism in which objects take on the appearance of subjects and subjects—men and women—are treated as things. He switches around the positive and negative signs in Marx's analysis of capitalism, while simultaneously demonstrating his inability to move beyond it. Of course, given what Baudrillard has to say about history turning back on itself in *The Illusion Of The End*, he arms himself against criticisms of this type by incorporating them into his theory."

"I don't know anything about this."

"But that's incredible," I exclaimed. "I've been

reading Baudrillard for nearly twenty years and you seem to be telling me that you've grasped all the issues he raises quite intuitively, and that you've done so working from a tiny fragment of his extensive output. You seem to have arrived at positions remarkably similar to my own, but without putting in the long and arduous hours of reading and thinking I've dedicated to this task."

"As I've already said, I did this because I wanted to learn more about Baudrillard, I really know very little about him. I found it arduous enough retyping his text."

"So now you've got the *BaudriR* project up on your web site, what else do you intend to do with it?"

"I want to find a publisher who'll put it out as a book."

"But that's impossible!" I cried. "This is a massive project and reproducing it in book form would be very expensive. It's unlikely that any publisher with the money to do it as a book would touch it, because it so blatantly infringes copyright."

"I don't think copyright is a problem, Baudrillard's writing constitutes only a small part of what I've created, it's broken up by a mass of other people's comments and there are errors in my transcription. The question I'm asking is who really owns this text?"

"Of course, from a Socratic point of view, what you've done is completely valid, but the international laws concerning intellectual property are very strict. The copyright status of the text you've used will be quite complicated. *In The Shadow Of Silent Majorities* is translated from

French and consists of essays from a number of sources. There is Baudrillard's original copyright, then that will be held through at least one French publisher, on top of which Semiotext(e) will have licensed the copyright in English and their licence is clearly non-exclusive because other American presses have published parts of the text in other forms and other translations, and then there's the question of the copyright on the translation."

"I wrote to Columbia University to ask if I could use the book, but I didn't hear back from them."

"That's because Jim Fleming who runs Semiotext(e), and Columbia University who he used to work with, had disagreements over some of the stuff he was publishing and got divorced. This, of course, makes the copyright situation even more complex. Fleming is keeping the old Semiotext(e) books in print, but it seems to me that Columbia might legitimately lay at least partial claim to the copyright on this particular translation."

"But surely they won't mind that I've used the text?"

"To persuade any commercial publisher to touch your project, you'd actually have to clear the copyright, which looks to me like it would be very difficult. I thought that was one of the great things about what you'd done, that you'd so flagrantly contravened the laws of copyright. I'm also curious about these America Online chat rooms that you've used to generate text that fragments In The Shadow Of Silent Majorities, since it occurred to me that as the carrier of these services, AOL might claim copyright on what goes on within them. I haven't checked this out, but if anyone is able to claim copyright on what appears in chat rooms, it would seem more likely that it would be the carrier rather than the individual participants. It would be rather amusing to see someone like AOL try to claim copyright on *BaudriR*."

"I wouldn't know about that, I haven't thought about it."

"The copyright status of text generated in specific chat rooms might be dealt with in their terms and conditions of use. Have you looked at these? I haven't because I've never used a chat room."

"You've never used a chat room?"

"No."

"I find them fascinating, I log on thinking I'll just go into one quickly, and then I spend hours and hours with it."

"What you reproduce from chat rooms is side-splittingly funny in the context of detourning Baudrillard, but it is also utterly banal."

"But the banality is its fascination."

The conversation could have gone on in this way for hours. However, having finished my coffee, I decided to leave. Despite allowing a few weeks to pass between interviewing Frearson and transcribing what took place, I'm still not sure whether she was self-consciously performing the role Baudrillard had allotted the masses in his theoretical work, or if she'd blindly stumbled into the part. My guess is both and neither, in a(n) (un)knowing post-modern sort of way. *BaudriR* is already a cult among a number of my acquaintances who regularly get high on theory. I can't imagine a single one of them believing me

when I tell them Frearson claimed to know nothing of Baudrillard beyond *In The Shadow Of Silent Majorities*. The "truth", of course, doesn't matter—whatever way you look at it, BaudriR is a triumph. Read BaudriR at the following web address:
http://www.baudrir.com.

The end of my Mute article is perhaps a little misleading, since when I left Messrs C., I did so in the company of Annabel Frearson. We were both heading east, so we cut across the City together. Strolling through Smithfield, Frearson told me about an acquaintance who'd bought a flat opposite the meat market—it had seemed nice and quiet when they'd viewed it in the day, and it was only after moving in that this unfortunate realised they would be disturbed by the noise of revving lorry engines all night. At this point, the Pharoah Sanders album I'd been playing as I was typing (or writing), came to an end, so I got up and put on a compilation CD called *Pulp Fusion*—which describes itself as "funky jazz classics & original breaks from the tough side," The featured artists included Johnny Hammond, Pucho, Reuben Wilson, Minnie Riperton and Idris Muhammed. It was the sort of thing that at one time might have been called acid jazz.

However, don't let this fool you into thinking I've any records by the likes of The Brand New Heavies. I don't, since if I was going to listen to anything contemporary it would probably be techno.

Annabel and I cut along Cheapside, through Aldgate and into Whitechapel. She was going to a bar close to Fieldgate Street, and I was going to The Tayyab on Fieldgate Street. The first time I'd met the novelist and psychogeographer Iain Sinclair, it had been at this location, but back then it had been a pub called The Queen's Head with an elderly Polish landlady pulling the pints. On another occasion, Sinclair had taken great delight in introducing me to Rachel Whiteread in this boozer. Whiteread was, of course, famous for obliterating the history of a terraced row in which I'd once lived by making a concrete cast of a house a few doors down from the one I'd occupied. Since Whiteread had no desire to meet me, and I certainly had nothing complimentary to say to her, we exchanged very few words. Strangely, I'm doing further corrections to this text after a night out drinking in The Royal Oak. At one point I was seated next to Fiona Banner, who told me an anecdote about how she'd been reading a satirical story I'd written about Rachel Whiteread when the object of my barbed words entered the room she was seated in and started speaking to her. Moving on, and bearing in mind that The Queens is now a restaurant, I got a table and before long was joined by novelist Tony White. I ordered sag aloo, Tony had chicken curry. We shared a dahl and rice, but had our own nan bread. We talked books and art, and by the time we were finished, I was stuffed.

Having paid for this repast, we headed up Brick Lane to buy bagels. The Lane was heaving, it had been transformed, and was filled with young kids who no doubt considered themselves trendy. Brick Lane was no longer the place I'd once known and loved. That was then, this was now. We did run into the artist Donald Parsnips and his wife Melissa who lived on Club Row. Tony hadn't met Mr. and Mrs. Parsnips before, so I introduced them. There'd been a power cut and Adam (that's Donald's "real" name) and Melissa had been unable to cook, so they'd hit a curry house instead. Melissa looked well, despite having just undergone an operation because she suffered from a rare eye disease. We talked more art, and also about what was happening in New York (where Donald was based part time). After this cultural exchange, and with bags of bagels in our hands, Tony and I headed east to his place in Shadwell. We sat up late chewing the cud over Wyndham Lewis, and other matters cultural and political.

I want to add here that I haven't marked that many corrections onto the manuscript of the first draft of *Memphis Underground*, and that the present paragraph is a spontaneous addition conceived after I'd already defaced this print out with an initial set of revisions. That said, I've also moved on, and as I type this accretion I'm listening to the early Upsetters album *Clint Eastwood*. I have the CD in question on the Jet Star label, hilariously repackaged as *The Best Of Lee Perry And "The Upsetters"*. I love cheesy reissues, and I also prefer Perry's late-sixties/early-seventies material to his dub works. If I wanted to listen to dub, I'd take King Tubby over Perry any day.

Stump Juice

I don't know how Claire Grogan found me. I was nursing a pint in The Palm Tree. I'd been staying at my mother's for six weeks and was feeling pretty sorry for myself. Whenever I managed to get some money together, I'd escape to points north, usually somewhere between Soho and Mile End. Grogan sat down opposite me and slid a fresh Guinness across the table. She was drinking chilled Becks straight from a bottle. I'd only met Claire once before, when Tony Cheam had marched us from The Masque Haunt to The Wenlock Arms. I recognised Grogan instantly, she was solidly built with black hair and brown eyes. You could tell she'd eaten well as a child, even if her behaviour hadn't been a dead give away that she came from a privileged background. Grogan picked my sunglasses off the table and checked out the make. Fortunately they were Ray-Bans, and this met with her approval.

"Tony's disappeared and I want you to take his place." Claire announced.

"Not again!" I groaned. "Besides, I thought you'd split up."

"Tony and I are soul mates, we are destined to remain together, but in the meantime I want you step into his shoes."

"You want me to be your boyfriend?" I joshed.

"Sure," Grogan replied, "if you're pretending to be Tony then we're an item, but you've also got to carry on with Tony's work."

"What's he got on?"

"He's had some funding through to make films, you got any ideas for art movies you wanna do?"

"Yep, I'm gonna remake avant-garde classics, starting with Warhol's *Sleep* and Debord's *Screams In Favour Of De Sade*."

"How you gonna do that?"

"Both are easy. With *Sleep*, instead of eight hours of a human asleep, I'm gonna shoot a dead dog in a ditch for eight hours. With *Screams* it will be a colour remake, where Debord had blackened stock, I'll have TV colour bars. Then when he had white light, I'll have TV snow. There were no images in Debord's feature, and there won't be any in my colour remake. The random dialogue accompanying my TV snow will be in English, a straight translation from the original

French. The final twenty minutes of TV snow will, of course, be entirely silent."

"Brilliant," Grogan observed. Then she added: "Do you want another drink?"

"Sure," I replied.

"You won't get brewers droop?"

"Would that bother you?"

"Well, if you want to take Tony's place, you have to come home with me tonight, so we can fuck. After all, Tony was my boyfriend."

"In that case, forget the drink."

We took a cab to Grogan's place in the wilds of Tufnell Park. Claire couldn't wait to get home, so she unbuttoned my flies in the taxi and took my soul finger out.

"It's swelling." Grogan remarked superfluously.

"I don't wanna blow my own trumpet, so get it in your mouth and feel it grow and grow." Even half-cut I thought this sounded a bit childish. "Afterwards, I'll be able to see what it looks like smeared with your lipstick."

Claire was eager enough to show what she was capable of sexually, so my crass dialogue didn't put her off. She didn't even spit out my spunk, she swallowed it. Once I'd come, Grogan suggested I go down on her. After I'd used my tongue to bring her to orgasm, she paid off the cabbie and we went into her house, where I had her over the Aga.

Afrodesia

I could have taken a bus but I preferred to walk. The stalls were still being laid out as I cut through Watney Street Market, a designed-for-pedestrians simulacrum of classic brutalism, less celebrated than The Brunswick Centre in Bloomsbury but to my mind the pre-eminent example of modernist architecture in Shadwell. Of course, it wasn't as impressive as the Tricorn Centre in Portsmouth, but as a small scale exercise in twentieth-century retail architecture, only the Anglia Centre in Norwich rivalled the Watney. Turning left out of the shopping centre, I walked the short distance to Sidney Street, famous for being the location of a shoot out between cops and anarchists a hundred years previously. From Sidney Street I cut across Whitechapel Road and up Cambridge Heath Road. Before long I'd passed Bethnal Green tube station and was heading up to Hackney. Mare Street had changed. It had become trendy since I'd first started visiting it regularly as a callow youth of sixteen for various parties against racism. However, being a tad further out from the centre of town, it was still preferable to Shoreditch or Brick Lane, which were considerably more fashionable than Hackney. I cut through the churchyard just before reaching the top of Mare Street, and around to Homerton Hospital.

My friend, underground film-maker Mick Cohen, was lying in a hospital bed with Dani Behr watching over him. I don't watch the box, but I'm told that Behr is a well known and much loved television presenter. I wouldn't know about that, but I can say with a reasonable degree of certainty that she's an admirable human being. Between Behr and Mick's parents, there was a constant vigil at his bedside. I hadn't met Behr before, but I knew she'd shared a flat with Mick for a year or two and that they'd become fast friends. I'd phoned the hospital and asked if it was okay to visit, Behr took me into the corridor to talk this over.

"I'm the wicked witch," she explained, "when Mick's parents aren't here, it's my job to discourage visitors. Mick took an overdose and needs a lot of rest, so we're not keen on his friends coming here. Since you got here on the hospital's say so, you can sit by him but you can't wake him up. Do you know anything about suicide? Things can get mixed up in anybody's mind, I've worked with The Samaritans, and we're all potential suicides when things are going wrong. Rather than dropping in at the hospital, the best way for you to get news of Mick is to phone his flatmate, she'll keep you up to date. Let's go back in to the ward, if Mick wakes up then you can talk to him."

So I went and sat in the chair Behr was occupying when I arrived. At my feet was a chill box, Bear's emergency supplies. She poured herself a fruit juice as I sat there. Mick didn't wake. When I left, Behr took my place. I walked back through the churchyard, down Mare Street, then cut across London Fields and Broadway Market onto Hackney Road, coming out by the City Farm. I was running late, so I picked up a passing 55 bus and got off at the top of Charring Cross Road. I walked down to Trafalgar Square, down Whitehall, I was slowed by the hoards of tourists in Parliament Square, but once I was on the other side of The Houses Of Parliament, I was able to make my way to the Arts Council headquarters on Great Peter Street at a brisk clip. I ran into Tony White on my way in, I said I was going for lunch with Mark Waugh. Tony said he'd see me at the Literature Department's reception that night. Taxis were being ordered to take people from the Literature Department to the other side of Trafalgar Square for this reception. The receptionist told me I could call Mark up on the internal phone while she was busy organising this transportation. Mark was surprised it was me who called him, I explained the situation. Once he was down from his office, we strolled to Fiesta, an Italian café on Horseferry Road. I had mozzarella and tomato in ciabatta, Mark had mozzarella and spinach.

"Have you seen the *BaudriR* project that's up on the web?" I asked.

"Yes, Baudrillard typed word for word into chat rooms, it's amazing."

"Last night I interviewed Annabel Frearson who did it and I was flabbergasted, she didn't know anything of Baudrillard beyond *In The Shadow Of Silent Majorities*."

"Never! It's such a brilliant piece of work, surely she knows more than that one little book."

"That's all she knows, the piece is pure intuition, an extraordinary achievement."

We ate and we talked; we talked, ate and drank tea. I asked Mark what he was doing with his second novel, since it was a few years since he'd published his first, *Come*, with Pulp Faction. He didn't seem very interested in finding a publisher for his completed but unpublished second book, he was more drawn towards film as a form of expression. The publishing industry lacked the velocity Mark craved when he was working as an artist rather than as an arts administrator. He found publishing too slow, too insipid, I didn't have a problem with Mark's preference for film over book production, but since he had a second novel written, I thought it was a shame he'd lost his enthusiasm for pursuing non-linear forms in the print medium.

After lunch, I walked up to Berwick Street where I visited Malcolm Norris. Malcolm ran the London end of Youth International, a rag trade operation that exported British subcultural clothing to the US. Punk, skinhead, mod, teddy boy, these were all styles with a specialist market on the other side of the pond and from which a shrewd entrepreneur could make serious money thanks to the fetishisation of London labels. Malcolm was much too nice a bloke to make his own tidy pile from teenage dreams, he worked long hours for a minimal wage, it was his bosses in California who were coining it. I chatted to Malcolm about the latest situationist publications, and showed him the proof copy of the Debord biography I was reviewing. I told him that biography was not a genre well suited to the collective practice and left-communist politics of the Situationist International, and while Hussey had done extensive research and produced a perfectly adequate journalistic account of Debord's life, the book was still far from satisfactory. There were plenty of biographical details that would be new to English language readers, most obviously about Debord's childhood and family background, but these did little to enrich our under-standing of the Situationist project. Malcolm asked me if I'd read the Rebel Inc. biography of Trocchi, and when I replied negatively he gave me a copy he'd picked up as a remainder for a couple of quid. Shortly after this, I split for Marylebone. Nuccia answered the door when I rang up to her flat, Sophie was in the bath. I didn't want anything to eat, but Nuccia made me a pot of tea and among other things we conversed about an article in a women's magazine she'd been reading that suggested ingesting chocolate in moderation boosted one's health.

I'd left my suit in Nuccia's apartment, and once

Sophie had done her make up, I went through to a bedroom to change into it. It was an eighties silver suit which I'd bought in a charity shop in Corby for a fiver. The girl who'd sold me the suit, perhaps ten years my junior, had informed me it was cheap because it was utterly unfashionable and she'd been horrified when I'd insisted on buying it. I'd worn the suit when I'd appeared in the Channel 4 film *The Falconer* made by Iain Sinclair and Chris Petit, and it had occasioned much comment after the programme was screened. Sophie though it was a terrible suit, but that it was typical of me to wear such a thing. She politely informed me I looked extremely arty in it. Other people had suggested I looked like a mad professor, especially now that I'd grown my hair out and it was somewhat unruly. I'd a white shirt and black tie to wear with the suit, but at the last minute changed my mind and decided to keep on the black and white checked Ben Sherman shirt I was already wearing. The Bennie had a button-down collar, so I decided I didn't need a tie. Sophie was wearing a new, and very expensive black dress. After Sophie had exchanged a few sentences in Italian with her mother, we left the flat and walked over to Soho, where we met Rob McGlynn in The French House. Sophie and Rob hadn't met before, but they got on really well. Rob talked about his writing, he was unpublished but had a big shot agent who I was certain would get him a decent book deal. Sophie talked about her art, she had an incredible control of line and a lot of talent, but needed to be more pushy if she was ever to quit her bilingual proof-reading job and go professional. After one drink, we strolled down to the National Gallery, where we found quite a mixed crowd. I ran into Pete Ayrton who'd published five of my books on his Serpent's Tail imprint.

"Are you getting an award?" Pete asked.

"Apparently," I told him.

"What do you get?"

"Seven grand."

"And you're going to shake Salman Rushdie's hand?"

"If he'll shake mine."

"I have to see this."

There was a jazz band playing in an alcove, not the type of jazz I like, but it was a nod in the right direction even if it wasn't free form. The canapés were considerably better, I lifted one off a tray and could see fresh flowers beneath the clear glass that until a moment before had been covered by an avocado snack. Various people greeted me, it was incredible how many people I knew at the Arts Council. Tony White was just one of those present. Cultural theorist Judith Williamson popped up and said hello, asking me if I'd seen George and Melinda recently and wanting to know how they were. Speeches were made about the importance of the arts and more specifically literature. I actually thought Salman Rushdie gave the best of the three speeches—but then I really am rather too fond of damning with faint praise. When Rushdie finished rambling, I was among the fourteen writers and one literary agent who were invited up to shake his hand. When I took his paw in mine, I though he looked wearied. Regardless of what I think of Rushdie as a person, and to be honest it isn't a lot, I have to admit he looked like he needed a good rest. He appeared to be that most elusive of creatures, a thoroughly mediocre novelist who'd actually suffered for his art. Rushdie had made a miscalculation when he wrote *The Satanic Verses*, and so many years latter he still looked very sad and sorrowful. I've no idea what the other writers who shook Rushdie's hand thought of his prose, or if they considered this an honour, but for me it was a joke. The fact that I'd just been given seven grand made the raillery even better. Seven grand is seven grand. It would enable me to ease off on the amount of journalism I hacked out, and instead concentrate on writing a book. Perhaps even this book, *Memphis Underground*.

The Gigolo

I didn't get to sleep much that first night I spent with Claire Grogan, but I did get a lot of fucking in. Or rather, what I enjoyed was pretty much non-stop sex until the alarm went off at eight the following morning. After that little bell rang, everything changed. Claire pushed me off her, telling me she'd had enough of a shafting. We got up, showered, had breakfast. The food we ate was very good. Expensive bread, a load of different cheeses including goats cheese, olives. Grogan had a fancy coffee maker too, so I had several strong espressos. While we were eating, Claire was running me through this whole number about Tony and his involvement with the Neoist movement in the nineteen-eighties. I had to repeat all this shit she told me as though I was Tony. There where quite a number of different routines. One was about how I'd hitch-hiked to Italy to take part in the Ninth Neoist Festival. The first ride wasn't bad, straight off the boat at Calais and I was picked up by an English guy with a van travelling to the south of France to see his girlfriend. We motored all night, getting stopped once by armed cops, and taking occasional breaks for coffee. I had about twenty quid on me, so I was running through the money fast.

I didn't sleep that first night and I was already short of shut-eye since at that time I was homeless and kipping on friends' floors. After the English guy dropped me off in the morning, it took a long time to get another lift. Thankfully, after a short ride from a thirty-something bleached blonde in a red sports car, I got taken to Geneva by a Swiss couple calling themselves Ronnie and Bonnie. They wanted to practice their English on a native speaker. Ronnie and Bonnie took me out clubbing, and introduced me to some of their English friends. I got to sleep in their flat, and in one version of the story I slept on their sofa, and in the other—well, you can imagine what happens in the alternative rendering of this tale. In the morning Ronnie and Bonnie took me to a café for breakfast, then dropped me off at the best point for hitching a lift through Mt. Blanc. Later, after nightfall, I walked across Milan in the pissing rain, laughing at the people huddled in phone boxes because they were afraid of getting wet. In the morning the sun came out and it got very hot. Dripping wet, I couldn't get a lift, but once I'd dried off things picked up. I headed back into the Alps beyond Bergamo. At one point I stripped off and plunged into a mountain stream to get cool. I was so out of it my memories are all fucked up, and I can't fit them together in the correct sequence. I was dehydrated and at the top of a hill a middle-aged woman gave me glass after glass of water. The days I spent in Ponte Nossa were exactly what you'd expect at an avant-garde art festival in a tiny mountain village. Egos were falling in the street, and a lot of locals were puzzled by what was going on. Somehow I missed the civic reception, cum opening, of this Neoist meet.

The journey home was pretty much like the one out,

except that Tony slept in at least one garden shed. He, or I, also suffered a series of bum rides. One guy offered me a lift when I wasn't even hitching, and after I stopped him feeling me up, made me get out of his car on motorway hard shoulder, so I had to spend an hour walking to the next exit from where I'd be able to thumb a ride. I sat on a fence for hours, when a French lorry driver finally gave me a lift, I fell down on the way to his cab and tore the knee of my trousers. Another lift was from a bunch of hippies, and their car broke down on a motorway, so I had another long walk before I was able to thumb a fresh ride. I had a bit more luck as I made my way up through France, a family who picked me up insisted on taking me back to their farm house and feeding me. The last ride into Calais was from a youngish couple who were Jesus freaks, and they informed me God told them to stop and give me a lift. I had a return ticket for the boat, and bunked the train back to London. Once I reached the city of my youth, I walked to Hackney and crashed exhausted on a friend's floor. A few days after this, a room came up in a housing co-op in Stoke Newington, so at last I found myself with somewhere cheap to live. The only downside to life in my own pad was the water was busted. I had to piss in the garden and it was a five minute walk to the nearest public convenience when I wanted to drop a log. However, I only lived like this for six weeks until the plumbing was fixed, then other people started moving into the Victorian town house to share it with me.

"Do we have to go through Tony's life in this kind of detail?" I demanded, after Claire made me repeat to her the anecdotes I've just retold here.

"Yes, yes," Grogan snapped, "we have to do this, it turns me on big time."

So that's how we spent the morning, going over and over different stories, which Claire would relate in the third person and I'd retell in the first. For lunch we went out to an Italian restaurant, and after pasta and ice cream, we made our way to a sex shop in King's Cross.

"I want you to choose a blow up sex doll." Grogan told me. "I'll pay for it, but you have to select one."

It wasn't difficult for me to make my choice. I picked the cheapest doll because I was completely indifferent about the purchase. The box had a photograph of Linda Lovelace on it, and according to the copy with which this packaging was emblazoned, the doll who was also called Linda enjoyed giving blow jobs. Since the sex toy was inanimate, this claim struck me as fraudulent. Customers were forbidden from undoing the cartons and looking at the dolls prior to making a purchase. Therefore, it wasn't until we got Linda home and took her out of the box that I discovered she looked nothing like the picture of Linda Lovelace on the wrapping. Lovelace had brown hair, whereas the rubber hair on my love doll was blonde. Linda had cost £15, a special discount offer. I could have had a Pamela Anderson rubber dolly for £50 and I rather suspected that once I'd removed the outer packaging, she'd have been identical to Linda. I'm not up on contemporary porn stars, but their blow up doubles were even more expensive than Pamela, although I'd imagine that the only material differences between them and cheapo Linda were the pictures and copy on the boxes they'd been stuffed in.

"Tony had this thing about a girl he'd once known called Sophie," Claire explained. "We bought a blow up doll, and I'd watch Tony having sex with her, while we both pretended she was this girl Sophie."

"What happened to Sophie?" I asked.

"Tony had a huge row with her, then she disappeared."

"No, no!" I exclaimed. "I didn't mean what happened to the girl Tony was fixated on, I meant what happened to the rubber dolly he used to pretend was Sophie."

"She disappeared," Claire whispered, "at the same time as Tony. Sophie ruined our relationship, after a few weeks of rampant threesomes, all Tony ever wanted me to do was watch as he made out with his blow up doll."

"So why do you want me to pretend I'm Tony, while I use this rubber dolly to simulate having sex with his ex-girlfriend."

"Because I want to work through what went wrong with our relationship, and see if it could have gone differently. That's why I want you to step into Tony's shoes, you've not only got to fuck Linda—sorry, I meant Sophie—several times a day while I watch, I also want you to continue with his artistic projects."

I looked at Linda and I didn't find her in the least bit attractive, then I thought about what Claire wanted me to do and I knew it was totally fucked up. Grogan told me to strip and by the time I'd taken my clothes off I had an erection. I guess I was getting off on the fact that Claire was watching me, since I wasn't excited by Linda's rubbery curves. I kissed Linda on the mouth, then I played with her tits and her clit.

"Stop farting about," Grogan bellowed, "you're teasing Sophie, and you're teasing me. I want you to get on top of her and ride."

I did what I was told, and five minutes later I'd come.

Blow Your Whistle

I'd gone to ground for six days, I'd been working on my book—this book—*Memphis Underground*. When I broke cover, I walked from King's Cross to Rob McGlynn's flat on the Golden Lane Estate between Old Street and The Barbican. We sat on Rob's balcony looking west towards Centrepoint and the post office tower. We drank beer, premium bottled lager from Belgium. McGlynn had only been living in this pad for six months, and he absolutely loved the view. He was on the twelfth floor, and the prospects to the north and west were spectacular. I'd lived on the eighth floor of a tower block in Poplar from where I'd cultivated a studied indifferent to sublime cityscapes. You can get used to this kind of view and the aesthetics of tragedy that often accompany sublime enthusiasms for urban living are, to say the least, problematic. What I appreciated about being high up was the light that came into the flat, and the fact that the noises of the city weren't as harsh as at ground level, they became muted as they rose higher and higher.

Eventually, we left McGlynn's flat and cut southwest through the City, crossing the river at Southwark Bridge. We walked along the South Bank. The National Film Theatre was heaving, but we resisted the lure of the French new wave and pressed west, past the Houses Of Parliament. We were on a mission of sorts. I thought of times past. I'd tried to sleep on a bench by the river here in the late-seventies and got moved on by the cops. On another occasion in the early eighties, I'd sat here during the day and was starring at the river when a uniformed cop sat down beside me to make friendly conversation, like this was the most normal thing in the world. I'd got up and gone back to where I was living in Kennington, shocked and speechless. The river, the stretch of The Thames from Richmond to Greenwich, carried so many memories for me—carried so many of my memories, and was so over burdened with history, that the way the water just kept flowing sometimes surprised me. We walked on and were up on the road by the time we passed Jeffrey Archer's flat. The disgraced Tory MP and best-selling author inevitably became a subject of our conversation. Rob said that if Iain Sinclair had managed to keep his contempt for Archer a little more under control, the interview he'd conducted with this john would have been much more effective as a demolition job. I countered that Sinclair was probably more controlled than I'd have been if I'd had to meet Archer.

McGlynn's mobile rang, it was Marvin Schwartz, he wanted to know where we were. Having decided to walk rather than take the bus, we were running late. We were only a few minutes on foot from the Milch Gallery where we'd arranged to meet Marvin. When we arrived, we found Schwartz standing on the steps up to the gallery. I went inside and bought bottled lager. In the twenty-first century these little galleries rarely gave booze away free, sponsorship for operations like Milch was thin on the ground. We stood on the steps leading up to the gallery and talked about the various places we where headed. Marvin was going to Vienna, Budapest and Prague, in his capacity as an arts administrator—he was also, I should add, a practising artist. Rob was hot-footing it to France, a holiday. I was going to Liverpool as an artist and Berlin as a writer—consecutively, although attempting this feat simultaneously might have proved more challenging. Since we were attending a Jonas Dahlberg opening, we eventually went inside the gallery to look at the art.

There were two video pieces being shown, and Rob pointed out that they were being projected into mirrors. I explained this was to maximise the size of the image on the walls, in effect making the placing of the projectors much further back from the "screens" than would have been possible otherwise. The work was slow pans around architectural interiors, Rob liked the work, I was indifferent to it.

From Milch we headed down to Little Portugal to eat tapas. The cluster of bars and restaurants serving London's Portuguese community are located conveniently close to the MI6 HQ in Vauxhall, and many a spy can be spotted getting pissed in these charming establishments. We dined al fresco at Estrella on the South Lambeth Road, and as far as I know we didn't meet any spooks, but McGlynn's sister Mole did wander past. She sat with us long enough to consume a can of 7-Up. Mole lived a couple of streets away, and was on her way elsewhere, I forget her exact destination. Melvin asked some people on the table next to ours what they were eating, and they insisted on giving it to us. We drank bottled beer and my recollection of our conversation is hazy. I do, however, recall that some of it revolved around Marvin's plans to test the humour levels of ethical avant-gardists such as Alexander Brenner.

Funky Wah Wah

I was churning out experimental film, or rather video, at a phenomenal rate. I'd remade *Sleep* and *Screams In Favour Of De Sade*, and a whole bunch of other stuff from the fifties and sixties. I'd just redone *Gilbert & George In The Bush* as *Punch & Judy In The Bush*, which consisted of a single shot of a naked twenty-something's crotch with miniature marionettes in her pubes. Get this, since I had my model standing up for a fifteen minute take of her quim, she would move slightly and cause the puppets to shake. It was a minimal piece and the movement was rather subtle, but I was as pleased as a perforation with the results, and I just knew it would get the critics raving about my art. I was also busy reworking a lot of Neoist material with which I'd actually been involved, or rather in which Tony Cheam—who I was pretending to be—had been implicated. I'd been remaking Pete Horobin and Stewart Home's *Pram 84* as *Pram 69*. The original had been shot around Lumsden in Aberdeenshire, with Horobin pushing a pram filled with his camping gear along country roads in imitation of old-fashioned highland tramping. I'd crammed a pram with dead pea fowls and lacy black underwear, which I filmed being pushed along canal banks in Hackney by a dosser I paid in cans of strong lager. That was, until my mobile rang.

"Hello," I said as I put my phone to my ear.

"It's me," it was Claire Grogan, I don't know why she would never say her name when she called.

"What's happening?"

"The leaves are happening, season of mists and mellow fruitiness..."

"Close titted friend of the maturing sun," I interrupted.

"That's not quite right," Claire snapped, "Keats would never use a term like titted."

"Fuck it," I said.

"Anyway, that wasn't what I phoned to tell you. I

need you to get your ass back here, so we can put your passport in order."

"But I'm filming," I protested.

"How much time you got on the cam?"

"I dunno, twenty-five maybe thirty minutes."

"That'll do."

"What do you mean it will do?"

"I mean you've got enough material to run with, you don't need to edit, just screen it as it is, that'll save time and money on post-production."

"Sounds good to me, I dunno why I'm pissing about in Hackney when I got myself a fine piece of ass in Tufnell Park."

"Yeah, Sophie is missing you, and once we've got your photograph on a passport with Tony Cheam's name on it, you can give her some of the old push and pull."

"Groovy."

I got the dosser who'd been working with me to dump the pram and its contents in the canal, which made a great final shot what with all the panties and pea fowls floating off towards Islington, while air bubbled up around the wheels of the upside down and partially submerged baby carriage. I knew the short I'd just made was a real motherfucker, a massive improvement on the original I was parodying. I got the dosser to sign a release form saying he'd received ample recompense for his troubles, and gave him a four pack of super-strength lager as a parting gift. On the bus back to Tufnell Park, I went over some of the things Grogan had told me about my—or rather Tony Cheam's—meetings with the mysterious Pete Horobin. I'd encountered the maestro on a number of occasions in London. Glasgow, Dundee and Ponte Nossa. He was determined to bypass the usual channels of publicity and establish his reputation as an artist purely on the basis of rumour. The strategy appeared to by working, since I'd just remade one of his more notorious art shorts.

When I got back to Sophie's place—I mean Claire's pad—I had to have a passport photo taken. Grogan had found a forger who made me up a passport with all Tony Cheam's personal details and my photograph in it. Once this was done, the document was perfect in every way, except—of course—that it was a fake. After the bloke who fabricated the dummy passport had been paid off, Claire urged me to give Sophie a ride. My blow up sex doll was beginning to sag a bit from heavy use, so once I'd breathed some life back into her, we made the beast with two backs. At first I'd been sceptical about the fun to be had with a rubber lover, but by this time I was convinced it was the best sex going. I never had to worry about Sophie's needs, since she didn't have any, I could just get on top of her and bang away until I came—which rarely took longer than five minutes. That left me with a lot more time to get on with my film work than if I'd had a regular flesh and blood lover with her own wants and desires. My new autosexual proclivities were simultaneously a practical demonstration of my stature as an artist, since as I've made clear, Sophie really wasn't much to look at, and my getting off in this way was a major feat of human imagination.

Natural Soul Brother

I slept on Rob McGlynn's floor, and woke before my host. When Rob woke he made pancakes, I'd already made coffee and we consumed this fare at a table on his balcony. McGlynn had writing to do, so I split at eleven. The stall holders were still setting up on White-cross Street, but the market wasn't what it used to be. There were no exciting soul CDs, the blokes who'd specialised in cheap music had partially switched to computer games, DVDs and videos, so I wandered up Clerkenwell Road to the street market at Leather Lane, and things were no better there. I had a piece in the new issue of *The Idler*, so I rang the bell to their office to see if I could blag a copy of the magazine, but no one was in. I walked on to Soho, and naturally enough gravitated towards Berwick Street. I tried the record shops but didn't turn up much. I already had the CD reissue of The Monks official sixties releases, and decided to give a secondhand copy of their demos a miss. Eight quid was too much to make this a bargain, even if it contained songs that were previously unreleased in any form. The CD was a German import and a new copy cost fifteen quid. The Monks shifted in Berwick Street, since the retail record outlets catered for specialist tastes—soul, reggae, jazz, psyche, punk, rockabilly, sixties garage, all this and other musical groves that bypassed best-seller channels. If I was looking for something, like the narrator of *Cain's Book*, I didn't know what it was. I bought some black bread and called on Malcolm Norris. He made me a cup of coffee and we talked about Lee Perry. Then Malcolm told me about a Manchester United football match he'd recently attended. Time was passing by, so I left for Euston. I could have taken a bus or tube, but I preferred to walk.

The three o'clock train to Liverpool was crowded, so I was glad I had a reserved seat. I was still working on the lecture I'd be giving the following morning, so I had papers spread all over the table I was sharing with three other people. I had an aisle rather than a window seat, and from time to time I found my attention somewhat distracted. A woman in her early thirties who looked like she was half-Italian and half-Chinese, kept getting up from her seat and pulling a suitcase down from an overhead rack to take things out. She was wearing a slit skirt and had fantastic legs. I tried not to let my jaw drop when I looked up from my papers, and was confronted by large portions of her bare leg. I'd booked a seat in what was allegedly a quiet coach, where the use of mobiles was officially banned. This official ban was, of course, meaningless. The guy sitting opposite me had his phone on, and answered the calls his wife made to him. There was a party of school children in the carriage, and they weren't exactly quiet either. Still, none of this was quite as beguiling as the woman a couple of seats down from me who just couldn't leave her suitcase alone.

There is a standing joke about travellers coming out of Lime Street Station, jumping into a taxi and asking to go to The Adelphi. I walked to the hotel, which took about a minute. I'd stayed at The Adelphi before, and knew exactly where it was. I checked in and was pleased to get an old room at the far end of one of the wings. One of the main door panels had been replaced with a piece of wood that wasn't quite the right colour, but the bedroom retained something of its original opulence. There were mirrors in three corners of the room and gilt on the ceiling. I would have preferred it if the old-fashioned duck print that decorated one wall had been removed. The bathroom suite was modern, although I'm assured there are still marble baths in some of these old rooms. I sat down at the dressing table, spread my papers out and continued to work on my lecture. By eight o'clock I realised I wasn't going to spent the evening socialising. I ate three slices of the black bread I'd bought in Soho, made a cup of tea and got back to my lecture notes. These would have to be completed to my satisfaction before I went to bed.

Bill Drummond was reading in Liverpool that night, but I didn't know where. The last time I'd spoken to Bill he'd told me he was reading with Irvine Welsh and Kevin Simpson. I'd got the date but Bill had to hang up before telling me the location, because his baby son Flint needed attention. I sat at the dressing table until after midnight working up my lecture notes. Whenever I looked up, I'd see myself reflected infinitely, since the mirror in front of me was directly opposite the large glass on the wardrobe. From time to time I would raise my head, take delight in the formalist perfection of this infinite regress, and think about the notes I was working on. Occasionally, my thoughts wandered onto other, vaguely related, matters. For instance, the last time I'd seen Bill Drummond had been in Hull when we were both participating in Root 2000. My train had been much delayed, and about five minutes after I'd got into the hotel, Bill knocked on the door of my room. It was good to see him and we'd gone out for an Indian meal, which helped me relax after the rigours of my journey. That said, I couldn't relax completely since I still had work to do on my Root 2000 presentation. In Hull I'd also had the morning after my arrival to finish arranging my notes and had been able to do so to my satisfaction the day after going out with Bill. In Liverpool I was giving an early morning lecture, so once the preparatory work on it had been completed, I took a bath and went to bed—forgetting to mark the summer solstice in any way whatsoever.

Green Tambourine

One morning I decided to give up writing. Claire thought I was pulling some kind of Samuel Beckett routine, that I was sick of film-making and was going to switch to fiction. She imagined I'd spend my days composing lures of the following type: "I have nothing to say but I've yet to run through the effluvium with which I might describe my taste for dissipation. My contribution to avant-garde fiction is to announce its exhaustion, which is merely another way of proclaiming it must live out it's own death, since there is exhaustion and exhaustion—as well as lethargy, languor and lassitude. My predilection for indolence is not yet identical to the enervation of anti-writing. I don't so much as possess a pen, but enough of nostalgia. I plugged in my computer because I wanted to collect my email. I don't write, I type. I have nothing to say beyond the fact that I'm embroiled in a bare faced lie. For reasons that elude me, I can't help signifying a great deal more than I consciously intend. Debility is my message, and since I've gone to the trouble of pointing this out, I guess the bulk of my readers will recognise that fragility is almost and already a synonym for subtlety. My computer is black and sleek and obsolete—a PowerBook 1400 that isn't even compatible with the latest Mac peripherals. I went from the word processing package to the email package, and from the email package to the word processing package, and so forth, and so on, and back again, breaking off very briefly to look at the system tools. Did I have anything to say? I wasn't sure, all I knew was that there was no beginning, there was no end, it went forever. That's why I had decided to give up writing, and it is also what made the resolution essentially meaningless. The point was that there was no point, that giving up was essentially the same as carrying on. It's hard enough to find critics who understand what I'm banging on about, but hasn't it always been this way? Not only have I immersed myself in the anti-traditions of the avant-garde, I'm also very much aware of the Black Atlantic and the stake of those who live outside the overdeveloped world in modernism. Newspaper reviewers don't have a clue where I'm coming from, they might be perfectly well qualified to judge chick lit and lad lit, but they have no points of reference when it comes to my novels, I leave them all at sea. Even those who've read in the right areas to make some sense of my activities all too often miss the point, since as a good Afro-Celt I've crossed stylistic experimentation with popular story telling. After re-reading the preceding line with something approaching disdain, I got up and made myself a sandwich. Wittgenstein on steroids. Rancid cheese. I once tried explaining to a publicist that my problems began with my father. He refused to get a job, and slobbed around the house all day experimenting with make-up and women's underwear. No one seemed to understand I found this funny, or that I'd laughed my cock off when I'd read Wittgenstein and Hegel. I rather liked Jarry's *umour* but was far more impressed when rib-tickling effects were realised without conscious effort on the part of the author. I guess that was why I had so many problems with Gertrude Stein. So I got up and got myself another drink, since as far as my father was concerned there was nothing worth reading other than The Bible, except—of course—for back copies of *Women's Wear Weekly*. I remember going into our house one time with my childhood buddy Sticky-Wicket Jim and finding I was unable to explain why my dad was buck naked and lying on top of a lady I'd never seen before. Perhaps it is not so much that I have nothing to say, but rather that I am unable to articulate the pain of being forced as a child to walk about in public with a paper bag over my head and etcetera, and so on, and etcetera, for at least another forty thousand words, blah, blah, blah..."

Grogan must have been out of her mind if she thought I was more interested in parodying avant-garde prose than remaking avant-garde films. Writing was too much like hard work, especially prose of the type parodied above that doesn't even use normal paragraph breaks. If I was going to write stuff intended for publication, I'd use short paragraphs because that would bulk out the finished product. You'd be amazed how many extra pages are created when you use short paragraphs, those little indents at the beginning and the space on the end of the last line will make a book look much longer than it really is. What's more, the reader is left feeling they've really achieved something by reading to the end of a 300 page epic, when much of what they've worked through was actually blank space. Dialogue is a particularly good way of fostering these illusions..

"Well fuck you too!" Claire was screaming.

I'd just accused her of murdering Sophie. I'd had a heavy session with my sex doll the night before, and had fallen asleep with my rubber lover in my arms. When I woke in the morning, Sophie was deflated. During the night she'd been stabbed with a pair of scissors that were still lying at the foot of the bed. Grogan told me I was behaving just like John Johnson. I informed her I was John Johnson, but she insisted I was Tony Cheam. She told me that if I checked my passport or my diary, I'd see that she was right. When I reread my day book, it seemed to be written in a whole bunch of different hands. Claire said this was the effect of all the cocaine I was snorting. However, I'm convinced that Grogan was adding entries when I wasn't around. That was why I decided to give up writing. I didn't need to write because Claire was doing it for me, and this actually gave me more time to concentrate on my film-making. There were some pretty surreal entries in my diary, and I knew I hadn't written them because what they describe never happened to me. For example, there was an account of how in my early twenties I'd been homeless and had walked from East Dulwich to Bethnal Green. It was February and it was snowing. I'd gone into The Museum Of Childhood, and sat down on a bench to get warm. I had half-escaped from this world when I was shaken back by an attendant who wanted to know if I was okay. The museum was closing up for the night, and if I couldn't get out on my own two feet an ambulance could be called. It said in my diary that I just wanted to be left alone, that I was ready to die at that moment, and that if it hadn't been for the intervention of the museum guard, I'd no longer be alive. Death was described as being like entering a golden light, it was splendid and enticing. When I read this, I knew Grogan was faking the entries in my diary. The fictitious incident I've just related is pure romanticism, and definitely not something that could have been experienced by me. I wondered if Claire was trying to drive me mad. I knew she was jealous of the way I'd got so involved with Sophie—but then she'd wanted us all to get involved in a threesome. My rubber doll was damaged beyond repair, and that night I had sex with Claire for the first time in weeks.

Live Injection

I woke at six-twenty, got up and had a shower. I'd had a bath the night before as a way of relaxing, but I still needed to wash my hair. Breakfast was a typical hotel buffet with nothing quite hot enough by the time I'd got it on my plate. I started with fruit juice, yoghurt and muesli, then moved on to fried egg, mushrooms, beans, tomatoes and toast. This was inevitably accompanied by a retired cockney geezer seated at the table next to mine complaining about what a terrible holiday he was having in Liverpool. I went up to my room and gathered my lecture notes together. It took me ten minutes to walk to the art school in Hope Street. I'd timed it so that I'd arrive just before nine, since I was scheduled to kick things off at nine-thirty. As is usual with these conferences—and this particularly conference was called *Work, Talk, Rest & Play*—things ran a little late. I was given a conference pack and a coffee, then sat waiting for people to arrive. While I waited, conference organiser Colin Fallows came over to say hello. We'd first met eight years earlier, when I'd accidentally run into Sex Pistols biographer Jon Savage on Portobello Road and Colin was with him. I already knew of Fallows, since I possessed a copy of the album of avant-garde sound works he'd compiled entitled *Dada For Now*, and had asked him how he'd managed to collect the material together. Moving away from Portobello Road in the early nineties in terms of both time and space, Colin introduced me to Baroness Mary Warnock who was chairing the conference.

After a brief introduction from Warnock, I delivered my lecture thirty minutes behind schedule. I began by addressing the premises of the conference, the role of the artist today and the effects technology was having on it. I pointed out that while the conference literature suggested new communication technology character-ised the twentieth-century, we should not forget that the same was also true of the nineteenth-century—which saw the development of railways and the telex, amongst other things. Technology is a big subject, and I used Walter Benjamin as a starting point for looking at it. I then explained that where the pre-conference lit-erature talked about the expanding globally dominant cultural industry, this could only be understood as a part of global capitalism. I also suggested that Stalin-ism and Maoism had imposed capitalism on what had been peasant societies, and so what characterised the twentieth-century was a shift from the formal to the real domination of capital on a global scale. As a result, industrial production had been shifted around the planet, and some of the most advanced industry is now found in what were once considered "backward" countries, just as regions that were previously heavily industrialised—such as the American Mid-West and British Midlands—had become rust belts.

I then went on to look at how some of the declining industrial nations had transformed cultural production and real estate into key generators of wealth. I spelt out that as well as being global, the cultural industry was also highly localised—being both centralised and localised in places such as Los Angeles, New York and London, Furthermore, cultural production was closely tied in with the gentrification of what were tradition-ally working class areas in these cities, and the meteoric rise of property prices had destroyed much of what had given such areas their character, and thus what initially made them attractive to the artistic vanguard among the gentrifiers. From here I moved on to the rather one-sided suggestion in the preliminary material for the conference that the practice of the early twentieth-century avant-garde had been normalised within contemporary art practice. I pointed out that while the technique of bricolage, and the treatment of the entire history of art as source material for the production of new work had become normalised, the critique of the institution of art that accompanied it had been jettisoned. I talked of Hegel and Peter Bürger, the involvement of the Berlin Dadaists and the Situationist International with the communist left. I spoke about the avant-garde's desire to integrate art and life, and of how art gains its appearance of ideological autonomy from its commodification.

I am greatly condensing my argument—and quite deliberately stripping away specific citations from both classical avant-garde sources and my own oeuvre—the gist of my speech was that if capitalism provides the material conditions for art, then German idealism supplies it with its ideological legitimation. Drawing on the same sources, Marx concluded that human activity constitutes reality through its praxis; truth is process, the process of self-development; or, as Marx more famously put it, the rounded individual of mature communism is a hunter in the morning, a fisherman in the afternoon, and a critical critic at night—without being hunter, fisherman or critic. Since it is shackled by commodification, artistic practice is a deformation of the sensuous unfolding of the self that will be possible once we've achieved real human community. The goal of communism is to abolish the reification of human activity into separate realms such as work and play, the aesthetic and the political. Communism will rescue the aesthetic from the ghetto of art and place it at the centre of life. Where then, I asked rhetorically, does this leave the role of the artist? I said it was a banality to state that under capitalism everyone reproduces the conditions of their own alienation, therefore when arts money is available it is unrealistic to expect those who might bag it not to go for it. However, while it is desirable that arts money should go to those with progressive views, progressive artists must always keep in sight the goal of self-negation, aiming in the long term for the abolition of their role as specialist non-specialists.

I could, of course, provide a less condensed version of my talk—but to do so would unnecessarily replicate words, sentences and even whole paragraphs I have written elsewhere. While I produced a new lecture to deliver at Liverpool, I was still drawing on work I had done before. Much, if not all, of this will be accessible to those readers of *Memphis Underground* who wish to pursue it. What I am trying to do here is illustrate the ways in which theory—or more specifically, constantly reforging the passage between theory and practice—provides me with highs similar to those described as being junk driven in *Cain's Book*. After my talk there were a few questions, followed by a coffee break. On my way out of the lecture hall, I was introduced to Max Wigram, the next speaker, who'd missed my talk. I was still holding my lecture notes, and I was asked if I could summarise what I'd said. So I ran through the material I've outlined above.

"What, did you read all that?" Max said pointing at the sheaf of papers I was holding in my hand.

"I didn't read this, these are just points to expand from, they provided me with a structure for my talk. I believe that a certain amount of improvisation helps when one gives a lecture, I find it rather boring when people bury their head in an essay and read word for word something they've prepared earlier."

217

"I got pissed last night and I've got a hangover, I haven't prepared anything. How long did you spend on that?" Wigram asked.

"Altogether, it took me about fifteen hours to prepare this particular lecture, but I'm drawing on stuff that I did as long as twenty years ago."

"Bloody hell!" Max wailed. With that this close friend of today's top art stars, a much loved gallerist and curator of the *Apocalypse* blockbuster exhibition, stalked off.

After the coffee break, I went back into the lecture hall to see Wigram talk. Max, it transpired, was very angry. Quite what he was very angry about wasn't always clear, since his passion on those subjects he addressed seemed to inhibit any ability he might have had to articulate his views. Max didn't give a lecture, he talked for a few minutes, then invited questions from the floor. As time went by, it became apparent that among other things Wigram felt very angry about any restraints whatsoever being placed on artists. He was a romantic and what he had to say thrilled most of the many art students in the audience.

Next up was John Fox of Welfare State International. Fox was a professional dissembler, a veteran of community art from 1968 to the present. I enjoyed his feigned amateurism, feigned as only a consummate professional could fake being inept. To some observers, Fox's positions appeared vaguely similar to my own, but his theoretical points of reference—Ruskin and Morris—are indicative of the sharp differences that exist between us. Fox took a few sideways bashes at me in his presentation—he hadn't quite grasped the full import of my rhetoric about the sensuous. I view wo/man as both rational and sensuous, and given the setting I was speaking in, I'd felt it appropriate to approach the sensuous from the perspective of the rational. I'd used words and words alone for my talk. Fox used music, slides and his own life to illustrate his notion of the social role of contemporary artists. Despite my distaste for Fox's threadbare anarchism, I appreciated his accomplished presentation, which stood in sharp contrast to both his opinions and his "art". Welfare State International worked very hard at being slackers.

I'd eaten too much for breakfast, so I didn't want lunch. While most of those present went to a nearby café, I headed for Hairy Records where I checked out the secondhand James Brown and Isley Brothers CDs. The afternoon session was kicked off by Eddie Berg, a man who clearly knew a lot about making successful grant applications. He was followed by Tim Eastop from the Arts Council. Among other things, Eastop was arguing that arts funding was currently being directed towards politically radical work. I didn't find Eastop's examples—these included Michael Landy and Jeremy Deller—particularly convincing, but I did think his choice of argument entertaining. Judith Palmer was next, she works part-time for the Arts Council, and part-time as a freelance journalist. She got everybody's attention by giving a talk about the social ranking of artists in consumer surveys. In the plenary session I got to speak about the obsession with audience that had been evident in much of what had been said during the day. I suggested that audience hadn't been an issue with innovations in Afro-American music, since this musical culture emerged out of a specific community and what was important about it—at least initially—were the social relations formed in and through its practice and development.

I went for supper with Colin Fallows and his girlfriend Julie, who also taught at the art school. The restaurant was two minutes walk from the art school. I ate aubergine pate with salad and crusty white bread. Colin and Julia ate something else, at this distance, I'm writing almost four weeks after the events I'm describing, I don't remember exactly what. I do, however, remember enjoying my food. We talked about the conference, clothes, art and music. That is, until a middle-aged man came up to our table and asked if he could join us. I pushed out a chair, and he sat down.

"You looked like you where having such an interesting conversation, I wanted to join you. What were you talking about?"

"We were discussing the William Burroughs cut up tapes, Colin has them all in his possession and is planning to issue the complete set on CD." I explained.

"Right. So what do you think of those people who view humanity as a cancer on the face of the earth?" the man asked.

"You mean people like deep ecologists?" I said.

"What?"

"Deep ecologists."

"I've never heard of deep ecologists.".

"They think humanity is a cancer on the face of the earth."

"What do you think of them?"

"That they're misanthropic."

"What do you mean?"

"That they hate people."

"Do you agree with ecology?"

"I've no sympathy for deep ecology. It views humanity as separate from nature, whereas we're a part of the natural world but we also act upon it. I think deep ecology is a product of scientific dualism?"

"What?"

220

"Look," I said, "we were about to leave when you came over. Do you want to come to the Unity Theatre with us?"

"I don't go to the theatre very often."

"Well, you can come with us if you want."

"No, I'll stay here."

So we got up and left without the guy who'd wanted to join us. A few minutes later we were in the bar of the theatre. I drank lager. Colin and Julie had soft drinks. Other people joined us, including John Brady from North West Arts who conversed with me about my involvement in the Karen Eliot multiple name project. There was a tannoy announcement about the film programme starting, so we trooped to our seats. We were watching a series of short films designed to be viewed on home computers, but projected here onto a big screen. Too many of the shorts recycled ideas from sixties experimental films or pop videos, relying on soundtrack beats to hold them together. There were, however, notable exceptions. Chang Young-Hae's *The Perfect Artistic Website* used text instead of images, and the longer it went on, the better it became. A series of banal statements became hilarious because parts of the "argument" had been emphasised by varying the size of the letters and the length of time particular sentences, or parts of sentences, where shown on the screen. *Video Hacking* was a fake documentary by Manuel Saiz about an artist who rented videos and returned them with minor alterations, so the next viewer would be confronted by sublime and surreal effects.

After the screening, I went back to the theatre bar where I talked to Judith Palmer about what we'd just seen, until this evolved into a discussion of the viewing culture developed around the Exploding Cinema. Just before midnight I made my way back to The

Adelphi with a bunch of conference delegates. I took a bath before going to bed. I sat up in bed and channel hopped on the TV, hoping to catch a news programme. I ended up voyeuristically watching part of a documentary about voyeurism, which was itself extremely voyeuristic. After ten minutes I gave up on the TV, as inevitably happened when I was provided with a set for my entertainment, I found the programming bored me. Instead, I read *A Life In Pieces: Reflections On Alexander Trocchi*, edited by Allan Campbell and Tim Niel, for an hour then went to sleep.

Haunted Castle

I wasn't sure whether I was John Johnson or Tony Cheam. The American who'd just introduced himself as Mr. Bradley certainly took me for the latter. Bradley said he'd met me during my residency in Orkney. I had no recollection of this momentous encounter, but then I'd probably been smacked out of my mind when it occurred. Bradley mentioned that my behaviour during our first meeting seemed a little erratic. Bradley announced he was working with someone called The Colonel, and offered me an all expenses covered trip to Finland to meet his employer. Scandinavia was as good a place to go as Morden, for me the journey was of more consequence than the destination. Our route was circuitous, it would take days—possibly even weeks—to reach our destination. We left in the morning, I don't recall what we did the previous night. Bradley told me later that we'd stayed in a guest house in Hounslow, but I don't know whether I believe him.

We flew from London to Naples, from where we caught a connecting flight to Sfax. It was when we arrived in Tunisia that we ran into problems. For some reason as a British national, I didn't have to pay tax to get into the country. Mr. Bradley was travelling on an American passport and the officials who waved me through would not accept payment from him in either dollars or sterling. It seemed he must pay in the local currency, of which he was entirely bereft. There had been a whole group of us on the plane going to a cultural conference, but rather than following the others onto the bus heading east, I waited for Mr. Bradley. He emerged from immigration two hours after me, saying that he'd had to bribe the guy checking his passport with a considerable sum to change a few dollars into local money. We found a few more stragglers, and eventually someone phoned ahead and was told the bus we'd missed would return to pick us up later. On the way into Libya, an official took my passport and told me I'd get it back later. When we finally arrived in Tripoli, the hotels that had been booked for delegates to the cultural conference we were attending were full, so we had to sleep in the corridors. Or rather, I failed to sleep in a corridor. It was a night of insomnia, of tossing and turning, as people trouped back and forth through the hotel without any readily apparent rhyme or reason.

Arriving at the conference I was unable to understand what the proceedings were about, despite the fact that they were conducted in English. My chief memory is of Israel being endlessly denounced as a bandit state, and of interminable standing up as the Libyan national anthem was played over and over and over again. When I wasn't thinking about getting out of Libya, and how I might reclaim my passport from the official who'd purloined it, I thought about Claire. I'd spent a weird few weeks with her pretending that I was Tony Cheam and I'd concluded she was crazy. Bradley had presented me with an opportunity to go someplace other than my mother's house in Morden. I was happy to take detours rather than fly directly to Finland, although I did object to going places where my nationality placed me under a cloud of suspicion and my passport was confiscated. Which is how I came to wish I'd stayed in London. Claire's sexual fixation with Tony Cheam might have been sick, but it was preferable to being a guest of The Colonel. At lunch time on the first full day I spent in Libya, I was offered a place on a coach trip into the desert. I refused to get on the bus because I was convinced I'd be killed and my body dumped in the shifting sands of the Libyan wastelands. As it turned out, those who accepted this offer I barely had the temerity to refuse, met The Colonel and were returned safely enough to our hotel later that night.

(Keep On) Bumpin'

I got up at seven, and the first thing I did was take a shower. Once I'd dressed I was ready to face breakfast. The buffet acted as a reminder that it was the weekend, when rooms at the Adelphi were available at ridiculously cheap rates. The range of food on offer was greatly reduced, there were no fried eggs or chips on a Saturday. I started my repast with yoghurt and fruit juice, then moved on to muesli, which I overloaded with prunes. I continued my victuals with scrambled egg, beans, mushrooms and toast. The couple at the table across from mine were talking about a visit they'd paid to The Cavern the previous night. This was not, of course, the venue at which The Beatles played early gigs, that was now a car park and the demolished pop shrine had been rebuilt next to the original site. John Lennon of The Beatles had attended the art school hosting the Work, *Talk, Rest & Play* conference, but no one was directing hordes of pop picking tourists towards it—which as far as I was concerned, was something of a relief.

Judith Palmer came down to the dining room with her boyfriend, and they sat with me. Before long we were joined by another conference delegate. Prior to the shindig in Liverpool, the last time I'd seen Judith I'd been standing in the doorway of The Foundry in Shoreditch. The Foundry is one of those places that, for me at least, is hard to avoid. A lot of my friends go to The Foundry, or at least walk past it, which is one of the reasons I like standing in the doorway, or sitting on the benches to the side of the public entrance. I stand in the doorway when it's raining, I sit outside when it's reasonably warm and dry. On the night in question it was raining sporadically, and I was framed by the doorway, when the conceptual artist Ceal Floyer walked past the bar and I called out to her since she hadn't clocked me. Floyer was on her way elsewhere, but she stopped for a drink and it was the first time we'd spoken since she'd moved to Berlin a year or two earlier. I've read at The Foundry with the likes of Nick Lezard and Billy Childish, but I wasn't reading that evening. I believe that earlier that evening there'd been a launch for the Matthew Collin book *This Is Serbia Calling*. Nights have been spent in The Foundry with the techno crew clustered around Praxis Records and Datacide magazine. On at least one occasion I've sat in The Foundry thinking the music I was hearing sounded like Lol Coxhill, then turned around and discovered it was Lol Coxhill playing his horn. Improvisation legend Coxhill is hard to avoid in London. I've seen him entertaining at parties thrown by John Williams and Charlotte Creig in Kensal Rise, I've even seen him busking. However, on the particular night I'm recalling, in the dog days of March 2001, I was standing in the doorway of The Foundry because the bar was crowded and it was raining outside. On that specific night, I'd told Judith Palmer that I'd never win an Arts Council Writers' Award. I'd explained that I'd applied every year for eight years for one, had seven rejections and was waiting for my eighth. I was planning to apply for twenty years, then I'd publish documentation of my inability to win the award. At breakfast on that other morning in Liverpool, Judith teased me for telling her I'd never get money out of the Literature Department of the Arts Council, then bagging seven grand a month later.

Once everyone had finished their breakfast, we went up to our rooms. Between breakfast and leaving the hotel, I took a shit. My bowel movements are something I've neglected to record, and writing this nearly four weeks after the events, I find it impossible to recall when most of them occurred. After dropping a log, I wandered along to the art school. Roy Ascott was on first, and he was talking about the way he'd bagged big bucks for research in the art and science crossover field. Ascott read very proficiently from a prepared paper, and I could see why he'd become a dollar magnet. As Ascott's lecture went on, it became increasingly deranged, with much wild talk of shamanism greatly agitating his audience. I was impressed, Ascott got himself taken seriously within academia despite being immersed in discourses that would have caused most people to be dismissed as nuts. Tomas Roope of Tomato Interactive was somewhat less imposing. Roope was an upper middle-class kid selling his interactive designs to corporations on the basis that they somehow emerged from street culture. He was the Byron Lee of interactive design, successful and prosaic. He claimed that play was part of his artistic process, that his highly paid work funded his unpaid creative experiments, but I'd have described the latter activity as pitching.

Last up that morning was Keith Khan. He talked about his involvement with the Notting Hill Carnival, the Tate Modern and the Millennium Dome, as well as the institutionalised racism he'd encountered in the art world. His presentation was brilliant, with fine modulation of his vocal tones and a very rational approach to the issues he addressed. I learnt later that Khan's mother had sent him for elocution lessons, but it was very much his choice to present himself in a way that quite self-consciously challenged racial stereotypes. Colin Fallows grabbed me on the way out to lunch, and I insisted we go to Marks & Spencers before finding a café, since I needed to buy some new socks, having omitted to bring sufficient clean ones with me. I bought a three pack for a tenner, or rather a penny less than a tenner. Then we went to eat, or rather Colin ate and I drank an espresso. I'd overloaded my stomach at breakfast and didn't want lunch. We discussed the presentations we'd seen that morning, then Colin told me about the work he was doing at the art school.

When we headed back for the afternoon session of the conference, I got a craving for grapes, so I went to a greengrocers and bought this fruit, a food that signified opulence in many a Northern European still life painting of the early capitalist epoch. In the twenty-first century grapes were readily available in England, but three or four hundred years ago, they'd been a luxury. *Art Monthly* editor Patricia Bickers had cancelled her appearance at the conference due to overwork, and when I returned Colin Fallows was chairing a panel session about the Arts Council sponsored Year Of The Artist. This was followed by Ilyana Nedkova speaking about a show she'd curated that addressed the gendering of technology. John Byrne—who lectured at Liverpool Art School—gave a wrap up session, in which he suggested that perhaps it was time to abolish the role of the artist.

After a break, there was a final plenary session, which I got roped into, since most of that day's conference participants had pissed off. The chair and panellists advanced divers obsessions. Mary Warnock was worrying over government policy on the arts, and also—perhaps not unsurprisingly given her age—death. I complained that the discussion of death was far too narrow in its orientation, and pointed out that in many traditional African cultures someone was not considered to be dead until they'd passed out of living memory. No one, and that includes me, picked up on the implications of such a world view within digital cultures, an immortality of the sort desired by those members of the Neoist Network who in the eighties proclaimed they wanted to die in the TV. From the floor, someone suggested that art ought to be professionalised, since anybody could wake up in the morning and decide they were an artist. I jumped right in there, since I'd woken up one morning in 1982 and decided to be an artist. I'd thought that becoming an artist was a matter of bureaucratic manipulation, and I'd wanted to test my theoretical understanding of the matter against cultural practice. Having received public funding and been reviewed in the art press, nearly twenty years on I could conclude

I was right. I went on to explain that my situation was relatively unusual, most people who work as artists have an art school training. As far as I was concerned, the art world was already fully professionalised, and a requirement for paper qualifications would only further entrench vested interests. Personally, and as I'd already made clear, I wanted to see the art world replaced with sensuous human self-activity.

Once this final plenary session was over, I walked to John Foster Gardens for the conference buffet with Mary Warnock. Mary asked me what I'd thought of the event, and I'd told her I'd found most of it very interesting. Even where I disagreed with the views being put across, the bulk of participants had argued intelligibly and intelligently. Although I didn't say so, Warnock herself was my best example. She'd taken her job as chair very seriously, and was clearly passionate about the arts. I didn't share her perspectives or enthusiasms, but the energy she put into encouraging state support of culture was quite astounding. When we arrived at the buffet, I grabbed some ciabatta that had been filled with mozzarella, and purloined a bottle of red wine. Warnock got deep into conversation with someone else. When I'd finished eating, I sought out Keith Khan. I told him I'd been particularly interested in his critique of unconscious racism manifested at an Edge performance art festival held around Brick Lane in the early nineties. Having lived in this area, I was able to enumerate other examples of art world bigotry against the local Bangladeshi community that Keith was unfamiliar with. We chatted about this, and various other matters until someone else came along wanting to speak to Khan. I ended up going to a bar called The Magnet with Jenny Rutter, Victoria Munich and another girl whose name I didn't catch.

Jenny had attended art school but now worked in an administrative capacity with a theatre company, Victoria had a background in drama. Both were based in Manchester. Munich had spoken from the audience during the final plenary session, saying that she was leaving the conference feeling empowered and able to call herself an artist. I'd clocked the younger women sitting with her, and I don't recall either of them making interventions from the floor. It was Victoria who popped the question that all three of them wanted to ask me, and over which they'd been arguing for two days.

"We've been trying to guess how old you are," Victoria said, "and you're obviously not as young as you look, because you've done a lot of things in your life. We think you could be anything between twenty-six and forty, so how old are you?"

"Thirty-nine," I said.

"Jenny thought you were thirty-nine."

Rutter smiled, at twenty-four she was the youngest of the three women. She'd grown up in Norwich, and we talked about the town, since I'd visited it on a number of occasions. I'd friends from the south coast who'd moved to the city and bought a house in Silver Street. Rutter knew exactly where my friends lived, immediately identifying it as being close to the Anglia Shopping Centre.

A Sack Full Of Soul

After the first session, I didn't bother going to the cultural congress. Some cats from Australia had agreed to let me use their room during the day, since I wasn't getting any sleep in the hotel corridor at night. I slept when the sun was up, and at night I'd read whatever English language books I was able to borrow—stuff like the Miles Davis autobiography, and several novels by Clarence Cooper Junior. I got breakfast and supper at the hotel, I snoozed while most of the delegates were getting their lunch at the symposium. Bradley had appropriated a broom cupboard, and this retreat enabled him to dream of well-stacked blondes at night, while during the day his attention was held by The Arabian Basis Of Post-Modern Culture convocation. On the last day of the congress my passport was returned to me with the compliments of The Colonel. Early the next morning we were driven by bus to Sfax airport, when we arrived it transpired we'd hit a Muslim holiday, and there were no connecting flights to Naples. We had to sleep overnight in the departure lounge. By means of a route that is too torturous to describe, Mr. Bradley led me not as I had expected to Scandinavia, but Minnesota.

"One day," Mr. Bradley remarked as we boarded a boat at Duluth, "you will meet Mr. Warhol. He is a first class artist, a very remarkable person indeed."

We moved slowly up the North Shore of Lake Superior. Sometimes we would see a deserted trading station close by the bank, clinging to the skirts of the unknown. The remains of tumble down cabins and enclosures seemed to be held in place by a spell. The plural term "furs" would ring in the air for a while—and on we went again into the silence, along empty reaches, round the silt bends, high walls of forest to one side and the waters of Lake Superior on the other, the ponderous beat of the stern-wheel reverberating in hollow claps. Trees, trees, millions of tress, massive, immense, running up high, and at their foot, hugging the bank crept the little begrimed steamboat on which I travelled with Mr. Bradley, like a sluggish beetle crawling on the floor of a lofty portico. It made me feel very small, very lost, and yet it was not altogether depressing, that feeling. After all, the grimy beetle crawled on—which was just what I wanted it to do.

As we trundled past French River, Palmers, Knife River, Larsmont, Two Harbors and Flood Bay State Park, I thought of other journeys I had made. I remembered an overnight ramble from Belfast to Dundalk at the height of the troubles. My intention had been to put the psycho back into psychogeography, and I think I succeeded in my own modest way. Psychologically, and perhaps even literally, I risked death. I wanted to see whether there would ever be an end to anything, or if the matters I felt unable to resolve would run on interminably. Given my eventual return to London, I concluded that I was fated to live out my own death, neither earth nor gun fire swallowed me up. I imagined Artaud in Ireland, and fantasised my demise as being very different to muddling along in the fashion I'd adopted until then. I wanted to vanish, I wanted to start again, I wanted somewhere to live since I was homeless at the time. I was sick of wandering across London and sleeping on a different sofa every night. I had plenty of friends who'd put me up but I needed a pad of my own. I was twenty-three, and knew I wasn't going to make it as a musician. It was in Ireland that I decided to break with Neoism. Unfortunately, I don't recall whether I was in the occupied territories or the Republic when I determined to have done with the rearguard and strike out on my own. For those not in the know, Neoism was a prefix and a suffix without a signifier. Neoism has also been interpreted, somewhat controversially, as an avant-garde movement in the tradition Dadaism, Surrealism, Lettrism, Situationism and Fluxus. At the time I went to Ireland, I'd been involved with Neoism for about a year.

I'd left Belfast in the afternoon, I arrived in Newry at four in the morning. On the way I'd only been stopped once by the cops, and they lost all interest in me when they heard my London accent. I hadn't slept for days, I was hallucinating figures in the landscape as a result of my fourteen hour peregrinations. I wanted to see how far I could push myself before dropping from fatigue. The army checkpoint at Newry was the best crack on my travels. As I approached it three squaddies raised their riffles and aimed them at me. I just ambled towards them wondering if they'd kill me. Someone asked me what I thought I was doing and the guns dropped when the squaddies heard my accent. I'd announced I was walking to the Republic. The squaddies couldn't believe someone who was English would turn up at this border post, twelve or so miles from the actual border, in the middle of the night. They thought I was mad. Told me I couldn't walk across "bandit country" to Dundalk. I assured them I'd be okay, since I wasn't running around dressed in fatigues intimidating people with guns. It was they, and not I, who had to answer for their cruel deeds, not to mention those of Oliver Cromwell and William Of Orange. Then I left them at their post, freaked out of their minds, they didn't try to stop me strolling on. My walk hadn't been particularly eventful, and I was tired, so once I was safely in the Republic I hitched a lift to Dublin. I could have continued on foot, but what was the point? There was no beginning, there was no end, my travails went on forever. Since I'd lived, I determined to go on with my cultural activities for another five years, before embarking on a three year Art Strike. In the meantime, and while I was in Dublin, I visited various sites associated with James Joyce.

"The traditional way of life here," Mr. Bradley mused as he gazed across endless water and sparsely populated land, "was destroyed even before the white man arrived. Trade changed everything, furs were sent out and guns came in. A lot of Red Indians were killed by diseases like small pox which arrived in North America via Europe, and this sickness reached these more remote areas before any of the corrosive bearers of capitalist "civilisation". The population was decimated, and fur trapping became their principal means of support."

The steamer seemed at her last gasp, the stern wheel flopped languidly, and I caught myself listening on tip-toe for the next beat of the boat, for its sober truth. We passed Castle Danger, a place named after a boat called Castle that was wrecked on the off-shore reef. I expected our dilapidated ship to give up at any minute. It was like watching the last flickers of a life. But still we crawled. Sometimes I would pick out a tree ahead to measure our progress towards Finland, but I'd lose my bearing before we came abreast of it. To keep the eyes so long on one thing was too much for human patience. We passed Beaver Bay and Silver Bay, docked fretfully at Ilgen City. The first settlement on the road into interior was Finland. The area was originally resettled by Finns, and numerous farms dotted the countryside.

The distant view was of mile upon mile of forest that extended beyond the boundaries of Minnesota and on into Canada. Much of the land around Finland has been painstakingly cleared, but it was once heavily timbered with tall thin spruce, tamarack and birch with its accompanying underbrush. The jack pine that was once scattered about was mostly removed by lumber companies in the nineteenth century. Much of the land was originally swampy but an abundance of moderately sized streams made drainage relatively easy. Many boulders were scattered about, left as glacial deposits after the last ice age. Finns were first attracted to the region as timbermen and miners, but many moved into rented homesteads or bought land as soon as they had the money to do so.

It was dusk when we arrived by taxi in Finland, our final destination being not the town itself, but a farm lying close to it. Upon our arrival, the housekeeper informed us that Mr. Warhol was away on business, but would return before the week was through. I was tired, and after a light supper of black bread and salad with Mr. Bradley, asked to be shown to my room. I flopped down on the bed and fell asleep without so much as undressing. I dreamt of the streets of a town that were particularly well laid out, with a beautiful esplanade lined with lime trees, which ran north and south across an isthmus through the centre of this miniature metropolis. It was a summer evening, and the central street was as crowded with promenaders as any Parisian boulevard. The gleaming light of the dying day played on abysses and ridges, painting them with all the subtle mystery of colour and shade, with darts of the cloud-piercing sun alighting upon high-tossed hissing spray and over this canvas painting the rainbow of a moment. When the night blotted out the filigree of the forest, with cloud-help, the moon lay over all this innumerable fleeting and ever-varying mosaics.

Dread Ina Jamdong

While I've been reconstructing this narrative, or rather when I've been taking breaks from reconstructing this account of my rather brief passage through a certain space and time, I've been reading *People Funny Boy* by David Katz—a biography of the renowned Jamaican music producer Lee Perry. It is one of the worst music books I've read for some time, since the author throws in too much detail and loses the plot in minutiae. Since biography and autobiography are always and already fictional, I've deliberately simplified my account of the time I spent last month in Liverpool, and I've quite consciously omitted to mention many of the people I met there. Likewise, I've said nothing of the view I enjoyed from my hotel window of assorted ventilation shafts, and am skipping all descriptions of waking, breakfast and checking out on my last morning there. I arrived at the train station, which as I had time to kill was by an indirect route, at 10.50 am. On the concourse, I ran into Keith Khan. We were travelling on the same train and got seats together. I'd planned to use this journey as an opportunity to begin correcting a print out I had with me of the first and second sections of *Memphis Underground*, but as it turned out, I didn't commence this work until I was in Germany. Instead, I chatted to Keith about his cultural activities, and the ways in which I thought it might be interesting to relate them historically to classical avant-garde concerns about everyday life.

Once I was in London, I went to a pub in Euston Street where I had several pints with Richard Marshall, who'd written an essay about me for the 3:AM website. We talked about Hazlitt, and Richard suggested my plagiaristic tendencies made me a far more typical representative of English literary traditions than jokers like Julian Barnes or Martin Amis. Richard enjoyed being simultaneously provocative and supportive, and this was one of the many things that endeared him to me. I walked Dick down to the Three Greyhounds in Soho, which entailed navigating the entire length of Tottenham Court Road, a street with which I am overly familiar. I left Marshall with a couple of his friends, and located a phone box. I left an answer phone message for Richard Essex, who'd I'd last seen on the day I'd gone underground to work on this manuscript. I called Rob McGlynn and he invited me over to his flat. After a brisk walk to Clerkenwell, I found myself sitting on Rob's balcony. He drank Bloody Marys, I drank mineral water. We talked about Robbe-Grillet. There were a lot of Robbe-Grillet's novels in McGlynn's flat, since my host was good at languages, I was surprised most were English translations. It got late, and as Rob was going to France, he suggested I sleep in his bed while he packed. I was woken at six by Rob calling from Stansted Airport, when he'd left the flat he'd forgotten to change the message on his answering machine. He wanted callers to know he was away.

I went back to sleep. When I woke at eight, I tidied up and watered the plants on the balcony. For breakfast I had coffee and toast. I walked to London Bridge train station, and caught a suburban service to New Cross. I met Pil and Galia Kollectiv in the main entrance to Goldsmiths College of Art. If their surname sounds a little strange, that is because they'd changed their names by deed-poll. I was giving these two post-graduate fine art students a tutorial. We went up to the library and used a video room to look at some of their animations. The funniest of these was a remake of Kenneth Anger's *Scorpio Rising*, which used jelly beans for its characters.

We spent three hours viewing and discussing this work, then I caught a train back towards the centre of town. I decided to alight at London Bridge and walk along the Thames. On the bookstalls outside the National Film Theatre I noticed a hardback copy of *Negrophobia* by Darius James. The novel had never been published in the UK, and this is the only time I've seen a first edition of it offered for sale anywhere in London. I'd picked up a copy of the American paperback in the now defunct Compendium Bookshop in Camden Town when that was issued.

I crossed the Thames at Hungerford Bridge and cut up to Soho. I changed twenty pounds sterling into Deutschmarks, then called on Malcolm Norris in Berwick Street. We talked about various Soho pubs we both frequented, and it quickly became apparent that Malcolm didn't share my aversion to The Coach & Horses, which was always too crowded for my liking. After two cups of coffee, I left Malcolm and walked the short distance to Marylebone where I called on Sophie and Nuccia McNeil. Nuccia had made gnocchi, one of my favourite Italian dishes, and I ate a huge portion despite the temperature having hit thirty in London that afternoon. There were news reports of dolphins frolicking in the Thames around London Bridge. I'd not seen them when I'd walked past, but then I hadn't been looking. Feeling stuffed, since the gnocchi was only the first part of a three course meal, I waddled away from Marylebone around ten, and called Richard Essex from a phone box on Oxford Street. We talked about John Dee and Amadeo Bordiga. Richard wanted to meet up, but I was flying out of London in the morning, so I'd said I'd give him a call when I got back the following week. I had the keys to Rob McGlynn's flat, so I walked to Clerkenwell and crashed there.

INTERLUDE

MEMORIES AND TRACES: LIZ YOUNG'S ESCAPE FROM THIS WORLD

The deaths of writers Robin Cook, Kathy Acker and Laurence James were all deeply upsetting for me, and made my shock at the passing of Elizabeth Young in March all the more traumatic. Liz read compulsively and when a new book came out by someone we both admired—say Bridget Penney or Darius James—we'd spend hours discussing it. Not that Liz restricted her interests to books: alongside well thumbed tomes her Ladbroke Grove flat was filled with some of the most unbelievable kitsch I've ever encountered—brightly coloured cushions, garish clothes and novelty knick-knacks. Typical of the things Liz bought is a key ring with a miniature leather jacket hanging from it that she gave me one Solstice. Presents were very important to Young, and her friends were constantly amazed by her ingenuity and generosity with regard to them. That said, Liz's love of curiosities wasn't limited to trinkets. She was the first person to offer me smart drugs—at one time her fridge was filled with bizarre "medicines" she'd mail ordered from the US which allegedly boosted one's intelligence. More to my taste was the weird range of herbal teas I'd be offered whenever I went down The Grove—not to mention the latest developments in health food. Young was always on top of consumer trends.

I first met Liz when she came to the launch of my bildungsroman *Pure Mania* at the now sadly defunct Compendium bookshop in Camden Town. Young was notoriously retiring but we immediately struck up a friendship because she was intrigued by the sexual imagery I was using in the novel. Liz knew well enough that what I was doing was developing and exaggerating the kind of metaphors that are found in pulp fiction, but for years she would tease me by saying "do you really imagine mudflats, amphibians and the big bang when you're having sex?" I suspect that the Goth in Young was secretly disappointed that I wasn't quite as mad as my books, while her more respectable side was quietly relieved that I am no more than half-insane. We had rather different relationships to the notion of capital "L" literature. Liz saw me as too antagonistic towards what I refused to accept was "the" canon, although she also greatly appreciated the fact that my fictional practice emerged from extensive reading both "within" and "around" "it". We rubbed along very well since among other things we shared a relish for both horror fiction and conspiracy theory as forms of unintentional humour. We also tried and usually failed to maintain a polite silence over differences of taste. Young had little time for what she viewed as my "ironic" immersion in dialectics, and I was always astonished by the amount of true crime she gulped down.

Reading a proof copy of Liz's forthcoming collection of journalism *Pandora's Handbag: Adventures in the Book World*, it was as if she'd been conjured back from the dead and was lounging on a sofa across from my chair. Young was very much given to taking to her bed, but when she received visitors she'd sprawl on her sofa with her much loved cat. Liz was a long term sufferer from hepatitis C and if she didn't feel well enough to receive people, she'd lie in bed and talk on the phone. Young rarely called earlier than ten or eleven in the evening, and the conversations could go on till dawn. *Pandora's Handbag* is very much like a marathon phone conversation with Liz, although obviously the collection is also shaped by the demands of jobbing journalism. Young was always very adept at working her interests into review and feature formats—and as a result landed regular work from national newspapers (which if not always better paid, were certainly more prestigious than the magazines she also wrote for). The constraints imposed by these forms of writing, pressures of "space" and "time", certainly produced curious effects when Liz was struggling both with and against them. There is a provisional feel to everything gathered in *Pandora's Handbag*; opinions are revised and even almost imperceptibly reversed between the articles and the introductory sections. Further eddies and crosscurrents emerge from the tension that also exists between Young's love of narrative, and simultaneous attraction to theories that undercut narrative. Negative spaces emerge that are every bit as fascinating as anything Liz states explicitly.

That said, *Pandora's Handbag* also shows Young very gracefully coming to terms with her life. She was often upset by the way her journalism was edited, and in this collection—which she was working on right up to her death—cuts are restored, and in some places records set straight. The introductory sections also show Liz as a little less unwilling to be overtly critical than in the past. One of the things fellow literary critics never allowed Young to live down was that in her twenties she appeared in the film *Rude Boy*—based around jock rock band The Clash—giving roadie Ray Gange a simulated blow job. Liz may have been quiet and understated in the way she addressed the baroque mythology surrounding her insignificant walk-on part in a fifth-rate film, but she was also unflapped and unembarrassed. Introducing a review of Johnny Green's book about The Clash *A Riot Of Our Own*, she reproduces the words Green claims were exchanged immediately after this scene was filmed. Gange is alleged to have propositioned Young as follows: "How about doing it for real?" To which she is said to have responded: "You must be joking." Liz comments wryly: "Actually the conversational interchange wasn't quite like that and that's why we have 'Rashomon'." Quite.

Despite coming from a very privileged background, Young also moved in what might quaintly be described as "low-life" circles for the whole of her adult life, and partly as a result of this she wrote from a liberal position that was on the whole to the left of her broadsheet colleagues. Liz had a difficult existence and hard drugs, as well as books, were her retreat from the world. It was typical of Young that if something didn't interest someone, she'd try to keep the subject out of her interchanges with them, no matter how important the matter was to her. While I agree with much of what Liz wrote about the persecution of heroin users, I have never found drug rushes very enthralling. Once Young realised this, she rarely spoke to me about narcotics. That said, I do think it was direct experience of repressive drug laws that served as one of the well-springs of Liz's instinctive sympathy for those she perceived as dispossessed and persecuted. Her outrage at her black brother-in-law being continuously stopped and searched because he drove a decent car was completely instinctive. However, the pressure of working to tight deadlines for the liberal press could take its toll. In an interview with T. Coraghessan Boyle collected in

Pandora's Handbag, Young quotes this sound bite sensationalist as saying: "If I wanted to use all my gifts to write extravagantly beautiful novels in praise of Hitler, then it is my right and my prerogative..." I always found Liz at her most elegant and eloquent when she addressed post-modern "blank generation" fiction, perhaps because our understandings were at their closest in this area. I didn't share Young's patience with "the great American novel", nor its transatlantic equivalent—"the great British mistake." Indeed, when we strayed into this area together disagreements inevitably arose. While it is unlikely Boyle would seriously consider writing a book praising Hitler, his overblown rhetoric is an example of precisely the sort of thing I felt Liz should have been deconstructing, whereas she would run with it.

However, Young understood long before any broadsheet hack why writers as diverse as Irvine Welsh, Iain Sinclair, Dennis Cooper and Lynne Tillman were significant. Indeed, her reviews of Cooper, in particular, played a pivotal role in breaking him in the UK. Books were important to Liz but as she makes clear in *Pandora's Handbag* while introducing a piece on the rise of biography, what she enjoyed much more than criticism were literary anecdotes. Given this, it is almost inevitable that I should pause here to provide some gossip about the time I turned up to visit Young shortly after Will Self had arrived unexpectedly at her flat. Rather than buzzing me in as she usually did, Liz came down the stairs looking flustered. After Young had explained that Self was upstairs, and I'd solemnly promised to be polite to him, I was ushered into her quarters. Liz liked Self's work but knew I had a low opinion of it. Self lay sprawled on a sofa, while Young spoon-fed him Weetabix in an attempt to coax him out of a torpor. As time passed, Will cheered up and even became curious about me. Liz was asking me a few questions about my writing because she was preparing a piece on my books for *The Guardian*. Self hadn't heard of me, which Young clearly found embarrassing. I simply took this as proof he was poorly read. Anyway, Liz pulled a selection of my paperbacks from a shelf and handed them to him, saying he ought to know my writing. The books Young had grabbed included my novel *Red London* which carried the following citation from a Steven Wells *NME* review: "Stewart Home's sperm'n'blood-sodden scribblings make Will Self's writings read like the self-indulgent dribblings of a sad Oxbridge junkie trying to sound hard." After absorbing this, Self slumped back against the sofa moaning: "but it's true, I am a sad Oxford junkie", while Liz began the process of cheering him up once again.

Needless to say, Will Self and I have not enjoyed the best of relations since this incident. It is therefore very much a tribute to Young that when I encountered Self at the Austrian Cultural Institute in London shortly after her death, we succeeded in being polite to each other for the first time in seven years. Liz had so many unlikely friends and enthusiasms, and I don't think there is anybody else who—without even being present—could have inveigled Will Self and I to speak courteously to each other. Thus Young lives on in memories and the innumerable social relationships that both shaped her and which she had a hand in shaping. Since only the history of a writer's influence can be addressed by consistent materialists, a more substantial treatment of what Liz achieved will to have to wait. For the time being it is fitting enough that while her *Times* obituary stated she was born on 6 February 1951, *The Guardian* placed her birthday on 6 June. This is a mystery that I prefer to leave unresolved; it is enough to state that all the obituaries agreed Young died in London of liver failure on 18 March 2001. *Pandora's Handbag* is available from Serpent's Tail.

PART 4
MESSAGE FROM A BLACK MAN

Thinking Of One Thing & Doin' Another

I woke up with Cleopatra in my arms, or rather with a love doll crushed against my chest, a very different sex toy to the one with which I'd had a fling in London. The inflatable I was embracing hadn't been made in the image of one of Yakub's Frankenstein creations. My new sweetheart was a Pearl of Islam. Man, she even had realistic black hair and not just on her head, rather than a pathetic rubber barnet coated with yellow colouring.

"As salaam aliekum," I greeted Cleopatra.

"Wa 'liekum salaam," she replied.

"What am I doing here?" I asked.

"Fuck me and I'll tell you later."

I didn't need a second invitation. It was good to have my pelvis wedged between those strong black thighs, and feel Cleo's large but light as air brown knockers bouncing off my chest. I brought my paramour to orgasm before I allowed myself the luxury of coming. After this, we spent some time gazing into one another's eyes, and eventually Cleopatra spoke.

"You find it very difficult to separate policy from justice, but in the political world they have frequently been separated with shameful dexterity. For example, according to the limited views of many self-interested nineteenth-century politicians, the abolition of the infernal slave trade would not only have been unsound policy, but a flagrant infringement of the laws (which are allowed to have been infamous) that induced white motherfuckers to purchase plantations in Africa and the Americas. Despite it being all along consonant with justice, with the common principles of humanity, not to mention Islam and Christianity, to abolish this abominable mischief."

"Uniformity is the characteristic of brute creation," I shot back. "Every species of bird build their nests with the same materials, and in the same form—the genius and disposition of one individual is that of all, and it is only education that raises us to fresh heights. It is the glory of human nature, that the operations of reason, though variable, and by no means infallible, are capable of infinite improvement. We are perpetually deriving happiness from new sources, and even before we leave this world are capable of tasting the felicity of angels."

"Why was the life of soul singer Marvin Gaye divided between ecstasy and misery?" was Cleopatra's rejoinder. "Can any other answer be given than this, that the effervescence of his imagination produced both, but had his fancy been allowed to cool in the love of Allah, he would have undoubtedly acquired more strength of mind. Still, if the purpose of life be to educate the intellectual part of man, then Marvin's task was to move on from Christianity to Islam. Had not death led to a nobler scene of action, it is probable that he would have enjoyed more equal happiness on earth, and joined the Fruit of Islam. Instead, Marvin was prepared for another stage of existence by nourishing the passions which agitate the civilised man.

"Little did the founder of our Temple consider the unspeakable importance to the interests of religion that the ambition of those that rise inside our organisation be circumscribed within narrow limits—instead they have been left unbounded scope for courting prefer-ment. These Fruits should be reminded that there is no God but God, and the wisdom of the world is nothing when placed against His wisdom.

"Weak minds are always fond of resting in the cer-emonials of duty," Cleo charmed me, "but prudence offers much simpler motives. It would be better if superficial moralists had said less respecting behaviour, and outward observances, for unless virtue, of any kind, be built on knowledge, it will only produce a kind of insipid duty."

"Which reminds me," I put in, "I've been paid to come here and make a number of art works. I wanted to shoot some hardcore pornography with a fine look-ing bitch, and you've got everything I'm looking for in the curves department. My yet to be made classic of avant-garde indecency shall star the two of us, and three or four other Pearls, with some exquisite Gospel music placed on the soundtrack that I will synchronise with our bucking. The art house crowd can never be righteous, and I want to let those blue-eyed devils know that regardless of whatever fine sentiments they preach, they are the evil creation of a mad scientist."

"Oh baby, make love to me again," Cleopatra panted, 'but this time with your movie cameras run-ning!"

I'm going to use subtitles and everything in the film we're making, " I divulged dramatically. "I'll use boards to explain the difference between blue-eyed devils, and blue-eyed Afro-Celts."

"Darling, I'm so glad to be making love to a real man."

"Did you know that it has been argued, mainly on the basis of the similarities between Irish myths and

The Kalevala, that the Finns are a Celtic, that is to say an African, people?"

"Kid, that really turns me on, it makes me ache to feel your pearl jam squirting between my thighs."

"Lights, action, cameras!" I shouted in my triumph. Then added as an afterthought: "Do it, sister, do it!"

I'd been worried about my ability to get it up when I had someone in the bedroom filming me having it off with various love dolls. Rather fortuitously, I discovered I got off on this voyeuristic addition to my cavorting. The resulting frolic turned out to be the most fun I'd ever had with my clothes off. Perhaps it is superfluous to add that it also created an instant classic of avant-garde pornography.

Trouble Funk Express

I arrived at Berlin Tegel at 15.35 local time. After clearing customs, I still had five hours to kill before catching an overnight train from Berlin Zoo station, so I decided to walk into town. I didn't have a map, but this wasn't a problem, the stops for the 109 bus marked out a route for me. It was hot, but I enjoyed my deliberately slow stroll. Close to the airport, I passed over and alongside various stretches of wood and water. As I approached the heart of the city, the spaces between buildings began to diminish and graffiti appeared on various walls. To begin with the graffiti I clocked was always on the walls of buildings numbered 16. I followed the 109 bus route as far as Charlottenburg, then I cut left and not long afterwards found myself at the Zoo station. I still had three hours to wait until I could board my train.

I skirted around the Zoological Gardens until I found a bench by a river five minutes walk from the train station. I sat down and got some food from my rucksack. I'd brought black bread and oranges with me from London. I ate several slices of bread and three oranges. I also drank a bottle of water. On a bench beside mine, two besuited male office workers were getting pissed. Dozens of people walked and cycled past me as I sat consuming my modest fare, there were a surprising number of conversations being conducted in English, mainly by youngsters with American accents. I pulled a copy of *Eros & Civilization* by Herbert Marcuse from my bag and set about re-reading it. The substance of Marcuse's argument was extremely familiar to me. I'd brought this book to Germany because it was a pocket-sized paperback and thus light to carry. I'd wanted a work that was easy to follow but that would bear immediate rereading. Marcuse was perfect, since he provided light reading but was not too frivolous. The book provided me with entertainment until just before nine, when I made my way to the train station.

The City Night Line sleeper to Zurich was late. The German railways are partially privatised and the trains don't run on time: profits come first. I got to my compartment and was surprised to discover I was sharing it with a woman in her sixties. We tried to communicate but failed miserably. I don't speak German and the woman didn't understand English. I went to the wash room and got cleaned up. I had to stand on the sink to clean my feet, which were sweaty after my walk across town in heavy shoes that weren't at all suitable for urban strolling on a hot day in June. My ticket was checked shortly after I got back to my compartment, so I lay down on my bunk and tried to sleep. The woman I was sharing the quarters with read for several hours, but eventually stretched out on her bed. She clearly didn't feel comfortable about the sleeping arrangements, and got up every so often to pace about, waking me when she did this.

I got up at seven, washed and got my shit together. I alighted from the train at Basel Badischer Bahnhof at quarter to eight. Wolfgang Bortlik was supposed to be on the platform to meet me, but there was no sign of him, so I walked through passport control without anyone checking my papers, then sat waiting for him in the ticket hall. Wolfgang appeared shortly after eight, looking flushed. He'd been running late and had cycled to the station, so we walked back to Erasmusplatz with my host pushing his bike. Bortlik lives in a large house with his family, the last time I'd stayed it had been autumn and I'd been housed in a spacious attic room. During the summer, the attic was considered too hot for guests, so this time I had a room in a downstairs flat that was rented out when I'd been there six years previously. We had a breakfast of bread and coffee, then I read before taking a shower. Bortlik had work to get on with.

Around noon, I strolled along the Rhine to the Museum Jean Tinguely. As well as the permanent exhibition of Tinguely's work, there was an extensive retrospective of Daniel Spoerri. The best thing about the Spoerri display was that in an extremely flash private museum, the artist had placed some colour photocopies and posters in clip frames, which appeared to be his way of putting two fingers up to the institution (of art). The exhibition was exactly what I'd expect from Spoerri, endless examples of unwashed crockery glued to boards. Of more interest than these annotated typographies of chance, were various reworked found objects. Spoerri is neither as consistent nor as careful as Asger Jorn in his production of detourned pictures, indeed many of his works are merely decorative, Spoerri is, of course, obsessed with breaking the picture plane—and adding "real" tails to mice in a painting, so that these hung down beneath the frame is a serviceable enough joke. A shower unit attached to an appropriated river painting had a certain ontological right-onness, whereas taps attached to a print of a woman's face is mere formalism. However, even Spoerri's weaker pieces were preferable to Tinguely's machines, which looked horrendously old-fashioned.

I walked back along the Rhine, stopping at one point for an iced coffee. The drink I was served rather surprised me, since it came in an ice cream glass which contained considerably more dairy product than coffee. I hadn't considered ordering a desert, but the sweet was pleasant enough. I let myself into Bortlik's house; he'd given me a set of keys since he'd been planning to go out. I sat in the living room and flicked through various art books until Wolfgang came home. We took a tram to the Basel SBB station, where we bought food to eat during our train journey to Zurich. I had a ciabatta sandwich with mozzarella filling, I don't recall what Wolfgang ate. I was reading at Paranoia City on Bäckerstrasser, a short walk through the rain from the train station. The bookshop was exactly as I remembered it from my last visit to Zurich in 1995, when I'd stayed overnight and later heavily fictionalised this experience in my novel *Come Before Christ & Murder Love*.

We were greeted at the shop by its proprietor Tommy Geiger and Susann Zahnd, who'd read a selection of my work in German the last time I'd been in Zurich. Tommy made me an espresso, while I caught up with Susann, who told me that she'd given birth the day after she'd appeared on stage with me in 1995. After introducing himself as my German translator, Wolfgang gave a ten minute introductory talk about my work. I read and spoke in English for forty minutes, then Susann read a chapter from my novel *Blow Job* in German. After a break, during which I chatted with members of the audience, I read and spoke for another forty minutes. After further exchanges with those who'd turned up, including a couple of journalists, Wolfgang and I headed back to Basel at eleven. Tommy presented me with a couple of English language spoken word CDs by William Cody Maher before I left. The last time I'd been in the city, Tommy had given me a photography book and a satirical pseudo-academic work about Lenin and Dada written in French. Tommy is a good guy.

I Got Ants In My Pants

The Foundation I was working with really had a lot of bread, it was a tasty set up. I'd been hanging around Finland for a few days, with a telephone wired into a digital recorder and a two-way mirror from behind which various salesmen were shot on digital video as they made their pitches. Bullshit merchants were perfect victims for a performance artist. Just then, the phone rang.

"Hello."

"Hello, is that Mr. Cheam?"

"Yes it is," I lied, "where's that girl you were meant to be sending over?"

"I'm Ryan from Dataview Research, we're conducting a survey about television advertising."

"Dataview Research? That's the corniest name I've ever heard for a whorehouse."

"If you could just tell me how many hours television you watch a week."

"I'm really itching to take off my clothes in front of that hot piece of tail you're sending over, then allowing her to rub oil all over my body. It's a hand job I'm after."

"Mr. Cheam, I'm not from a whorehouse, I'm conducting a survey about television advertising."

"Well why the hell didn't you say so earlier? Are you tryin' to embarrass me or something?"

"I'm not trying to embarrass you."

"You're not from Embarrass? Let me tell you that Embarrass is one of the most historic places on Iron Ridge. The name comes from the French for blockage, but otherwise the locale is pretty much a Finnish enclave, with masses of old homesteads dotted about. The Finns up there were involved in a lot of working class resistance and played a major role in the 1907 Mesabi miners' strike. The only reason I agreed to talk to you was because I thought you grandpa was a militant and had lost his job for fighting the bosses."

"Mr. Cheam, I'm calling from Duluth and I'm conducting a survey into television advertising for Dataview Research."

"Don't bullshit me, you're reading off a script and after you've got me engaged in some cock and bull conversation, you're gonna try to sell me a new kitchen—and that, boy, is a mug's game, because you're not even on a wage. I know for a fact you're only getting a commission, that you've been conned into working for what will probably turn out to be a whole lot of nothing. I know how they get you all excited, saying you could make a hundred thousand bucks a year, which maybe one salesmen in a thousand hits. Most people don't last three months in your line of exploitation, they get starved out cos they can't make it on commission only employment."

"So are you interested in having your kitchen refitted?"

"As a matter of fact I am, but only if you'll answer a few of my questions."

"Fire away."

"Are you standing buck naked on top of a desk with nothing but a ginger wig on your head?"

"As a matter of fact I am, but how did you know?"

"Well, the way you allowed me to lead you off the track shows you're new on the job. You've got a script and you're supposed to stick with it. All the new salesmen are made to stand buck naked on their desk with a ginger wig on their head. If you make enough sales you'll be allowed to wear your clothes. If you become very adept at your job you might even get to take the wig off and sit down. But you're no good, you've let me lead you astray, you'll never make it, you might as well quit now."

"Everybody needs a job."

"Not if they're rich, or they've cracked the secret of claiming welfare."

"Well do you want me to come over and give you a one hour presentation about our fitted kitchens?"

"Don't bullshit me, it isn't a one hour presentation, you'll take four hours, but come over anyway."

"When?"

"This afternoon."

After I'd phoned through to The Foundation to book an assistant to film Ryan's sales pitch from behind the two way mirror, Cleopatra walked into the room. My blow up sex doll was putting me off my stride. Earlier on I hadn't really thought about it, but after we'd made our classic of avant-garde pornography—which incidentally, I'd decided to entitle *How Sweet It Is*—it struck me that a sex toy shouldn't be holding conversations with its owner.

"Cleo honey, what the hell is going on here?"

"What do you mean?"

"Why are you talking to me? A love doll isn't supposed to get up and walk around, let alone hold conversations with its owner."

"Don't worry about it."

"What do you mean don't worry about it?"

"I mean don't worry about it."

"But I am worrying about it. What you're doing makes no sense whatsoever."

"I thought you were an intelligent guy, so why are you so hung up on rationality."

"What?"

"Do I have to spell this out?"

"Spell what out?"

"Look, you're dead and The Grim Reaper figured that having a love doll interact with you would be one way of drawing this fact to your attention."

"Death is not true. And while I'm on the subject, why are you acting as a mouthpiece for some clown dressed in a hooded-cloak and carrying a plastic scythe?"

"The Grim Reaper has a macabre sense of humour but that doesn't make him a clown and incidentally his scythe's not made from plastic."

"Your chum is a complete prat, he's the sort of person who listens to heavy metal music."

"Pray tell me, what's wrong with being dead?"

"Nothing, but let's look at this another way. If you're the cipher through which Death has chosen to manifest himself to me, I'll live forever anyway because I'm ready to fuck you both up the bum hole."

"Regardless of whether you dream on or get real, there's nothing that can be done about the fact that you've stopped living."

"If I've stopped living how is it that I'm still able to imagine my own death?"

"Death lies beyond the limits of your puny imagination, which as you well know is completely shackled by a rather too self-conscious post-modern solipsism. If the fundamentally anti-productive vignettes you claim to have been living through were unreservedly self-referential, Death would have orchestrated our love sessions with a backdrop in Baltimore, or Portland, or some other American city both he and you have passed through."

"He hasn't visited the north?"

"He's been to Vancouver, he's been to Seattle, he's been to Boston, he's even been to Providence."

"Big deal, what about the south?"

"Atlanta, New Orleans."

"Has The Reaper ever been to Grimsby?"

"Death hasn't been to Minnesota, but I know for a fact that he's planning to visit the North Star State. He's also considering acting out an allegory about an archetype whose fictions invariably turn into truths.

"The Reaper may well imagine he can provide a credible description of Minnesota based on his experiences of Finland and New York, but he'll change his hard rock tune if he ever gets to within a hundred miles of the North Shore."

"A number of observers have commented that the landscape here is remarkably similar to that of Finland."

"There isn't anything in this twice told tall tale relating to the Memphis of Chuck Berry, Willie Mitchell and Booker T.—or indeed, the Egyptian Memphis. Death simply assumes anyone who comes across his fabulations will make the necessary connections."

"Death is real but he simultaneously functions as an allegory that enables us to explore the idea of America, a subject on which you exhibit considerable ambivalence. The issue The Reaper wants the living to ponder is whether America is a geographical location, a state of mind, a way of life, or even all three of these things and much more to boot. Perhaps he even believes that the dead are all Americans now, since military devastation has become Washington's way of providing the wider world with the gift of democracy."

"This bozo's japes will backfire on him. I can't see him making much impression on the North Shore and Arrowhead. If I was The Grim Reaper I'd make sure this allegory included some action set in Minneapolis. Your head banging friend is making a mistake just plonking us out in the country."

"You're bored, you wanna go to St. Paul!"

"There must be a decent record shop down there, I could do with some good music to liven me up."

"Why don't you ask Death if you can have your record collection transported here?"

"What?"

"Go on, just ask The Reaper to move your record collection from London. I'd imagine that in a couple of aeons he might be happy to have you wake up with your CDs mysteriously strewn around you, since this would be a suitable way of reintroducing Claire Grogan into our allegory."

"Why would we want to do that?"

"Look, although Death takes us beyond rationality and to the outer limits of any notion of narrative, The

Reaper still requires a sense of closure at the end of the numberless allegories he acts out. Death draws everything together and we have yet to resolve what Claire Grogan was about. Just look at all those celebrity phantoms in the earlier parts of this tale, they were introduced as the living dead but we still attained a blatantly false sense of closure by killing them off."

"I didn't murder Richard Edwards."

"Edwards disappeared in real life, so it is only just he should vanish from the allegory we've been acting out with The Reaper. That's the poetics of doubling."

"Poetics?"

"There is a joke in there somewhere about murdering the dead."

"What?"

"Look, just do what I've suggested. You'll probably have to holler a bit when you ask for your records, Death tends to blast James Brown way too loud and he won't hear if you don't shout."

"What vintage James Brown is his favoured groove fest?"

"Heavy funk, *The Payback* album."

"I like that record."

"Well, since your musical tastes aren't so different from those of your master, why don't you just ask him for your records?"

"HEY YOU OUT THERE ON THE OTHER SIDE OF HELL," I shouted at the two-way mirror on the wall of my studio, "I NEED SOME DECENT SOUNDS. YOU WOULDN'T COME OUT TO THE NORTH SHORE AND LISTEN TO NOTHING BUT BIRD SONG. SO I WANT YOU TO TRANSPORT MY RECORD COLLECTION OVER FROM LONDON. I KNOW THERE ISN'T A LOT OF POINT THREATENING YOU, BUT IT WOULD BE A

GOOD WAY OF MAKING IT PATENTLY OBVIOUS TO THE HANDFUL OF MORALISTS WHO MIGHT MISS THE POINT THAT THE INCONSISTENCIES IN WHAT YOU'VE CHOSEN TO REVEAL ABOUT THE MYSTERIES OF LIFE WERE DELIBERATE. THAT YOU HAVE NO INTEREST WHATSOEVER IN NATURALISM, AND YOU FEEL QUITE AT LIBERTY TO DO WHATEVER YOU WANT ON THIS ISLAND EARTH. SO GET ME SOME SWINGING SOUNDS!"

Having said this, I left The Reaper to stew in his own juices. I figured he'd come through in the end, after all he didn't want a full scale rebellion on his hands, with the "dead" refusing to stop living. I'd decided to give the dude a day to think things over.

In the meantime I had to deal with the salesman I'd invited over. He only lasted about ten minutes. I had recordings of amplified jet engines blasting out on my hi-fi, and hardcore gay porn on the widescreen TV. When I announced that I was obsessed with serial killers, Ryan flipped and left. The film that we shot through the two way mirror looked good, but it was shorter than I'd expected. Not to worry, there were plenty more salesmen where Ryan came from, and I fully intended to pursue the fine art of winding them up—since I was, after all, being paid to do it. I spent the rest of the afternoon making passionate love to Cleopatra, then I got drunk on finest Ardbeg malt whiskey. I felt good and wanted to sleep through till morning, when I had high hopes of waking up to find my record collection sharing the room with me.

Chicken Strut

I'd spent the morning in downtown Basel, on the wrong side of the Rhine, trawling discount shops since I needed new clothes. I didn't buy anything. Even in the sales the Swiss prices were too high for my liking—despite being reduced, much of what I looked at was still expensive because fashionable labels had been attached to it. Bortlik told me later that I'd been scavenging the traditional red light district. I'd spotted some sex shops. The whores sat discreetly in bars, waiting to be picked up. I didn't see any junkie prostitutes, who apparently worked a different beat. We caught an afternoon train from the Badischer Bahnhof. The express had come from Milan and was going all the way to Hamburg. Wolfgang found some abandoned Swiss newspapers by our seats, and both contained decent sized stories about my appearance at Paranoia City in Zurich. This got us talking about book promotion. Bortlik had two novels of his own published by Edition Nautilus, and he travelled all over the German speaking parts of Switzerland to promote them. In the smaller Swiss towns, any author doing a reading was guaranteed expansive coverage in the local press. Three hours after catching the train, or to be more precise three hours and two minutes after we'd boarded the express, we alighted at Mainz. Ingo Rüdiger from LiteraturBüro Mainz greeted us on the platform. I'd first met Ingo six years earlier, when I'd done an extensive three week promotional tour for my German publisher and he'd organised the reading I did in Münster, he'd been a student there at the time.

Bortlik and I were staying at Hotel Hammer, which was located across the street from the railway station. Rüdiger checked us in, then said he'd wait in the Italian café next door while we freshened up. The hotel was a good three star, with a pleasantly modern—that is to say eighties—interior. On the wall of my bedroom was a print by Barlie L. Andria entitled *Il Colossea* and numbered 364/1000. The picture showed a modern city, in the form of slightly abstracted tower blocks, emerging from behind and to the sides of a Roman amphitheatre. This summed up the two thousand year history of Mainz, which was founded as a Roman town and is now an important media centre, with one of the main German television stations being based in the city. The headboard of my bed was a retro-constructivist work of art, featuring buildings at the top which had been made from shaped metal blocks of blue, yellow and grey. The lower parts of the headboard had a light natural wood finish. The curtains were striped in red, purple, white, yellow, blue and green—with the edging of the colours deliberately left rough. There were bedside table lamps, and a larger free standing floor light, in silver and gold with their stems twisted in modernist curves. I had a glass table, rounded wooden chairs, and even a leather topped bench that had been set into the dresser. The carpet was a fantasia of blue and grey swirls, overlaid with hammers in yellow, red, navy, green and orange. There was air conditioning, and the bathroom was designed along equally tasty retro-futurist lines. I was in seventh heaven, and it was rather a shame I had to go and do a reading, I'd have been quite happy just to crash in my room.

After dumping my bag in a wardrobe, I washed my hands and face. When I joined Ingo at the café next door, he ordered a coffee for me and we spoke about the Situationist International. More specifically, we talked about why there was considerably less interest in the situationists in Germany than in French or Anglo-

American cultural and political circles. When Bortlik joined us I asked him about the decor in his room, and it transpired he only had a single bed, whereas mine was a double. Since I'm a vegetarian, Rüdiger said there wasn't anywhere suitable for us to eat around the station. In the end, we wandered down to Hafeneck where I was reading. I wanted spaghetti and pesto, but Wolfgang and Ingo insisted I should consume something more substantial since the LiteraturBüro was paying for my meal, so I had pasta overloaded with vegetables. We sat at a table outside the pub, and as we ate we were joined by an assortment of Rüdiger's friends. One of the bar staff gave me a fortune cookie, and inside was a message that read: "No one can spoil your good luck." This was printed in English on one side of the slip of paper, and in German on the other. I could hear the strains of rock music being played very loudly inside the tavern. The friendly landlord had sung with German fun punk band Die Frohlix in the eighties, he came out and introduced himself, then gave me a CD reissue of an album by the group.

Later, we went inside and Bortlik said a few words about me, then I read selected pieces of my fiction written in the third person. I had a microphone to work with, and as a result I was able to make my performance a little stronger than in Zurich. Unfortunately, the audience didn't have as firm a grasp of English as those who'd come to see me in Switzerland, so I cut most of the explanatory chatter between the excerpts from my books. I performed for half-an-hour, then put down the mike so that Bortlik could read a chapter from my novel *Blow Job* in his German translation. I lay on a bench beside the stage during my break. There was a silk screened portrait of Che Guevara pinned to the wall above me. As I looked up at Che an overhead fan was causing the portrait, which had been printed onto thin cloth, to flutter about. When I closed my eyes I had visions of Che as a zombie who'd risen from the grave in a futile attempt to save capitalism from the onslaught of revolutionary workers. Fortunately, I'd recovered from this upset by the time Wolfgang finished reading in German, I got up from the bench and recited some examples of my first person fiction. Afterwards, several people asked me how I managed to recite my texts from memory without the assistance of books or papers. I explained that everyone has the capacity to memorise in this fashion, but in literate societies very few people make use of such abilities. Memorising texts is simply a matter of understanding how the human brain functions and making use of this knowledge. We forget more in the two hours that follow learning something, than we do in the following two days. I learnt my texts a paragraph at a time, taking each section in by returning to it for a few minutes once an hour over the course of an evening. I learnt one paragraph a night until I could recite the entire text from memory. Anyone prepared to persevere with this technique could do what I did.

When I'm reading, or rather reciting from memory, I rarely drink alcohol until the performance is over. Prior to completing my second set in Mainz, I'd been drinking a mixture of coffee and sparkling water. Once I'd finished my act, I had a beer followed by a treble whisky. Around midnight, Bortlik announced he wanted to go back to our hotel, because he was returning to his family in Basel on an early train. I said I'd go with him. Wolfgang told me to stay if that's what I wanted to do. A girl in her late twenties clad in wet look denim jeans offered me a lift to the hotel. I was happy enough to walk, it was only a ten minutes on foot. Besides, I was tired, I'd been travelling around for days, weeks, months, years. I wanted to make the most of this opportunity for sleep. I'd enjoyed the evening but wasn't inclined to prolong the night's pleasures.

Slow Down

I woke up. Okay, so I don't really sleep because I'm in a permanent state of suspended animation, but let's pretend I woke up feeling pissed off. I had good reason to be out of sorts, you see The Grim Reaper had failed to transport my entire record collection from London to Finland, Minnesota. What did I get in the end? A handful of my CDs, that's what. Clearly that cheapskate Death was trying to save on shipping costs. I didn't understand his problem: he was registered with the Internal Revenue Service as a self-employed archetype, so any shit like that was tax deductible. Even if he had to front the money, it ain't like it was completely written off. To make matters worse, the Grim Reaper kept putting thoughts in my head. Even more annoyingly the blow up babe I'd been shagging just wouldn't stop bending my ear about getting married. It's bad enough when a flesh and blood bitch starts hitting you up with this shit, but coming from a sex toy it really stinks. So I told Cleo to shut the fuck up, since she ain't even s'posed to speak. She got all upset and after a furious argument lay down on the bed and fell asleep. It was at this point that I finally went through the CDs Death had sent over. What I'd got wasn't so bad but it still left a great deal to be desired in the quantity department.

I kicked off by blasting out *The Baby Huey Story*.

Baby Huey died while Curtis Mayfield was mid-way through making the first Babysitters album for his Curtom record label, so the band's only full length work out had to be pieced together from the unfinished sessions. Add to the original long player three bonus tracks, and you've got a mean bunch of psychedelic soul bone shakers to reissue on CD. I once played this delight to a journalist from a national newspaper and she mistook it for hard rock, which just goes to show how low down and nasty the press can be. Next up I got my Curtis Mayfield proper, two Impressions albums on one CD—*This Is My Country* and *The Young Mods' Forgotten Story*. In my humble opinion, these tracks rock harder than the solo material Mayfield did shortly afterwards, and of course on this reissue you got plenty of class tunes like *They Don't Know* and *Mighty Mighty (Spade & Whitey)*. Then I found myself getting joyous because The Grim Reaper had mailed over *Shorty The Pimp* by Don Julian & The Larks, a late-nineties compilation of classic seventies lounge funk.

Later I slapped *Donny Hathaway Live* into my beat box, and this platter features my two favourite tracks by him—*The Ghetto* and *Voices Inside (Everything Is Everything)*—plus some nice covers, so all told it provides a better mix of material than his studio albums. Then I went for a couple of Bar-Kays albums reissued on a single CD—*Gotta Grove* and *Black Rock*. This is absolutely classic Stax material, so it is a shame some of the tracks are shoddily digitised (presumably because the master tapes are lost or damaged). One of my favourite tunes on this Bar-Kays collection is the ballad *How Sweet It Would Be*, and the sound on that is really fucked up. However, I still enjoyed great numbers like *Don't Stop Dancing (To The Music)* and *Grab*

This Thing. There were also a couple of burlesques of Beatles songs, which undoubtedly helped shift units of the original vinyl pressing to Fab Four fans, while showing a healthy disrespect for Mersey beat. Afterwards, I moved on to the classic James Brown album *The Payback*, we already mentioned this one yesterday, so no need to go into details here. However, it is worth pointing out that no one can accuse me of having unnecessarily subtle taste when it comes to music, *Stone To The Bone*, I just dig that monster beat. Which brought me to *Droppin' Bombs: The Definitive Trouble Funk*, a majestic compilation of tracks by DC's joint greatest Go-Go band (the other, of course, being The Soul Searchers).

When I wanna go back, way on back, to the soulful sounds of the swinging sixties, then compilations really are the best way of doing it, and Death had given me a couple of goodies in this department. *From Route 66 To The Flamingo* mixes King Curtis with The Soul Sisters and operates as a guide to what would have got original mods finger poppin'. *The Twisted Wheel Story* is a supposedly representative selection of what was played at the legendary northern soul club of that name but then who cares about accuracy when you got the likes of Jerry O and Ronnie Milsap to shake your tail feather? You've probably guessed that when it comes to northern I vote with my feet for the first flush of the rare soul revival. I ain't got no arguments with The Mecca but I've always rated groove over obscurity. Which probably accounts for why The Reaper had shipped me *Booker T & The MGs Play The Hip Hits*, which was a bunch of sixties covers by the Stax house band that went unreleased until the mid-nineties. I'd also been air mailed Jr Walker & The All Stars' *The Ultimate Collection* and a similarly raw compilation by The Temptations entitled *Psychedelic Soul*, both of which go to show Motown could play it rough as well as smooth. Never forget song writers and producers like Norman Whitfield. Man, I really dug relistening to those melodies. I'd also been blessed with *Trouble Man* by Marvin Gaye, which I like a whole lot better than *What's Going On*—even if there is no one track that stands out like *Inner City Blues* on the earlier and more famous album.

You could tell Death was big on that Memphis sound because Hi Records were a force to be reckoned with on what he'd thrown my way. There was one of those two albums on one CD reissues by Willie Mitchell—*Ooh Baby, You Turn Me On* and *Live At The Royal*, as well as an Ann Peebles boxed set entitled *St. Louis Woman/Memphis Soul*. So Hi Records were as well represented as Stax and Motown in what had been plundered from the far more extensive collection that I'd temporarily abandoned in Tony Cheam's London flat. I could dig it, and aside from a CD reissue of *Workin' Together* by Ike & Tina Turner, that was pretty much it as far as down home soul went. A couple of classic jazz funk platters had been thrown in for good measure—*Head Hunters* by Herbie Hancock and *I Need Some Money* by Eddie Harris—and it was good to hear them again. There was also a solitary CD reissue of two Idris Muhammad albums, viz *Black Rhythm Revolution* and *Peace & Rhythm*. As for free jazz, there was *Nothing Is* by Sun Ra, *Black Unity* by Pharoah Sanders and *Slow Music* by Lol Coxhill and Morgan Fisher. I'd been allowed a single shot of reggae, two Lee Perry albums: *Scratch The Upsetter Again* and *Eastwood Rides Again* reissued on one CD.

I was pondering what to play next when there was a rapping sound from the large glass on the wall of my studio. The Reaper, it seemed, was getting wound-up by my refusal to do his bidding. What he wanted me to do—and I knew this because like I've said, he has the ability to put thoughts inside my head—was go and freeze my bollocks off outside, so that I could describe the landscape and some Finnish farm buildings. Well stuff that for a game of soldiers, I was going to do what I sodding well liked. I grabbed a copy of *Rockit*, a Columbia hip-hop compilation. I skipped Grandmaster Flash and The Sugarhill Gang, going straight to the second CD and slamming *Jam On Revenge (The Wikki-Wikki Song)* by Newcleus through the speakers of my beat box at high volume. I figured this would really destroy the mood Death was trying to create. I was determined to fuck shit up.

I looked into the mirror and there was The Reaper gazing back at me as he banged away on a computer keyboard in a futile attempt to place ideas in my mind. Death is one of those creeps who learnt to touch type when he was teenage, which probably accounts for his decision to purloin someone like me who did crap office jobs for the lead role in this current allegory production. I'm sure he must have done some shitty clerical jobs in his time and I know for a fact that The Whore Of Babylon worked as a typist during one of those periods in which secularism was ascendant. However, either the hip-hop I'd been playing wasn't having the desired effect or else The Reaper was deliberately ignoring me. He must have been out of his mind if he imagined that psychological tricks of this type would work on me. I wasn't a three year-old any more. Indeed I was by now almost convinced I was dead and fully determined to overcome this minor inconvenience so that I might live my life to the full. I tried shifting gears, pulled *Rockit* out of the beat box and slammed in Glenn Gould's recording of Bach's *The Well-Tempered Clavier*. After the first disk of the two CD set I switched to *Piano Music* by Cornelius Cardew. That didn't get any response either. I gazed into the surface of the mirror on my wall and Death was no where to be seen. I figured he'd probably got up to score coffee. In desperation I tried spinning *Gaelic Psalms From Lewis*—now these are pretty mental and they got the result I desired. The Reaper put down his coffee and came charging through the mirror at me. It was like an effect in a David Cronenberg film and as Death approached he diminished in size, until he was little more than an inch bigger than I am.

"What the fuck do you think you're doing?" The Reaper demanded as he waggled a finger at me.

"Fucking shit up," I replied nonchalantly.

"The time sequence in this allegory is going to pot!" Death went scarlet as he screamed this banality. "It would take several days to listen to all the music you claim to have reviewed this morning. Worse yet, you're supposed to be tramping around outside. I gave you some records to keep you amused while I was busy harvesting souls and now you're turning my psycho-drama into some ridiculous Bret Easton Ellis parody."

"My musical taste is much better than Bret Easton Ellis," I insisted, "if I was one of his characters, I'd be having ecstasies over the worst seventies prog rock you could imagine."

"I don't have to imagine it, all I have to do is flip open *American Psycho*."

"Do you think you could give me a copy? I haven't read it yet."

"You can't do this to me!" The Reaper was literally tearing at his hair as he said this.

"What do you mean?"

"I made you!"

"No you didn't," I corrected, "you killed me."

"For fuck's sake!"

"Don't swear, you'll ruin your chances of winning the Booker Prize.'

"Will you please go outside!"

"You were supposed to reply that swearing didn't prevent James Kelman from winning the Booker."

"That's ridiculous. I don't give a shit about the Booker, I don't write novels and I'd never say that."

"Who's scripting this allegory, you or me?"

"You're right, we're getting our roles confused here. As a personification of the negative I'm not supposed to be interested in consistency. I've had a bad day. Cleopatra keeps hassling me about starting a family."

"Have you been screwing Cleo?"

"I wanted to understand how you felt when you were shagging a love doll."

"Look, why would I care that you've been shagging that piece of plastic? You can keep Cleo if you'll agree to move things along by giving me a real flesh and blood woman to knob."

"I'll provide you with a girlfriend," Death replied slyly, "if you'll agree to go outside and take a look at some typical Finnish farm buildings."

"Okay," I acquiesced.

"And if you meet anybody while you're out there," The Reaper added, "I want you to allude to some of my Finnish experiences, which you're to pass off as recollections that Claire Grogan heard from Tony Cheam and then forced you to learn by heart."

"Look, I'm getting very confused by all this, am I supposed to be John Johnson or Tony Cheam?"

"The way I see it, you're actually John Johnson, but you've started to believe that you're Tony Cheam."

"Clear as mud, so what are these false memories?"

"The first time I went to Finland," Death explained, "I got off the plane in the morning and spent the day in Helsinki. In the evening I was driven up into the middle of the country to a former railway station that had been converted into a house. So we drove and drove and the sun didn't go down because it was midsummer. When we arrived at where I was staying it was midnight but still light. To make me feel at home my Finnish host put on a Cock Sparrer album but hearing music that was so self-consciously rooted in an East London imaginary, the very place I'd travelled from that morning, was the weirdest and most alienating experience of my life. I stared out of a window at the pine forest which surrounded the house with Cock Sparrer doing my head in."

"Is that it?"

"It was an intense moment for me."

"You probably had to be there."

"If anyone was going to say that it should have been me," The Reaper screeched angrily. "Will you just go outside and look at some Finnish farm buildings instead of attempting to sabotage everything I try to do with you."

"In a minute."

All the time Death had been in the room with me, Cleopatra was crashed out on the bed, but just then she started stirring. The Reaper freaked out at the possibility she might wake up and find the two of us in the room together, thereby destroying whatever belief she still had in the idea that he respected her privacy as regards her relationships with other men. I suggested that Death hide in a wardrobe but he claimed to be agoraphobic because he'd spent much of his childhood locked in a laundry cupboard with nothing but dirty underwear for toys. In the end, I climbed in beside my clobber and let The Reaper shut the door to hide me. I couldn't believe it, Death had forgotten the C. S. Lewis novels he'd read as a child but they'd undoubtedly had a detrimental effect on his unconscious. I fell through the back of the wardrobe and found myself in The Reaper's office with his computer in front of me. When I looked at the mirror on the wall above the laptop, I could see Death getting it on with Cleopatra. The Reaper's notes on my life and death were lying beside his Mac PowerBook and I felt sick when I discovered how he'd planned to stitch me up. Fortunately, the boot was by this time on the other foot. Somewhat amazingly, I'd suddenly found myself in a position to make Death act out his own sick fantasies.

Shifting Gears

Breakfast at Hotel Hammer was pleasant enough, but forgettable in comparison to my room. I ate too much and waddled out feeling stuffed. To work off the effects of this buffet, I strolled down Augustinerstrasser and was bored by the half-timbered houses in the old town. I remained studiously unimpressed by St. Stephen's church with its Marc Chagall stained glass windows. Everything I saw palled in comparison to the decor of my hotel room. It struck me that there must be places in Mainz with Rosicrucian associations, despite the disappearance of The Temple Of The Sun. I knew that Johannes Gutenberg had been born in the town, but I made no attempt to locate the site of his original print-ing press. I gazed at Wiesbaden across the Rhine, and decided to catch the 10.22 express to Hamburg. If the surrealists imagined a crystal glass between the legs of the women they passed on the street, where the dadaists saw a monkey wrench, then one might well substitute a crevasse for those associated with fluxus. The 10.22 was the train I'd told my publisher Nautilus I'd catch, saying I'd phone if I decided to spend the day in Mainz and travel to Hamburg on an evening service.

The journey took almost six hours, and I used this time to revise the earlier parts of *Memphis Underground* from a manuscript copy I was carrying with me. I was met at Hamburg Hbf by Hanna Mittelstädt, who I'd not seen for six years. We took the S-Bahn to Blankenese, then a 189 bus to Wittenbergen. As we travelled to the cottage where I'd be spending the next few nights, we talked about the recent popularity of the French ultra-leftist Jacques Camatte amongst Anglo-American anarchists. Upon our arrival at Hanna's weekend home, I was greeted by Lutz Schulenburg, who owned Edition Nautilus and who I'd not met before. The last time I was in Germany, Schulenburg had been away visiting Subcommander Marcos and his Mexican rebels. After Hanna had introduced us, we sat on a terrace watching ships travelling between Hamburg harbour and the North Sea. The garden we were sitting in ran down to the banks of the Elbe, and some of the boats that passed by dwarfed our secluded retreat. As we consumed coffee and a fruit loaf, we talked about books and politics. Schulenburg's English was rudimentary, and I don't speak German, so Mittelstädt had to do a certain amount of translation. Citation of Camatte got a derisive laugh. Lutz was intrigued when I mentioned that the novels of mine he'd published in German translation were influenced by the *nouveau roman*, amongst many other things.

"Ah, so you've been stirred by Claude Simon, our German literary critics will not believe this. Simon is real literature, and the critics who admire him think you write pornography."

"The English writer who is most popular in Germany now," Hanna put in, "is Tim Parks. We don't understand this, we find his books boring. What do you think of Tim Parks?"

"I don't think anything of Tim Parks," I replied. "I once read the opening paragraph of one of his novels. After reading one line, I didn't want to read anything more. Life is short, I don't intend to destroy brain cells thinking about him."

Later, I went for a walk along the beach. When I returned, supper was ready. After our meal, we all went for a walk on the hill behind the cottage. I retired around midnight. I was woken in the morning by Lutz rattling around in the kitchen. I'd eaten half my breakfast by the time Hanna appeared on the terrace. After consuming a boiled egg, I left Mittelstädt and Schulenburg at the cottage, and walked along the Elbe to Blankenese. This Hamburg suburb had been founded as a town exactly seven hundred years earlier, and I found myself walking smack into the middle of celebrations designed to mark the anniversary. There was a street market selling the higher class of crap that is popular amongst the rich. Blankenese had once been an ordinary town, now it was a peculiarly wealthy suburb, with sailing and countryside distractions. Having had more than my fill of the delights on offer in Blankenese, I took the S-Bahn to Altona, where I fell in love with a delightfully proletarian pedestrianised shopping precinct. I bought a pair of sandals and some socks in Roland-Schuhe at 251 Grosse Bergstrasser. I clocked a chemist called Schiller Apotheke, then another called

Goethe Apotheke. In a clothes shop there were a lot of reduced Levi Sta-Prest, but the available sizes jumped from a twenty-eight inch waist to a thirty-four inch waist. Twenty-eight was too small for me, and thirty-four too large, so much to my chagrin I failed to bag a cheap pair of breeks.

Around three in the afternoon, I walked past Altona station and into the old town. It started to rain, and as the downpour became increasingly heavy, I sought refuge in a shopping centre. It was nearly four by this time, and many of the retail outlets in the mall were closing. I bought some drinking yoghurt, an apple, a banana and a packet of cashew nuts. The rain eased off, so I walked the streets and ate the food I'd purchased as I rambled around. Once I'd had my fill of the Altona district, I took the S-Bahn to St. Pauli. Coming up the steps from the station, I found myself close to the harbour, and on the edge of the biggest tourist trap in the whole of Germany. St. Pauli is where the Star Club was to be found when The Beatles were still struggling unknowns. Now that most people travel by air, passenger ferries no longer plough between Hamburg and Liverpool. St. Pauli is a district in which dozens of theatres put on big hit shows, everything from Andrew Lloyd Webber musicals to reviews of Beatles hits—and people are drawn to these attractions from all over Germany. There was little to interest me in the plethora of shops selling youth fashions, or even in the inescapable brothels and peep shows. The main drag in St. Pauli is the Reeperbahn, a street that is a byword for prostitution. Fans of the local football team are equally famous for being militant anti-fascists. I found a decent record shop and amused myself by going through its stock.

By catching a train from the Reeperbahn instead of St.

Pauli, I had an unbroken journey back to Blankenese. Teenagers were streaming straight out of the station at Blankenese and into Burger King. I bought a ten mark pizza from an Italian restaurant and ate it on the street. Once I'd disposed of the box, I took the 189 bus to Wittenbergen and wandered around the village. I got back to the cottage around ten, talked to Lutz and Hanna, and went to bed sometime after midnight. Breakfast on Sunday was a repeat, or more accurately an action replay, of Saturday. After my coffee, bread and single boiled egg. I went to the beach and reread the only book I had with me—*Eros & Civilization* by Herbert Marcuse. There were a lot of books in the cottage, mainly thrillers, and they were all German language editions. In my rereading of Marcuse, I paid particular attention to the chapter entitled The Aesthetic Dimension, since I thought it might be amusing to bamboozle a journalist by using this as a theoretical justification for my own work. After returning to the cottage, I drank coffee and ate salad. Hanna and I took the ferry from the Wittenbergen terminal to Hamburg Harbour. Lutz stayed behind to do some work in the garden. He would meet us later.

The trip down the Elbe took an hour. I enjoyed watching the Hamburg suburbs roll by. Hanna and I got seats at the back of the boat, but by the time the ferry stopped at Blankenese, the seats were all taken and those joining the service were forced to stand. As I enjoyed the views and the sunshine, I recalled another boat trip I'd taken from Mull to the neighbouring island of Staffa in the Hebrides. On that occasion the waters had been choppy, and the boat much smaller than the ferry I travelled on down The Elbe. On the trip to Staffa, various passengers had become hysterical, and began wailing that they were going to drown.

277

We arrived safely on Staffa, and the return trip to Mull was considerably smoother than the outward journey. After disembarking at Hamburg Harbour, Hanna and I walked through St. Pauli to an Italian restaurant called Rocco's. I ate gnocchi with a walnut sauce and green salad. Hanna had gnocchi with a cheese sauce and red salad. The food was excellent, as it had been the last time I'd eaten at Rocco's in 1995, the main difference between then and this more recent visit was that the restaurant had moved to new premises. Lutz joined us for coffee, then we walked to the Schilleroper where I was reading, or rather reciting. That night I read the same pieces in the same order that I'd recited earlier that week in Zurich and Mainz. However, in Hamburg, it was Hanna Mittelstädt who read a chapter from *Blow Job* in its German translation between my two sets—and not Susann or Wolfgang.

Groove Me

Death was in a tight corner but that didn't stop him pulling tricks he'd learnt from books about psychological warfare. The Reaper was pretending to be me and I'd imagine he did this in the hope that I'd start thinking I was him. I was already confused about who I was supposed to be. I hardly knew whether I was John Johnson, Tony Cheam, or even some self-styled avant-garde pornographer who'd joined the ranks of the reforgotten. However, if I was to retain any semblance of sanity I had to hold onto some salient and incontrovertible fact, and for me—at that moment in time—the only truth I had to go with was an indomitable conviction that despite the evidence piling up to the contrary, I was not and never had been a deranged serial killer. I was determined to do everything in my power to prevent Death using my life to enact one of his meaningless allegories since I felt success in resisting such a venture would at least prove I'd retained some level of autonomy and was not yet a mere extra in The Grim Reaper's carnival of lost souls.

Death was doing what I had been doing earlier, rifling through the CDs he'd sent over to Minnesota. As he did this he was listening to *The Bees Knees* by Dick Lee and Hamish Moore, an album that fused jazz and Gaelic folk music. Next he moved on to minimal techno, starting with *Vakio* by the Finnish group Panasonic, then spinning *Sheet One* by Plastikman. I knew exactly what The Reaper was doing since I'd read his plot outline after inadvertently escaping from his clutches. He'd made copious notes about how to deal with anyone deranged enough to break out from the lunatic asylum he called Hell. The long and the short of it was Death wanted to contain me by tricking me into diving through either a mirror or a still pool of water. What The Reaper wanted to avoid at all costs was having me walk away from his fetid fantasy world. Once I exited through Death's office door, I would be a free man struggling towards disalienation. The Reaper, of course, hoped to keep me mesmerised by pretending to have taken over my life and he knew I could see him in the mirror mounted on his office wall. He wanted to create further confusion in my mind about my identity.

The room Death operated from was pretty much what you'd expect. It was small with very little free space. One wall was lined with books, another with CDs and a hi-fi system. There was a beat box on the floor, but he also had a tape deck and CD set up with properly separated speakers. There were two bulging filing cabinets and a built-in cupboard inside which The Reaper had installed shelving that was crammed with yet more papers. Monitoring the movements of the dead was a bureaucratic business. There were two desks in the room, one with a Mac PowerBook sitting on it and the other graced with a PC. Beneath a small window there was an electric blue easy chair of Scandinavian design. I flipped through a few books—*Negrophobia* by Darius James, *Live From Death Row* by Mumia Abu-Jamal and *Black Power: The Politics Of Liberation* by Stokely Carmichael and Charles V. Hamilton.

By the time I'd exhausted my curiosity about Death's book collection, he was listening to those quintessentially crazed Americans in Europe, The Monks. The Reaper was playing my CD reissue of their only album *Black Monk Time* with four bonus tracks. The Monks had been formed by unwillingly drafted US servicemen based in Frankfurt. Their wacky music created quite a stir way back when and Polydor in Germany had released some records in 1966. However the band was dropped when these releases flopped. After The Monks, Death grooved to blue eyed soul in the form of *Detroit Breakout: An Ultimate Anthology of Mitch Ryder & The Detroit Wheels*. The pseudo-title track *Break Out* had been big on the northern soul scene but The Reaper's favourite seemed to be *Little Latin Lupe Lu*, since he repeatedly played it. Death was in something of a sixties garage rut since he followed Mitch Ryder with *The Boys From Tacoma: Anthology 1961-1969* by The Fabulous Wailers. Like The Reaper, I knew that The Wailers made their best recordings after they split from the Golden Crest label. It was at the beginning of this period that they'd cut the first cover version of Richard Berry's *Louie Louie* with Rockin' Robin Roberts on vocals, and it was their arrangement that became the standard one for this rock evergreen. Next Death went for a CD reissue with bonus tracks of Link Wray's classic album *Walkin' With Link*. This long player shits on everything else Wray ever did, as well as over-rated surf guitarists like Dick Dale. If you had *Walkin' With Link*, you really didn't need anything else by the Rumble man.

I've already mentioned that I had The Reaper down as being locked into some garage guitar groove, but then he surprised me by playing *Practical Time Travel* by Nocturnal Emissions. Don't be fooled by the band name, the record is late-nineties ambient and not mid-eighties industrial. Death followed this with his all time favourite Kraut Rock album, *The Man-Machine* by Kraftwerk. The Reaper, of course, was lulling me into a false sense of musical security. It seemed he wasn't so much orchestrating an allegory as providing a potted-guide to the freakiest sounds of the previous fifty years. Up to this point Death's tastes were pretty much in accord with my own but then he deliberately spoiled things by indulging his predilection for novelty records—in this instance *21st Century Boys: The Best Of Sigue Sigue Sputnik*. Within minutes of The Reaper being first introduced to me at a late night drinking party by the avant-garde pornographer Stewart Home, I had a row with him about this CD. Death disingenuously claimed Sputnik wrote nice tunes and seemed to find some kind of poetry in the fact that early copies of their debut album were shipped in a box, whereas their greatest hits collection came in a simple CD jewel case. Home was pretty irritating that night too since he was talking incessantly about the murder of his mother in some Notting Hill bedsit back in 1979. Indeed, he even whined pointlessly about the authorities failing to investigate her death properly. Cutting back to the present I knew The Reaper was playing Sputnik to wind me up, in the vain hope that I'd leap through his mirror because I'd want to change the record.

When I failed to fall for Death's initial bait, he tried spinning a CD reissue of the Graham Bond albums *Holy Magick* and *We Put Our Magick On You*. Now, I'd mentioned to The Reaper that I didn't like The Graham Bond Organisation and that to me albums like *The Sound Of 65* and *There's A Bond Between Us* featuring future rock superstars Ginger Baker and Jack Bruce were just so much bad blues boogie. What I hadn't said, mainly because Death had cut me off, was that by the time of *Holy Magick* Bond had found a style of his own that I liked a great deal. So not only did I know The Reaper's game I also truly believed that he was never going to succeed in his attempts to get me to jump back through his mirror and into the Valley of Death. It was time for me to bail out. I opened the door of the room The Reaper worked from and walked down a corridor. When I opened the front door I expected to find a stairwell that would lead me down onto the mean streets of East London. I was rather surprised to be confronted by a typical farm yard scene. There were hens running about. A digger was being used to load a trailer with what looked like cow shit. I could see two tractors and various other examples of agricultural machinery.

What particularly bothered me about the scene before my eyes was the sheer number of buildings dotted about, something that is typically used to identify Finnish farms in Minnesota. There was the first shack that had been built when the land was initially cleared and cultivated. A later log cabin. The recently constructed dwelling from which I'd just emerged stood behind me. There was a sauna, a cow barn, a horse barn, a root cellar, a woodshed, a tool house and hay barns scattered over the fields, not to mention other miscellaneous buildings. The clincher, of course, was that the sides of the hay barns slopped inwards with the flooring raised a foot above the ground. Spaces had been left between the logs from which the hay barns were constructed for air to circulate. Somehow Death had tricked onto a typical Finnish farm in rural Minnesota. I'd been conned.

"Greetings revenant!" The Reaper boomed as he emerged from a cow shed.

"What's happening?" I was puzzled.

"Convulsions, flesh, life, death, everything is everything!"

"What?"

"Parody, a bringing together of what some people might take to be divergent worlds when the factors being invoked are actually inextricably linked since modernism was shot through with all of them. All I had to do to signify this was place the word 'is' between the Anarcho-Futurists' repeated use of the term everything."

"You talk in riddles."

"Everything is everything, That said the Neoists took this commonplace of Afro-American slang and transformed it into 'anything is anything,' to give such banter a more obviously alchemical slant."

"Neoism, schleoism, ideology has fucked you up the gall-bladder."

"You sound like a cross between Gail Litvinov, who I first met at the Eighth International Neoist Apartment

Festival, and a character from Andy Warhol's *Flesh For Frankenstein*."

"That's because you've been telepathically placing thoughts in my brain."

"I've placed a coin under your tongue but don't flatter yourself with the anxiety of influence because what you say isn't even close to my position on the status of art within Hegel's system."

"What do you mean?"

"Isn't that obvious? The death of art spells the murder of artists and the real anti-artists appear. Burn the museums baby! Likewise, I'm still waiting to hear something substantial from you concerning the bogs, lakes and forest—not to mention the precipitation—that make this part of Minnesota very similar to Finland."

"But this part of Minnesota is Finland, or at least a place just outside the town of Finland."

"I know that, dummy. I was alluding to a more extensive area several thousand miles from here—with Russia to its east, Sweden to its west, the Arctic to its north and Estonia to its south."

"Don't call me a dummy! You're striving for an effect that I've yet to catch. You're the one who endowed me with these misunderstandings."

"You're intractable. Look at the efforts I've made just to make you realise you've stopped living."

"I'll never find the hacienda. The hacienda doesn't exist."

"Bringing you to the hacienda was easy. What I've found frustrating is getting you to acknowledge it exists. I had this fantasy of having my Andy Warhol zombie running a militia boot camp on the Iron Ridge and shocking you into accepting your own mortality. My initial plan for the finale included scenes of mass destruction drawn directly from *Heart Of Darkness*, *Aguirre, Wrath Of God* and *Apocalypse Now*. I guess I was thinking about *Cannibal Holocaust* too, and I was hoping to have some fun with the thought that death is a state of grace in which one can become properly centred. However I eventually abandoned these ideas as too subtle to get through your thick skull."

"One approaches truth by broken paths, which is rather different to imagining that one can embody or directly signify truth."

"Exactly, data can be falsified even if the notion of truth is problematic."

"You sound like Karl Popper."

"Just because Popper was a dick doesn't mean everything he said was wrong a priori."

"What are we doing in Minnesota? I thought the point of this psychogeographical exercise was to describe somewhere we'd never been?"

"We're not trying to describe Minnesota, we're invoking it. Those who learn of our activities will have to fill in the details. Anyone familiar with the North Shore will know we used real place names and they can patch in anything else they require from experience. We're attempting to delineate an America that is markedly different to the one Jean Baudrillard fancied didn't exist. American is dead. Long live America!"

"Fair enough, but you still haven't told me why we've come to Minnesota."

"We're not in Minnesota."

"We are."

"We're not."

"We are."

"We're in Hell."

"Let's not turn this into a pantomime parody of the Socratic method, just lay your position on me."

"We're trapped inside a rather complex web of social relations. We're not in Minnesota, we've never been to Minnesota. We're in Hell."

"So would you like to visit Minnesota."

"Yes, I'd like to visit Minnesota."

"Would you want to live there?"

"I don't know. I'd have to visit first but it's probably a cut above Hell."

"What do you know about Minnesota?"

"What do you want to know?"

"Celebrities."

"Bob Dylan, The Artist Formerly Known As Prince."

"Writers."

"F. Scott Fitzgerald, Sinclair Lewis, Garrison Keillor."

The World Is A Ghetto

I woke early, knowing as I raised myself from the depths of slumber that I was in a wonderland. After my performance and several drinks at the Schilleroper, I'd gone back to Lutz Schulenburg's Hamburg apartment. I'd slept on a sofa in the living room. Schulenburg's flat was stuffed with books, and the majority of these tomes were to my taste. The acres of print was dominated by theoretical works penned by key players of the communist-left, these had been spiced with classics of the twentieth-century avant-garde (a multi-volume edition of the complete literary works of Kurt Schwitters had caught my attention before I went to bed). The catch for me, of course, was that most of the books were

German language editions. An English translation of Barrot and Martin's *Eclipse And Re-Emergence Of The Communist Movement* was lying on the floor, but I was already overfamiliar with this text. I had my own copy of it in the same Black & Red edition. There were a lot of situationist books in both German and French on the shelves, so I leafed through some late works by Raoul Vaneigem that hadn't been translated into English. These were exactly what you'd expect from Vaneigem—who is a piss poor theorist, an atrocious dialectician and in his post-situationist works, politically dubious. I hadn't seen the handsome multi-volume hardback edition of the collected works of Franz Jung that Nautilus had published until visiting Schulenburg's flat. This achievement was impressive, although from my perspective it was a shame the set wasn't available in English. The Nautilus list certainly provided a context in which the novels of mine they'd done in German translation might be properly understood. Although, perhaps inevitably, alongside ultra-leftist and avant-garde works, Nautilus had published a few books of which I thoroughly disapproved—including biographies of Che Guevera and Mikhail Bakunin.

After I'd washed, Lutz took me up to Hanna Mittelstädt's flat, which was a couple of floors above his pad on the same side of the apartment block. For breakfast I had coffee, bread and a boiled egg. Afterwards we walked to the Nautilus office, and I helped break down and repack into smaller boxes a pallet of hardbacks that had been delivered that morning. I hung around the office for a while, then I took an S-Bahn to Hamburg Hbf, where I caught the midday train to Berlin. The journey took two hours and fourteen minutes. I was met at the Ostbahnhof by Darius James, Claudia Basrawi and Mario Mentrup. Mario had organised my last reading in Berlin in 1995, but I'd seen both him and Claudia more recently, since they'd stayed with me in Bethnal Green when they'd visited London in 1997. I hadn't seen Darius since January 1995, when I'd been in New York and had gone over to his apartment in Brooklyn to have dinner with him. It was Darius who recognised me on the platform, Mario and Claudia were flummoxed by my white Afro. The last time I'd seen Darius he'd had dreads and my hair was cropped. Now Darius had cropped hair and a moustache. He looked well and it felt good to see him, Claudia and Mario together.

We rode two U-Bahn trains to Mario and Claudia's apartment, where I dumped my bags, before departing almost immediately for a stroll along the canal from which Rosa Luxemburg's body was dredged in 1919. The café Mario wanted to stop at was closed when we reached it. There was a brief debate about going elsewhere for refreshments, but in the end we walked around for the fifteen minutes until the establishment which Mentrup favoured opened for business. Once we'd taken seats at a table on a waterside terrace, Claudia and I drank espresso. I don't recall what style of coffee Darius and Mario consumed. We sat with our beverages and conversed, or to say much the same thing another way, we discoursed as we sipped our drinks. I'm using these repetitions to act as a metaphor and marker for the ebb and flow of our verbal exchanges. Mario talked about his work as an actor, Claudia spoke about a TV project she was pursuing, and Darius was loquacious about how great it was to be away from the bustle of New York. He told me that before relocating to Europe, he'd spent too much of his time hustling high paid journalism, in order to make his rent. Having moved to Berlin where the living was easy thanks to a ready availability of cheap crash pads, Darius had been able to relax a little. He was also working on some new books.

As inevitably happens with Berlin café conversations between unabashed hipsters—or should that be cultural pimps?—the talk eventually shifted to Neoism. The style press in Germany was fascinated by Neoism, a neo-avant-garde movement of the eighties in which I had very actively participated. I mentioned that the Hamburg paper *Taz* had made much of my Neoist credentials when covering my reading at the Schilleroper, headlining its article *Die Gelüste Alternder Neoisten*. I also said that I considered nineteen-eighties style retro-futurism to have been very similar to Dada and Fluxus. A lot of garbage was produced under the aegis of Neoism, but there was some strong work too, and I cited the totally fried pulp-fusion prose of Blaster Al Ackerman as one of the high points of the movement. I also insisted there was much to be salvaged from the unbelievably sloppy output of tENTATIVELY, a cONVENIENCE. Mario said he didn't like tENTATIVELY, and had greatly angered him when he'd negatively covered his work for *Spex*. To my mind, tENT's problem was that his brain was on fire, so he was unable to slow down enough to think anything through. I then suggested Pete Horobin's *Data* output might be more to Mentrup's taste, and in particular the way in which this body of work was known principally through the agency of rumour, since Horobin quite self-consciously shunned publicity.

After a second round of coffee had been ordered, I'd mentioned that my paperback copy of *Negrophobia* had become very battered because so many people had borrowed it, so when we left Darius headed to his flat to get me a hardback replacement. Mario and

Claudia took me to their pad, where Basrawi prepared food. I took a shower, and by the time the meal was ready, Darius had returned. He gave me an inscribed first edition of his debut novel, and told me not to pass this one around, otherwise it would become as beaten up as the paperback I already possessed. As we ate pasta and salad, Mario talked about the unexpected death of Erich Mass from a stroke a couple of months earlier. I'd met Mass when I was in Berlin in 1995, he'd wanted to publish my novels but Nautilus had got to me first. Mario had worked very closely with Erich in an editorial capacity, and they'd included pieces by me in a number of their Mass Media anthologies. Once we'd eaten, we travelled en masse by U-Bahn to Kaffee Burger, where I was reading. The venue was run by Bert Papenfuss, a former star of the GDR underground, who wrote incredibly complex poetry addressing themes from German history. Papenfuss is a perfect example of the type of "dissident" who'd been blanked by the western press during the cold war, precisely because he criticised Leninism from the left. Although I'd corresponded with Papenfuss, I'd never met him. He'd translated some of my writing and published it in a left-communist journal he'd edited called *Sklaven*. I talked to Bert about Franz Jung; it was great to meet him.

The venue filled, and some of the faces turning up like bad pennies were familiar. I said hello to Christoph Fringli from Praxis Records and Rachel Zhark of the Home Wrecker Foundation. Claudia introduced me to her friend Melissa Logan from the band Chicks On Speed, and I inscribed one of my books for this rock goddess. I also spoke to Dunja Christochowitz from the monthly magazine *Style*, and a freelance journalist called Martina Gross. When it was time for the show to begin, we had a bit of fun with the introductions. Mario Mentrup got up and introduced Darius James in German, and Darius then introduced me in English. I recited the same two sets I'd done in Zurich, Mainz and Hamburg—but this time it was Mentrup who read a chapter of *Blow Job* in its German translation during my break. After my performance, I drank beers and gave press interviews. Dunja Christochowitz asked me if I wanted to be a writer or an entertainer. I told her that these days everyone was experiencing the effects of casualised labour, and so I had to be a jack of all trades in order to survive. The range of my voice is barely over an octave, but this hadn't stopped me from singing in public, and I'd do some dancing if that became necessary. Martina Gross had just discovered the situationists and was undergoing a crisis about her work as a journalist, since she didn't want to retrench the Spectacle. I reassured her that under capitalism all workers reproduce the conditions of their own aliena-tion. I rather suspected that she needed to supplement her readings of Debord with some Marx. I then spent far too long explaining to her why punk rock had more to do with Afro-American musical idioms than European avant-garde art.

Eventually, I managed to have a drink with Christoph Fringli. He'd been in Berlin for more than a year, after being forced out of London because he couldn't find anywhere affordable to live. Christoph's housing situa-tion was much improved in Berlin, but he said the city didn't compare with what London had been like from the mid-eighties to mid-nineties. Fringli's hardcore techno records had started selling in Switzerland, and he was thinking of moving there. I'd been to some great parties Christoph had hosted when he'd been based in the city of my birth. However, it wasn't only cutting edge DJs who were being forced out of London. I'd never known London to be as boring as it had become at the beginning of the twenty-first century, even the early eighties had been better. Christoph agreed with me about this.

"The initials of your name stand for shoot heroin," Rachel Zhark interrupted.

Rachel thought we were getting maudlin and should lighten up. The crowd at Kaffee Burger was thinning out, so a bunch of us piled into a car and headed to another bar.

Bustin' Loose

I'd deflated Cleopatra and stuffed her into a suitcase with some of my clothes. I don't know why I hadn't thought of doing this before, it was by far the best way of dealing with a troublesome love doll. If I got lonesome, I could always unpack my sweetheart and bring her back to life by the divine grace of my breath. I was lying buck naked on the bed in my room, waiting for the flesh and blood chick Death had promised to send. *AMMMUSIC 1966* by AMM was playing on my beat box. Now to someone unfamiliar with AMM, who might perhaps be hearing their brand of improvisation for the first time, it might not appear to be the perfect accompaniment for sex—but let's not forget the famous story of a couple turning up to an AMM concert and making love throughout their set. Such were the sixties, such is life. I lay back on the bed, my hands behind my head with my left leg resting on the raised knee of the right. The door opened, and Claire Grogan walked into the bedroom wearing little more than a negligee and a smile. The little more was a pair of stilettos.

"Mr. Warhol, he dead," she announced.

"What are you doing here?" I demanded.

"The Reaper sent me over, he said he'd promised you a fantasy flesh and blood lover."

"The double-crossing bastard," I murmured under my breath. Death had not only done what he'd promised, he'd quite consciously done it in a way that he knew was not at all what I wanted. The set up stank like the script of a long forgotten sexual hygiene movie.

Claire walked across to the bed, uncrossed my legs and fingered my balls. Once my shank was erect, she sat astride me and guided my manhood into the site of her mystery. She was bouncing up and down, and I was in two minds about what to do next. I could have told her to get off me, I could have simply pushed her off my loins but since my root knew nothing of shame I went carelessly with the flow of my desires. In this instance, inaction was the easiest course to follow. Consciously I knew it was a bad idea to have sex with Grogan. However, I didn't hold myself back, I spurted long before she'd had a chance to reach orgasm.

"You naughty boy," Claire giggled as my pearl jam filled her hole, "you didn't use any contraception. You've risked getting me pregnant. And now you've gone all limp, you'll have to use your tongue to get me off."

"What about if I tied you up then left you blindfolded on the bed?"

"What's that going to do for a woman?"

"I'd come back and fuck you once I'd got hard again."

"That sounds kinky. Me just lying here not knowing when I'm going to be pleasured."

"Are you up for it?"

"Yes."

So I tied Grogan up. Then I got a few things together and left the room. All I needed was my passport and plane ticket. I took a taxi to Duluth, then phoned Death while I waited for a bus to Chicago. The Reaper was out so I left a message on his answerphone.

"Listen," I said, "I'm running out on you. It was a low down nasty trick to promise me a real woman, and then send Grogan. I've had it with her, she's a psycho. To get away, I had to promise her some kinky sex, so she's tied up on the bed in that farm house you rented as a set for your allegory. You'd better get down there to make sure she's okay. I didn't tie the ropes tightly, so she should be able to free herself. However you sent her, so I want you to go and check she's got the horse sense to get loose. I'm not interest in Claire any more, so if you want to fuck her and she wants to shag you, go right ahead. And don't bother trying to find me, you never will."

My transatlantic flight was uneventful, that is until I got to immigration at Heathrow. The guy checking passports looked at my documents and asked me to step aside. The carpet in the small room I'd been led into was brown, the walls were off-white, there were a couple of grey plastic chairs, and a cheap brown chipboard desk. I stared at the floor, then the walls, then the ceiling. I checked my watch, and discovered half-an-hour had passed since I'd been corralled into the little cell. There were no windows. The door looked flimsy, but getting out that way unseen appeared unlikely. Eventually a policeman came in.

"What should I call you?" the cop asked.

"What do you mean?"

"The passport you're using has been tampered with,

the original owner's photograph has been removed and replaced with one of you. It's patently obvious that you aren't Anthony Graham Cheam."

"I am so!" I blurted lamely.

"No you're not," the cop boomed. "We've done a little checking, Cheam's body was dredged from the Thames a month ago. The file is still open on that one. We weren't necessarily looking for a murderer, since his death might have been a suicide, but if you killed him you might as well own up rather than force me to frame a guilty man."

"Tony was a lovely guy, I wouldn't have hurt him!"

"So you admit you aren't Tony Cheam. Now I want to know your real name."

"Just call me Tony."

"Okay Tony."

"Tony Cheam."

"Alright Tony, are you going to tell me where you got this passport?"

""It's quite a long story, and you'll probably think I'm crazy, but if you'll listen then I can explain."

"I'm all ears."

"A few months ago my name turned up in the Grim Reaper's little black book and ever since then he's been playing pranks on me because I refused to stop living."

"I'm afraid Tony that doesn't quite cut the mustard with me because if you're a already dead it is more than a little difficult to explain how you walked off a transatlantic flight with a doctored passport."

"But that's exactly what I was trying to explain when you so rudely interrupted. Death imagines that because he's claimed me as one of his own, he can do what he wants with me. I couldn't take any more of it, so I ran away. That's why I've turned up with a doctored passport. The Reaper's ridiculous obsession with Finland caused me to sicken of Minnesota."

"If Death is obsessed with Finland, what were you doing in Minnesota and why are you wandering around in the world of the living?"

"Don't you see, it's the consolation of influence, I blame Joyce!"

"Who on earth is Joyce and what has she got to do with all this?"

"I'm talking about James Joyce."

"Never heard of him."

"He's a famous modernist writer whose prose was haunted by Finnish culture."

"How so?"

"It's obvious in everything Joyce did from the title of his last masterpiece *Finnegans Wake* through to the significance he invested in the most mundane details of his life, such as the fact that he met his wife Nora outside the Finnish Hotel in Dublin."

"That doesn't explain why you were in Minnesota."

"Joyce didn't set his books in Finland, despite his obsession with Finnish culture. Under the code name *Memphis Underground*, the Reaper wanted to create a meaningless post-modern allegory using me as the canvas on which to paint this sick vision. After all there was significant Finnish emigration to Minnesota and I was staying on a Finnish farm."

"Okay, but then why is Death calling this allegorical work he's been constructing *Memphis Underground* if it's set in Minnesota."

"Don't you see? The flowing waters of the Mississippi connect Minnesota and Memphis and in the realm of mythology isn't that one of the major song lines for the spread of jazz, soul and the blues? That said, The

Reaper is also alluding to that other Memphis, the realm of the dead."

"You've lost me?"

"But don't you see, that's where I went wrong! I missed my line of flight, instead of travelling from Duluth to Chicago, I should have gone to St. Paul, and from there all the way down the Mississippi as far as New Orleans, where I could have got myself a jazz funeral. That way I wouldn't have used the dud passport that Death got Claire Grogan to palm off on me. Then there is the plane ticket from Chicago to London that Mr. Bradley gave me, if I'd thought this through, I'd have realised it was just another of The Reaper's cheap tricks to move things along. Wait a minute, if I'd gone down the Mississippi, I'd have passed through St. Louis, which is where William Burroughs came from, and didn't he have an evil composite devil in his novels called Bradley and Martin. The Mississippi must have been some sort of trap. My Times Square and Piccadilly. Possibly The Reaper is parodying existentialism. Maybe the freest people in the world are not so much those to be found in jails as those who are dead."

The rozzer clearly considered me deranged, and after taking fingerprints, blood and urine samples, he sent me off for a psychological examination. I impressed the shrink by catching and eating a fly as he examined me.

Soul Chills

Claudia had left Kaffee Burger with Darius and had yet to return to her flat. Mario's girlfriend had driven us back to the flat he shared with Claudia, but she'd left a few hours later to pick up her daughter and take her to school. Mentrup and I had a tête-à-tête over coffee, bread and cheese. After breakfast I said good-bye to Mario, and took a U1 train as far as Möckernbricke, where I changed onto a U7. Emerging from Jakob Kaiserplatz, I took a 109 bus to Tegel Flughafen. The flight back to Heathrow was uneventful, I was handed complementary copies of the *Telegraph* and the *Mail* as I got on the plane. Both papers devoted most of their home news coverage to the conviction of Barry George for the murder of TV presenter Jill Dando. I'd never heard of Dando until after she'd been gunned down, but according to the papers she'd been famous even before she was killed. To me this merely illustrated how fame was a relative concept. As far as I was concerned, it was only in death that Dando became a celebrity, famous for fifteen minutes and even as a corpse she was of no interest to me.

I dislike the tube, but find it the easiest way of getting to and from Heathrow. I got off at Piccadilly Circus and walked up to Berwick Street where I checked out the record shops. I'd thought about going to Richmond Park which is close to the airport, but hadn't wanted to lug my bag around all day. In the past I'd had access to more than one flat in Richmond, but not any longer. The rucksack on my back was a bit of a liability. I caught a 55 bus on Oxford Street, got off in Old Street and strode down Whitecross Street. In Safeway I bought bread and coffee, strawberries and orange juice. Rob McGlynn was in France but I had the keys to his flat, so I cut across to the Golden Lane Estate. I made coffee and watered the plants on the balcony. I ate half a dozen strawberries then split, leaving my rucksack behind me. I'd decanted a few things into a sports bag, and grabbed a couple of Rob's books to read. Since speed was of the essence, I took a circle line tube from Barbican to Bank, where I changed onto the Docklands Light Railway. I took a Lewisham train as far as Cutty Sark Gardens. Exiting the station, I was confronted by memories I'd rather forget. I dodged in and out of Essential Music and several bookshops. I had the misfortune to encounter a slew of remaindered Tim Parks novels, and even at a quid a shot they didn't look like they would walk.

From a phone box beside St. Alfege's church I made my arrangements for the evening, and several days to come. Later on I'd trundle up to Stamford Hill to see two different sets of friends, but first I wanted to take a stroll in Greenwich Park. I went up to the Observatory, where I'd participated in a Neoist Time Picnic in 1984. Somewhere I had a snap taken during the course of this do showing assorted retro-futurists, including myself, standing on the meridian line. A decade later I'd participated in a London Psychogeographical Association meet at this location, and it was at this latter function that I first encountered Rob McGlynn. I'd been a regular visitor to Greenwich Park over the previous twenty years, its dramatic rise and many curious features made it one of my favourite places in the whole of London. I took in the view across the Thames to the Isle of Dogs, then meandered past Queen Elizabeth's Oak and on to the gardens at the top of the park. After looking at the deer, and then the ducks in the pond, I sauntered along Charlton Way to Greenwich Point. Pausing on the way to enjoy the open view to Blackheath, I wondered if I'd ever realise my long standing ambition to spend at least a few years living in this area. There had been a time when it would have been easy enough for me to find a flat in East Greenwich with a rent I could afford, now even that was beyond me, and Blackheath? Well, I might as well forget about Blackheath, it had been expensive long before rising property prices made proletarian enclaves such as East Greenwich attractive to the upper-middle classes.

The view, or rather the lack of a view, from Greenwich Point was stunning. The City of London was wreathed in a miasma of smog. I could hardly make out the monumental architecture of the financial district. It was a shame I'd arranged to spend the evening in Stamford Hill, since the pollution that made my eyes sting and my throat smart also created spectacular sunsets. Rob McGlynn's twelfth floor west facing balcony was the best place I knew for contemplating the beauty of London's pollution—electric gashes in the darkening sky. From the Point I tramped down Royal Hill to Greenwich station, where I caught the DLR back to Bank. I took the Northern Line to Old Street, then hopped on a bus. I wasn't looking for anything. I just wanted to keep moving. I'd had my brief periods of instability, but for most of my life I'd a home to go back to when I felt like it, and despite this I'd never felt settled. I liked drifting around, but this shouldn't be mistaken for a love of adventure. I was finding it increasingly difficult to differentiate London and Basel, Zurich and Hamburg, Mainz and Berlin. Real life was elsewhere. Real life was everywhere.

I'll Never Sail The Sea Again

I was lying on a leather couch in a dimly lit room. The shrink was seated on a chair behind me, so that

I couldn't see him. I presume this was to prevent me gauging any bodily reactions he made to what I said. Unfortunately, there was no getting away from his pseudo-soothing voice. I found it hard to believe some people voluntarily placed themselves in grating situations like this. My one consolation was that while the soft cop was earning a good whack for the session, at least the bill was being footed by the state.

"I want to try some word associations," the doctor announced. "Every time I say a word, I want you to tell me the first thing that comes into your head."

"Okay."

"Father."

"Fender Precision bass."

"Mother."

"Peekaboo."

"Brother."

"Vox AC 30."

"Sister."

"HH Hundred Watt Combo."

"Grandfather."

"Plink plonk."

"Grandmother."

"Fire brigade."

"Uncle."

"Department store."

"Aunt."

"Insect."

"Son."

"Fender Strat."

"Daughter."

"Eerie Billy Haddock."

"Penis."

"Pecker, prick, sex pistol, water pistol, todger, soul finger, length, love muscle, love truncheon, love pole, cock, drake, dick, donger, ding-a-ling, bell end, meat, middle-wicket, shank, crank, handle, knob, protuberance, bulge, beef swelling, willy, wanger, fuck stick, chick spear, burning spear, hymen buster, weapon, lance, pike, javelin, dart, tool, rod, stalk, one-eyed trouser snake, serpent, viper, blood sausage, frankfurter, hot dog, periscope, phallus, pettifogger, wedding tackle, tuber, ass destroyer, plunger, tickler, stinger, junior, baby-maker, needle, pin, spike, skewer, stave, staff, wand, club, rigid digit, extremity, appendage, accessory, appurtenance, attachment, adjunct, creamer, stiff boy, big boy, rover, old faithful, ling master, sailor, shaft, John Thomas, John Bull, sex, stump, drill, jackhammer, screwdriver, organ…"

"That will do, I can see you're utterly fixated on this thing."

"But I haven't finished."

"That will do."

"Root."

"That's enough."

"Pork sword."

"Have you ever been sexually abused?"

"Manhood."

"Have you ever been sexually abused?"

"Rooster."

"Have you ever been sexually abused?"

"It depends what you mean by abuse."

"How old were you when you first had sexual relations with another human being?"

"Six."

"Six?"

"Yes, six years old."

"Tell me about it?"

"Well, there was this woman called Mrs. Smith who

lived down the street from me, she didn't have any kids of her own. She used to care for me after school. She'd take me up to her bedroom. She'd take her pants off, and hitch her skirt around her waist, then she'd pull my head into her bush and get me to lick it."

"And what did you feel when she did this?"

"It was boring, I'd have rather watched TV."

"Did you talk to anyone about it?"

"No."

"Why not?"

"Mrs. Smith told me not to talk about it."

"Did she talk to you about it?"

"Not really, she just said it was okay to do it, as long as I didn't tell anybody."

"So you didn't tell anybody?"

"No, not back then, but I've just told you."

"What is your earliest memory?"

"May 1964, when I was two, I was on a ferry going to see my dad who was in prison on the Isle Of Wight. It rained during the crossing and I was kept under a striped awning on the deck. The awning had blue, yellow, red and green stripes. I was attracted by the pretty colours and kept looking at them. Someone told me I'd see coloured sands as we approached the Isle Of Wight. I don't remember seeing the sands, I only remember being told about them, but I have a clear recollection of the awning."

"What other early memories do you have?"

"I don't know exactly how old I was, but this would have been in the mid-sixties, I went into a room in a house, and there was a multi-coloured carpet on the floor, all swirls. I turned around and around, watching as the colours blurred into each other and eventually I fell down because I was dizzy."

"Do you remember your first day at school?"

"I didn't have a first day, the first time I went to school, I only had to go in the morning. I hated it."

"Would you say you had a happy childhood?"

"No."

"Why was your childhood unhappy?"

"I didn't say it was unhappy."

"You said it wasn't happy."

"I said I didn't find it happy, it doesn't follow that my childhood was unhappy. Personally, I'd call it indifferent."

"Why was it indifferent?"

"Because my life was pretty much the same thing day after day and I found this incredibly boring. However, I'm not trying to put boredom down, boredom drives all sorts of people to do all kinds of incredible things."

"How is your love life?"

"I'm glad you asked me about that, because it's something I wanted to bring up. You see I'd already entered that state known as married patience when I got a job in an art school up north. So I'd be away from Balham all week and my wife was doing night work, taking calls for a mini-cab firm. I'd be home at the weekend but Beth always had to work then, those being busy days in the taxi business. It seemed like Beth and I hardly saw each other any more, and I got kind of lonesome. Of course, I had contact with plenty of attractive young women through my work but it is considered unprofessional to have affairs with students and I might have lost my job if I'd raised grades in exchange for blow jobs. One day I got it into my head that I'd buy myself one of those inflatable love dolls, you know, one made to look like the American porn star Traci Lords. In the end I decided to splash out on a deluxe model, with lots of special features, including a vibrating vulva. At first I kept Traci stashed in my room in Carlisle, but we were having uncommonly wild times together and eventually she persuaded me to take her down to London on weekends. Initially Beth didn't seem to mind too much about Traci but one Saturday night I came in drunk from the pub, only to discover Traci's batteries had been removed, so her cunt just wouldn't shake. If I'd not had a skinful I'd have managed to come without the aid of the built-in vibrator but after ten pints, I needed all the help I could get. So I sat up all night with Traci on my lap, whispering sweet nothings in her ear. When Beth got in that morning we had the most almighty row and pretty soon afterwards I took off for America on that doctored passport."

"You're bullshitting me, Bela."

"What are you saying?"

"You're bullshitting me, Bela.

"Why are you calling me Bela?"

"That's your name and you're not married either."

"Fuck you, I am too!"

"No you're not."

"Who told you that?"

"The cops. Once they had your fingerprints they quickly established that you are Bela Lugosi."

"Bollocks, if I'm not Tony Cheam, then I must be John Johnson."

"If you won't play ball with me, then I won't play ball with you. If you're not straight with me I'll file a report saying you're feigning madness and you're perfectly fit to stand trial."

Just then there was a knock on the door.

"Bela, I've got something to tell you," a disembodied voice announced, "there's a wasp in the kitchen."

"Give me five minutes and I'll be through," I replied in unison with the shrink.

"So now you've admitted who you really are," we both said together.

"You're Bela Lugosi!"

"No, you're Bela Lugosi!"

"No I'm not!"

"Yes you are!"

"Bela," a disembodied voice was screaming from the other side of the door, "there are now two wasps in the kitchen and if you don't come soon I'll eat them both myself!"

Long After Tonight Is All Over

I could continue almost indefinitely, since I will never quite catch up with myself. I'm still looking for my shadow, and if this phantasmagoria exists, then I am determined to jump over it. I could describe seeing John Eden, then detail my walk across Stamford Hill to George and Melinda's flat. I could just as easily write about my trip to Brighton the following day, or my meet with Richard Essex in King's X later that week. However, I want to justify my sudden and unexpected taste for the most bourgeois of literary genres—auto-biography. If many modernists and even post-modernists—where does someone like Burroughs figure on such an index?—used their fiction to provide a map of their minds, then in this there are many lingering traces of dualism. There is much talk of the body in recent theorising about this work but such discourse generally issues from the mouths of critics. Although it would be easy enough to play around with metaphors pertaining to bodies of work this would only obscure the fundamental problem which would necessarily remain unresolved. What I've just written—and it is not necessarily easy for all my readers to determine what I mean by this (and surely what I mean is of less consequence than what the reader understands me to be saying)—is in many ways more like a diary than autobiography. I've tried to exclude reflections about how random incidents on the road contribute to a general lack of pattern in my life. I've simply taken a slice of (un)reality, and what I've left out is just as important as what's been put in. For example, my encounters with Wolfgang Bortlik's family in Basel simply aren't detailed, and such omissions are every bit as political as they are aesthetic.

Among other things, I can't help inscribing into my books what goes on in and around my writing, since my fiction takes off from this. A lot of people imagine writers sit at home and write, but like everyone else they spend most of their time hustling. Since I am always and already writing about writing, I don't think there is much point in providing a long description of how I'm sitting on a blue and black office chair, dressed in a button down Ben Sherman shirt and Levi jeans with my PowerBook before me, bashing the keys of my computer. The words seem to flow out of my fingers. This fetish is something that has been with me since I began compiling my first novel *Pure Mania*, a concern with research that indicated memory is dispersed throughout the body rather than being restricted to the brain. My writing flows from my fingers, I don't draw it out from somewhere deep inside, that would be quite impossible since inside and outside interpenetrate each other and cancel each other out. This is what I do, what we do, it's as simple and mysterious as breathing. It's pure surface. Both reader and writer ARE "implicated".

The ways in which we'd bring a sense of closure to these interwoven narratives was resolved long ago—you were always and already complicit in this. Rather than looking forward to finishing my novel so that I can shoot up like the almost fictional narrator of *Cain's Book*, I'm going to sit down and write what you—if you started this book on page one and proceeded sequentially page by page to the end—have already read. This is not, of course, how what you've read will be written, or rather completed—but I will have remained true to the "spirit" of autobiography if I succeed in producing a self-consciously distorted account of my life. Slippages of time. Autobiography as science fiction. Journalism has always played a role in shaping my fiction. For many years I've modelled my prose on pulp styles that were in turn influenced by the popular press. Although I want a critical relationship to all modes of writing, this does not necessarily prevent me from being entertaining. I do what I do at least partially because I find it amusing. I want to combine critique, poetics and popular story telling.

If I was to continue in this vein and explain everything, this text would indeed go on forever. Instead of endlessly drawing things out, I offer you a necessarily false sense of closure, which even in my philosophy is not quite the same thing as a false conclusion. By deliberately leaving a great deal unsaid, I'm creating a sense of space. I have been told in the past that breadth and expansion are missing from my writing. Such misunderstandings may well arise from the fact that I'm seeking radical incompletion. I want to combine critique, poetics and popular story telling. I want to combine poetics, critique and popular story telling. I want to combine poetics, popular story telling and critique. I want to combine critique, popular story telling and poetics. I want to combine popular story telling, critique and poetics. I want to combine popular story telling, poetics and critique. I am Death. I am Undead. I stopped living. Ad nauseam.

one needle drops
all about music
american jukebox
little sister x2